TONI IS A COP WHO WANTS REVENGE.
SHE'S ABOUT TO STEP OVER THE LINE.
SHE'S GOING
UNDERCOVER

There were clusters of hookers on almost every corner. They came in all sizes, shapes and colors. Pimps in Cadillacs guarded the female merchandise. I tried to blend in, but it wasn't working. Even though I was dressed like one of them, they knew I wasn't . . .

There were three other girls on the corner, but the car stopped for me.

"How much?" he said as he leaned out the window.

My heart jumped into my throat. "A hundred," I said.

UNDERCOVER
Soledad Santiago

BANTAM BOOKS
TORONTO · NEW YORK · LONDON · SYDNEY · AUCKLAND

UNDERCOVER

A Bantam Book / February 1988

ISBN 0-553-26995-X

Published simultaneously in the United States and Canada

Bantam Books are published by Bantam Books, Inc. Its
trademark, consisting of the words "Bantam Books" and the
portrayal of a rooster, is Registered in U.S. Patent and
Trademark Office and in other countries. Marca Registrada.
Bantam Books, Inc., 666 Fifth Avenue, New York, New York
10103.

To Leylâ and Rocky
for passing through me
with visionary love . . .

y
Por esa canción en mi alma
Que ni en tristesa ni
en la profunda obscuridad
ha dejado de cantar

ACKNOWLEDGMENTS

With special thanks to:
My friends at the New York State Department of Law, among them Confidential Investigators, Alphonso Drafts, John de Rosa and Ana Nevarez and also to Assistant Attorney General Stephen Leon and, most especially, to Timothy Gilles.
To Andrew Daly for typing, typing, typing.
To my agent, Nancy Love, for opening the door.
To Becky Cabaza for editing with heart.
And to you Coleen O'Shea for wisdom and guidance.

AUTHOR'S NOTE

The Cobra's fangs are fairly short, but after it has struck the snake hangs on, chewing at the wound, injecting large quantities of venom. The seriousness of the bite depends very much on how long the cobra is allowed to chew.

The International Wildlife Encyclopedia, Vol. 4

UNDERCOVER

PROLOGUE

The last of the old man's cabbage soup crawled down the side of his mouth. The veined jowl fanned from his shoulder blades to his chin. He was a clarinetist who had played with the best. Now he enjoyed his one meal of the day in a place only losers would call a restaurant.

Jiggling the loose change in her apron pocket, Toni stood behind the counter. She looked young for her twenty-two years. Her auburn hair fell on a slightly chubby face, her full loveliness obscured by the ten pounds she should not have been carrying. Toni was waiting for the tip the old man gave her every night at this time. It was nine-thirty. The greasy spoon on Avenue A was beginning to empty out.

"Why don't you get going? That kid of yours probably needs you."

Toni shook her head. "That's okay, Zelda," she told the head waitress. "Kelly's asleep by now." Toni knew Zelda wanted her tip, but she was not about to let it go. Toni was saving her money to take Kelly out of this neighborhood, one day soon. A slice of noodle pudding beckoned from the cake display. She decided to take it as

1

a breakfast treat for Kelly. As she licked the sweetness from her fingers she anticipated the child's wide-eyed morning pleasure.

Four blocks and an avenue away, Kelly's small nose twitched. She was dreaming a dream she had been dreaming since before she knew words. It had colors and shapes. In her arms she clutched a pillow-sized Raggedy Ann doll.

On the street below, a car pulled up. Two men got out, and quietly they climbed the five flights of stairs to the only apartment on the top floor. One of the men was at least eighty pounds overweight. He huffed laboriously up the sloughed-off cement steps. The other man, young and well built, waited for him at the top of the stairwell. Then the fat man knocked.

Rumpled and ill, Kelly's nineteen-year-old uncle opened the door. The angry faces frightened him. In vain he tried to slam the door. The fat man pushed him to the floor.

"Where you goin' when you leave here?" the old man asked Toni.

"Maybe Queens," she said. "I heard they got some pretty good schools there. And the neighborhoods are better too."

"You're daydreaming," Zelda interrupted. "When you left Lenny you blew it. You're not going to make it out of here on two-bit tips." Zelda made a disparaging click with her tongue and shook her head.

"She wants to do it the right way," the old man said.

Toni thought about Lenny's threat. She would love him or die. Nervously, she rattled the change in her pocket some more.

"Where's the money, you dumb cocksucker?" The fat man picked up the sleepy-eyed occupant of the apartment and pushed him back toward the window and the radiator.

"I don't have it. I swear to God I didn't take it." The fat man threw a few more punches and under his breath he said, "This is no joke, Brian. This is no joke." He whispered as his fist knocked Brian's front teeth out.

Brian sank to his knees crying. He begged, "Don't do this to me. Please don't do this to me. Please . . . I didn't take the money."

The fat man lost himself in a violent fury. He knocked Brian down again and kicked him in the stomach and groin. The sounds of Brian's agony traveled down the long hall of the railroad flat, then died. Kelly opened her eyes. She thought that she was having a bad dream.

Toni wiped the old man's slobber from the counter, rinsed the rag, then washed her hands. She pulled her collection of coins from her pocket and spread them on the counter in piles of one dollar each. As she counted the change, she watched the desolate January night outside. It was now so cold only junkies and cops still moved. Toni caught her own eyes in the mirror behind the cake display. Her olive complexion was sallow; her green eyes had lost their shine. She pushed her bangs, which had grown too long, aside. Silently, she wondered, "Am I crazy to think I can make it out of here without Lenny?"

Kelly held her Raggedy Ann doll and walked toward the evil sounds. It was dark in the railroad flat. Only the front room, the kitchen, was lit. and only by the television.

"Mommy," the child said, "Mommy."

Toni rang the register open. On the counter she had made twenty piles of change. She said, "Zelda, I'm

3

putting in twenty dollars in dimes, nickles, and quarters. And I'm taking out a bill."

Zelda grunted.

In the kitchen of the railroad flat Brian's body began to break. The bones in his right arm cracked as he was thrown against a water pipe that ran from floor to ceiling. The back of his neck snapped. His forehead met the radiator and his brow parted to release his young blood with its deathly smell.

"Mommy! Mommy!" The child's cry became a long screech. The two men turned. For a moment the child gazed at the younger man. Then the fat man took the child's doll and pushed it down over her nose and mouth. Then he grabbed her by the throat. Her screams were quickly stifled. She flailed her arms and legs. Then she stopped.

"I'm leaving now," Toni told Zelda. She wrapped herself in her coat, hat, scarf, and gloves, held the bag with the noodle pudding close to her chest, and stepped out into the chill night air. It was a short walk to home but sometimes it seemed long. Tonight was one of those nights. It was so cold that the garbage in the gutter was stiff. There was no stink in the street. Her nose and eyes and ears hurt. There were no people in the street. The Lower East Side seemed like an abandoned graveyard. When it was dark as it was tonight, and when she felt alone as she did tonight, a terrible fear gripped her. A fear that she would never get out.

Some crawling thing rattled the garbage. As she began to cross from the corner of Tompkins Square Park to the south side of Seventh Street, a car, in the wrong lane, careened toward her. She felt it touch her coat. She stared after it for a moment, then kept walking. The bodega on the corner of Sixth Street was open. She stepped in for warmth. A radio on the counter was tuned to a Spanish station. As she bought the milk the man behind the cash register wrapped himself in a blanket and in the distance a siren called. The bodegero took her money and cursed the drug addicts who kept ripping him off.

"Dope fiends," he said, "I hate them, they lie, cheat, steal, and beat their own mother to get money for the cure."

Toni listened until her feet were warm again, then headed outside, where the siren screamed on. At first she thought it was the cops. Then she realized it was a fire engine coming from Fourteenth Street. The cold crawled under her coat and licked her spine with its icy tongue. The high whine of the siren seemed to oscillate behind her eyes, growing louder as it got nearer.

In the darkness behind her, another electronic scream began. Shining and screaming, the first engine turned the corner. The corner! Was it the corner to her home block? Could it be the corner to Fourth Street? She broke into a run without thinking, clutching her bags, running into the horrible heart of her terror, wanting to see for herself that she was wrong.

Toni turned the corner. Long evil flames licked the sky. They rose laughing from the windows. Her windows. The rest of the building was scorched and silent. To her breast she clutched Kelly's milk, Kelly's noodle pudding. Toni made it to the foot of the steps of her building. Blue arms stopped her. She tried to escape. But the arms would not let go.

"Lady, you can't go in there."

She screamed, she fought. She was stronger than four men. But there were too many of them. Too many men, too many arms.

"My little girl. Let me go. Let me go. My brother. My baby."

They had no ears. They did not let go. They held her. Watching. Watching. Watching as the flames danced into the sky and consumed her life in night. She screamed until there was no sound left. Nothing left in her. The blue arms had no ears. They did not let go.

"It's too late," they said. "Too late. There's nothing you can do now."

CHAPTER ONE

I opened the *Daily News* to the centerfold. The crease seemed to split me in two. The caption read: "Toni Conroy—Woman Graduates Top of Class—Police Academy First!" I studied my closely cropped hair and my new athletic frame carefully.

"Are you gonna pay for that paper, miss?"

I looked into the shadow of the underground newsstand. An old man returned my gaze. As I reached into my pocket for some change, his pale face opened in a toothless smile. He pointed to the centerfold. "Hey, that's you isn't it?"

I closed the paper quickly, handed him the coins, and disappeared up the subway station stairs into the June sun. How could he so easily have recognized me when I barely recognized myself? For a moment I wondered, had my ex-husband recognized me, too? My heart jumped in my chest. I comforted myself with the notion that he probably had not bought the paper. Or perhaps he was rotting in some jail and there were no papers. I looked at my watch. It was three o'clock in the afternoon.

Soledad Santiago

I crossed Astor Place toward St. Marks Place, passing the precariously balanced cube sculpture that was the gateway to the Lower East Side. St. Marks Place hadn't changed much. The patrons of the Gem Spa, a smoke shop on the corner of Second Avenue, were a little punkier than I recalled. Second Avenue seemed lazy and deserted. Shopkeepers waited for customers, and derelicts snoozed in doorways. In my T-shirt and faded jeans I fit right in. But in the cleaner's bag I carried slung over my shoulder was the uniform that would transform me.

On Fifth Street I turned east. The block was empty. Nobody hung out where the cops hung out. The old tenements with their empty stoops seemed to sway in the heat. Squad cars claimed most of the street and some of the sidewalk. A few old men played cards in the window of a first floor apartment. Mid-block the old precinct house nestled between two crooked four-story buildings. I stood for a moment at the foot of the short stairway that led up to the arched entrance.

To the left of the entrance a bronze plaque from the Marine Corps was dedicated to Patrolmen Rocco Laurie and Gregory Foster. I remembered them. In the neighborhood we used to call them Salt and Pepper because one was white and one was black. They were young, tough, gung ho yet kind, and everybody liked them. The two young patrolmen were best friends who had survived Nam together only to get blown away by a would-be revolutionary who didn't know how to pick a target. They had died on Avenue B on a cold winter night in 1972, the year my dad left home. I had stood on this spot and contemplated death before. But I shook that memory off. The block shimmered in the heat. I climbed the steps.

Inside the old precinct it was cooler. I passed the sarge at the desk. Behind him were seven more plaques dedicated to men who had given their lives in this precinct between 1964 and 1975. The sarge acted like he didn't see me. Even in the eighties women cops weren't too popular. I went down to the makeshift women's locker room to change. Mary, my partner in the Academy and now my roommate, had already changed. She was in uniform. As I walked through the precinct house basement with its steel gray walls and floors, Mary slammed her locker violently shut. It made a sharp cutting clang as her eyes searched mine. We had done better as partners than we were doing as roommates.

"Why did you do it?" she said.

I played with my lock, the combination momentarily eluding me. "Do what?" I turned from her gaze, my fingers felt the first tumbler click into place. "Besides," the lock came back the other way, "why should you be mad about it?"

Mary tugged on her uniform. "I hate this precinct."

"This is my old neighborhood."

"But you got out. What's the point of going backwards? I had no choice, I was assigned to this hell hole but you . . . you volunteered. If you had let them assign you to midtown like they wanted, maybe you could've helped me get a transfer. But no, you and that stupid social conscience."

I said, "Look, I explained this to you before. My kid brother Brian was a junkie, and he was only nineteen when it cost him his life. So I'm here for a reason. I know this neighborhood like the back of my hand. I'll do well here—I'll get rid of this monkey suit and make detective. Once I have my gold shield, you're gonna see some big dope busts with my name on them."

The second tumbler clicked into place, and as Mary brushed past me I saw the little vein on her temple throbbing. I tried stopping her, putting a hand on her arm, but she shook me off—her anger covering the deeper panic like a thick veil of ice.

The third tumbler clicked into place. As I watched

her womanly form disguised in the masculine cut of her uniform disappear around the curve of the stairwell, I heard her say "A one-woman war on drugs. You must be losing your mind." Then I removed the lock.

Mary was twenty-two and took things as she saw them. I was older, twenty-four, a whole life, marriage, and divorce already behind me, and for me it was different. But I couldn't tell her that. I kept my past to myself. Besides, what I told her was the truth. It was just that I left out a lot. I left it out because it was the hardest part. I didn't tell her about my daughter Kelly, who died with Brian because he had been so high that he nodded out with a cigarette in his hand and set his own mattress on fire—a fire that had consumed my apartment and my life. I climbed into my uniform. How could I have told her that I was not motivated by conscience or love or anything so noble? For me it was simpler than that. I had come back for my revenge.

I took off my jeans and my T-shirt and removed my uniform from the cleaner's bag. Then, I carefully put on the blue pants, the shirt, the tie, and the garrison belt.

I held my cold gun in my cold hand. It was a small, compact .38 caliber with a four-inch barrel that weighed about two pounds and fit snugly into my palm. I had learned to use it well at the Academy. Still, it amazed me that this instrument of deadly force fit so easily, so lightly, into my hand. Pulling the trigger was about as hard as lifting a gallon jug of juice with your index finger. I opened the cylinder to make sure every chamber was loaded. Pushing down with my thumb to activate the holster's safety latch, I placed the gun at my side. Then I ascended the stairs ready for the shift to begin.

I stopped at the bulletin board to see what sector I was assigned to and to take a look at my partner's name— *Errol Stutz*. I almost laughed out loud. What mother would pair such a romantic first name with such a ludicrous last name? But then mothers didn't pick last names, they gave them up. I tried to picture the man, wondering if he looked more like an Errol or more like a Stutz? I imagined him chunky, semiliterate, and sexist. Your average cop. We were assigned to sector B. I didn't know how the precinct was divided so it didn't mean much to me. Before I had time to study the map, I heard chairs scraping the floor behind me in the other room. Time for roll call.

The room was a sea of men in blue. I couldn't find Mary among the men. In front, a thin bespectacled sergeant propped a clipboard on his chest and smacked his lips. "All right fellas, simmer down." The room got quiet, and I found a seat in the back. "Item one—I wanna welcome our new recruits, Mary Montera and Toni Conroy. Why don't you new recruits stand up so we can get to know your faces."

Mary and I rose. A sort of mumble went around the room. I wasn't sure if they were welcoming us or if they were commiserating. I studied the men's eyes. They studied me. I tried to figure which one was Stutz but couldn't. Suddenly, I noticed that Mary had already sat down, and the sarge had begun talking again. I sat down.

"Item two—a little fire in the bodega on Seventh Street and Avenue D last night. The Fire Department suspects arson, so keep your eyes and ears open. Item three—it's hot out there now, the animals in the projects are still protesting. They don't want to move. They don't want those hell holes in Alphabet City torn down. Furthermore, the stoops are crawling with junkies. The hotter it gets the more of them there is."

He sucked on a tooth and tapped his clipboard with his pencil. "Major item—six weeks from now, they're gonna start shooting that movie about the Mafia. They're gonna turn Sixth Street into Little Italy the way it was in the twenties. There's gonna be plenty of expensive equipment down here. Paramount has its own security guards, but the mayor wants the surrounding area cleaned up and cleaned up fast. The city's gonna be watching us. So we're gonna sweep 'em up again tonight, fellas. We're gonna sweep the vermin offa those stoops. Bring those junkies in. And no head cracking. There's a new commissioner, and we don't wanna be hearin' them brutality charges. That means you too, Sevinsky." A heavy set bald guy with mean little gray eyes grunted. A chuckle jumped around the room. Apparently, this guy had a reputation.

Roll call began. A sandy-haired blue coat came in late and sat down next to me. He had wild blue eyes and stubble was growing on his chin. His uniform was just like everybody else's but it seemed to fit him better. The sarge went through most of the call, and this guy's name never came up. Neither did mine, for that matter. Mary was called and still not him, still not me. Mary was teamed up with Sevinsky. I was beginning to sweat it, worried that I would land Mr. Ivy League as my partner. Looking at him I thought there was nothing in the world we had in common. I was sneaking another peek at him when the sarge called, "Stutz, Errol." At first nobody answered, then the guy next to me turned with a Cheshire cat smile and said, "Here."

He said it louder than he had to. I was waiting to hear somebody else's name, anybody's but mine. Then the sarge yelled, "Conroy, Toni." I studied Stutz, trying to decide what color blue his eyes were. I never could read blue eyes. In my family, everybody had brown eyes but me. The white light in his button black pupils was flashing like a neon sign, and a smile played on the corner of his slightly crooked mouth.

The room was full of people noises—whispers, coughs, laughter, heavy footsteps—but between us it was very silent. He looked at me as if he knew me, had been waiting for me. As if this moment came as no surprise at all. Something about his smug, erect posture made me want to smack him in the face. Then he said, "I thought Toni was a man's name."

I didn't miss a beat. "I thought cops were supposed to shave."

He didn't bite; he just said, "I'm growing a beard," and touched his face. "The captain hates it."

Then he stood up. He had long legs and a nicely packaged ass. "Partner or driver?" he asked.

I got up myself before answering, "You drive," only because I wasn't ready to take the wheel. We headed out of the precinct house, down the old steps and to the squad car. I saw Mary walk off with Sevinsky. I wanted to wave but Mary looked too pissed-off to care.

It was after four, but it was still sweltering hot. The squad car's air conditioner wasn't working. We rolled the windows down.

"How long have you been down here?" I asked.

"Year and a half," he said, pushing his hat back with a proud thumb.

"Where you from?"

"Bay Shore, but now I live in Brooklyn. What about you?"

"Twelfth Street in the Village." I neglected to mention that I had moved there only two years ago.

"That's convenient," he said, "just across town."

I was staring out the window and I didn't answer.

"Easy commute," he reiterated.

I nodded my agreement but thought that it was another world from this. He made a U-turn. As the squad car pulled out toward Second Avenue, I began to feel a lack of air. When we crossed First Avenue, my hands clutched the dash board in front of me. I had not been back in nearly two years.

"Nervous?"

I shook my head, but my mouth was dry. The squad car radio crackled with messages that came and went. When we crossed Avenue A, a 10-13 came over, and it was for us. Stutz sped up and headed for Tompkins Square Park two blocks away. He parked hastily by the entrance, and bolted from the car. I was right on his ass. "Just follow me and take my cues," he said.

We ran toward a small crowd gathered at the park's band shell. Inside the circle of onlookers, a short angry Puerto Rican was puching a tall thin blond in the guts. She had a handful of his hair, forcing his head to one side. Then she buried her teeth deep in his neck. He moaned and twisted around to pound with both fists at her stomach. The blond hopped sideways; her stiletto heels flew from her big feet. The crowd was heating up and so was she. Deftly, she inserted her long fingers in his eyes. He hollered and knocked her off balance. She took him down with her. When he collapsed on top of her, she wrapped her legs around him. They rocked like they were dry humping until Errol managed to unlock her legs and pull the couple apart. He held the Rican by the collar, leaving his feet to kick in the air. I grabbed her. "Let him go you stoopid sonofabitch," she screamed at Errol. "He didn't do nothing. Let him go."

The little guy struggled against Errol's grip. The crowd swelled forward.

"Take your fucking hands off my wife!"

Errol winked at me. "Who's pressing charges?" he asked.

The blond nodded toward the crowd. "They all see what you pigs is doing. It's police brutality. We was minding our bidness, and you bastids butt in. Right or wrong?"

The peanut gallery chuckled. Errol rose to the occasion. "Are you guys through? Is this fight over?" he asked, and held his palms up in a gesture of supplication. Like a game show host on the jackpot question.

"We're not fighting," they chimed.

"What do you think?" Errol offered to take the

crowd's opinion. The tension broke, and a ripple of laughter punctuated a chorus of answers.

"Aw-w-w let 'em go."

"They love each other. Let 'em fuck each other up at home."

"It's they own bidness."

On Errol's cue I let her go. As soon as Errol cut the little husband loose, she jumped for him. He got her in the jaw. We separated them again. She played with the blood on her lip.

Errol said, "Look, if you don't cut the shit we're gonna hafta take you in."

They took a long look at each other, husband and wife. Then they both started cursing us for interfering in their private life. They studied each other's wounds. The crowd clapped. "Kiss and make up," they yelled.

The pair were hobbling off arm in arm when Errol's eyes met mine. "Welcome to the battle of the sexes," he said, and then the two of us just broke up. We were laughing so hard I forgot I had been afraid. Every time I looked at him I remembered how he'd played the crowd and I cracked up again. Finally, we were silent. In the distance, the lovers grew smaller.

As I watched them fade at the park's far exit, I thought about my mom and dad and the crazy shadow-box they danced when they were both drunk. But I didn't say so.

In the next three hours we rescued an old lady from a bunch of teenagers who were helping themselves to her groceries, stopped a fight at the welfare center, reunited a mother with a lost kid, and became the villains in a few more domestic disputes. In between we exchanged the kind of information partners do. I learned that his father was a cop in the small Long Island town where Errol had spent his childhood. The whole town was a town of cops. It was odd because Errol had this uptown air and nothing about him that spelled cop. He had two brothers, both younger, both cops. His mother was his mother; she kept a warm kitchen and a cozy home. He was following in his father's footsteps, but he also studied psychology in order to better understand the criminal mind. And he planned to study law.

As dusk fell, we were still cruising the neighborhood. The violet-blue air softened the edges of the burned-out tenements. From somewhere a sad bolero spilled into the street. Rivers ran from open hydrants, and children played in puddles of reflected light. On the corner a junkie drifted into this world, then out. Silhouetted in a bodega doorway, an old man brought a bottle of spiced rum repeatedly to his lips. Errol asked, "Why'd you join the force?"

"Good job, steady pay. Same reason as everybody else."

As the old man stepped out of the doorway into the oncoming night, he began to look like my dad the last time I saw him. I was twelve then. My dad, once a robust construction worker, had shriveled in alcoholism and pain. A cement truck had unloaded its wares on him and crushed every bone in his body. And even though he had eventually walked again, he had never gotten another decent day's work. And that broke him. Because my dad had been a hardworking Irishman and when he couldn't provide for us, he took up with the bottle and one day he just disappeared.

"I'm quitting, but tonight I need a cigarette," Errol said, pulling up in front of a bodega. "Come in with me."

Errol made a quick smooth exit on his side of the car. When I stepped out, I got nervous again. The bodega was only a few feet away. In the doorway a junkie and an old alcoholic glowered at us. I played with my garrison belt, avoiding their eyes. Errol and I hit the inside of the bodega at the same instant. I had been in a hundred bodegas. During high school I had worked in a bodega, and after my father's disappearance my mother had too. But in my uniform I no longer belonged. A group of customers stood around gossiping as they eyed us with naked suspicion.

"True Blue," Errol said putting his hand on his hips, trying to look at home. "What kind of night is it?" he asked the owner, who stood behind the counter. I knew the place had always sold not just food but numbers. I wondered if Errol knew.

"Hot," the owner answered. "It's hot for June."

"Not nearly as hot as it's gonna get," Errol said, handing the man a dollar and some change.

Errol and I looked at each other and I could tell we were both thinking the same thought.

They were afraid of us. I felt the discomfort of my new-found power and the way it separated me from the people who only two years before had been my neighbors. But when I remembered my purpose, the people didn't matter. "Ready?" I asked.

Back in the car I turned to him. "Let's go sweep the junkies."

"What's your hurry?"

"I wanna make a few good collars and get my gold shield . . . make detective."

We cruised deeper into the Lower East Side toward Avenue D. As we turned onto Fourth Street, I felt my lungs lock and my mouth go dry once more. My palms were damp, my fingers shook and a tic trembled in the corner of my right eye. In the soft beam of the weak streetlamps the school yard appeared out of the darkness. Errol stopped for a red light on the corner of Fourth Street and Avenue C. I wanted him to stop the car from crossing the street—from returning me to the past.

I stopped myself from reaching for Errol's arm and brought my hand back down into my lap. He had stopped at the intersection, watching the red light and the stragglers in the summer heat. Seconds began stretching into hours. His blue uniform became more blue. Then I heard him say, "You look like you saw a ghost. What are you staring at?"

His eyes reflected the changing light—red to green. "What are we waiting for?" I asked without answering him.

He touched the gas and we pulled into the intersection. Out there under the glow of streetlamps, long shadows and a bouncing ball preceded the sound of laughter. We entered East Fourth Street. In the school yard where I had last seen Brian and Kelly, other children played ball.

"You're looking the wrong way," Errol said. "Those stoops are crawling with junkies."

As I turned my head toward the stoops that lined the other side of the street, the whole world seemed to shift on its axis. The block was crawling with dope fiends; even two years ago it hadn't been like this. Some stood, some sat, some leaned on lampposts, and others nodded in and out of conversations. The windows of the now gutted building where I had once lived were still boarded up, but the stoop was now the most active on the block. The building's hollow interior made it ideal for shooting drugs or smoking the latest and most dangerous high, called crack. Several dealers had set up shop in the doorway. They operated as openly as if they had a license. Junkies climbed the stoops, pulled out their money, made their purchase and went inside to shoot up. I got so angry I thought I'd choke.

"Let's go back and crack some heads," I said.

Errol looked at me as if I were crazy and shook his head, smiling wistfully. "I guess all rookies are alike, the uniform makes you feel mean. But I expected you to be more of a woman."

That was a diversionary tactic I didn't appreciate. I opened the already open window further and glared out into the night. "I don't have to prove my womanhood to you."

I felt him realize his poor choice of words, but I didn't turn to face him.

"I'm sorry, I just meant you might have a little more compassion for these people."

When he said that, I had to see his face. What did he know about the real world? "Obviously," I said softly, "you've never had to live around these junkies, or tried to raise children in a place like this. There's a school across the street from there. A good cop would harass those fucks right off the block."

"They're victims," he countered, clutching the wheel, and I could feel him trying to get angry with me. "A real cop would go after the big guys."

I faked a bitter laugh. Slow and measured, I said, "You're right, let's just park the squad car right here and take our little bluecoat asses up the streeet until we find the Dope King of the Lower East Side."

He sank down in the seat, the anger seeming to seep from him. "One of these days I'm going to go undercover and do just that. Until then I guess it's all theory."

"Mothers used to sit on those stoops and watch their kids play before those junkies drove them inside." I rubbed my temples in frustration. "I guess it's different in Bay Shore."

He stopped for another red light. "I live in Brooklyn now."

We had come full circle. The car was again posed at the intersection. We stared at each other like adversaries in a duel. Finally, he put his foot on the gas. "What are you suggesting?" he asked.

I knew I had him.

"Nothing cloak and dagger. Let's just stop the car and pick up what we can. After all, it's the sarge's orders."

His smiling eyes told me I had just given him the opening he was looking for, but I had no idea what it was.

"Okay, we'll get them—but my way." He reached into the backseat for a bullhorn, which he dropped on my lap. "I'm gonna pull up across the street and just scare these fucks off the block.

"We're not going to try and make a collar?"

He smacked his lips. "Not tonight."

Satisfied for now, I just shrugged my shoulders. He wasn't the only psychologist in the car.

"Cover me," he said and got out, bullhorn in hand.

I followed and stood behind him as he took the middle of the street and shouted into the bullhorn, "All right, the party's over. I want you guys off this block. I want you off in two minutes. In five minutes we're gonna sweep these stoops."

At first, the junkies just stood there in paralyzed amazement. They stared at Errol and then they stared at each other. Then they started scrambling. Some headed inside the buildings; others ran off the block. Mothers, grandmothers, and children applauded from windows and fire escapes. Errol stood there for a while, a satisfied grin growing on his face. Then he shouted into the bullhorn, "All right, that's better."

We climbed back into the squad car and drove off.

"Hungry?" he asked, driving back toward Avenue A. I nodded yes. I was ready for a break.

We were eating pirogi at the table by the window when there was a commotion behind the counter.

"It's him. Is the order ready?" the waitress asked, sounding flustered.

I plopped a huge wad of sour cream onto my pirogi and watched as a brand new Cadillac pulled smoothly up to the curb. A man got out. At first I didn't recognize him. Then, as he stepped into the streetlamp's glow, I saw that he hadn't changed much. The door to the coffee shop was behind me, and I had my back to him as he entered.

"Do you recognize him?" Errol asked.

"Why do you ask?" I said, without turning around.

"The way you were staring, I thought . . ."

I shook my head, "No, it's just the Cadillac . . . in this neighborhood . . ."

As the old cash register rang behind me and the waitress giggled, I heard my ex-husband's mellow laugh join hers.

"He owns the Dragon. It's a swank after-hours joint that opened two years ago," Errol said quietly. "I'm convinced he's big-time coke, smoke, skag, what have you. I'll bet he's the source of half the drugs in the schools around here. I'll bet he's such a big dealer he gets his stuff straight from the Cobra." Errol's voice trailed off, his eyebrows furled into a vee in the center of his forehead. His eyes said that the subject of the conversation was headed our way. I felt the hair on the back of my neck stand on end. I kept my face tilted toward my pirogi, which now lay in the sour cream like pallid bodies in a sea of white blood. The name Cobra bounced around my brain. Then Lenny was behind me.

"Good evening, officers." he was as smooth as ever.

I felt Errol bristle. "Addicted any twelve year-olds lately?"

Lenny ignored him and focused on me. I looked into Errol's face and knew I couldn't escape. So I just turned to meet Lenny's hot, black eyes. A smile played on his lips, the square jaw set in mirth, the high cheekbones flawless as ever. I held my breath—waiting for him to give me away.

"I saw you in the *Daily News*," he said. Everything seemed to slow down as I fastened my eyes on his, waiting for his next line. "You looked good." Then, just before he turned to leave, he winked at me as if we were conspirators in some secret plot.

As the Cadillac pulled away from the curb, I shoved the pirogi around on my plate waiting for Errol to say something.

"Boy, I'd like to get that son of a bitch. Did you see the way he looked at you?"

I stuffed a pirogi in my mouth and shook my head from side to side. Then I took my time chewing while Errol kept talking.

"He uses flunkies for everything, never touches anything himself. That's why nobody's ever been able to nail him."

I stopped chewing, reached for my water glass, took a hefty drink, and let his words sink in. Lenny a dope dealer? How could he when he knew it was drugs that killed Brian and Kelly? After the fire, we had never really spoken. We blamed each other too much, the hatred between us was so great we couldn't even be in the same room together. I had never known him to be anything but a numbers runner. And in the neighborhood, numbers were considered a game. What had happened to him in these last two years? Had he lost every last bit of himself? I was dying to ask Errol for details, but I didn't want to seem too interested. Instead, I asked, "Who is this Cobra?"

"He's it. He's the man. He's the Dope King of the Lower East Side, and they say his territory keeps spreading. He sells that new Mexican heroin they call black tar."

As it occurred to me that exposing my past would not serve Lenny's purpose, I began to calm down. But how long before he tried to put me in his pocket again? Errol sucked angrily on a tooth.

"Boy, that pisses me off."

"Why don't we go after him?" I said as nonchalantly as I could.

"Who?"

"The Cobra."

"Can't. He's got no trail at all."

"What about this wise guy from the Dragon? What's his name?"

"Lenny da Rosa . . . But we can't get him either."

"Why not?"

"We're bluecoats, not narcs."

"What's the difference? If he can lead us to the Cobra, we should go for it." I laid six bucks on the table. "Let's start picking up these dope fiends. Sooner or later one of them is gonna give us something."

He studied my face in disbelief. "Some little thing," I went on, "some clue. Who this Lenny works with, where he keeps his stash, who's on the take."

"You're serious, aren't you?"

"Dead serious," I said, feeling a little crazy that my plot against dope now included targeting my own ex-husband. Errol pushed his chair back from the table. "I don't know anything about his modus operandi."

We got up to pay the bill. I looked at my watch, then studied the moon hanging red and low over the park. As the register rang for the second time in that half hour I said, "The answer's out there, and we're gonna find it."

CHAPTER TWO

It was shortly after midnight by the time I got out of my uniform and back into my jeans. Mary had left the precinct house without me. I decided to walk. Instead of going west, my feet took me to the east. I told myself I was just unwinding from the day. But inside I knew better. I knew I wanted to see the Dragon. I wanted to see Lenny's new world. The one he had built these last two years.

I walked toward East Tenth Street weaving my way through egg crates and card tables, through the groups of men playing dominoes, women watching children, and rushing packs of teenagers. The night was full of music—rock, Latin, and jazz—laughter, and intimate conversation. Faces young and old, cinnamon, bronze, mahogany, ivory, and russett reflected mellow in the streetlamp's glow. Summer bugs swirled around every light. Chips of glass studded the sidewalk. Children played a game of stickball. The ball soared high over parked cars and fell at my feet. I picked it up like old times. A fat-faced urchin reached his friendly hand my way. I handed him the ball. "Thanks, lady," he said with a smile. I stepped deep into happy memories of the past until all the bad things that had happened to me in this neighborhood were temporarily forgotten.

The Dragon was across from Tompkins Square Park on the best block in the Lower East Side. Brownstones with high ceilings and tall stoops overlooked the trees and the playground across the street. All through my childhood I had dreamed of living on that fairy-tale block. From the street you could see chandeliers in book-lined rooms. Expensive new cars were parked in front of brownstones, and the cops kept the block quiet and safe. These homes weren't part of the neighborhood scene. Rumor had it that one resident was a filmmaker, one a writer, and one a model.

Instead of walking where I might be spotted, I turned into Tompkins Square Park. It was more brightly lit than I remembered. Everytime I passed a lamppost, the shadow that trailed me would disappear under my feet, then reappear in front of me much larger than before. I watched it move like an independent being, passing under me then stretching in front of me. The playground was sheltered under the park's few large trees, their many leaves colored blue by the darkness. It was totally silent except for my own footsteps on the pavement as I headed for the children's swings. They had little red seats with green safety rails. I remembered lifting Kelly into those seats and taking turns with Lenny as we pushed her higher and higher into the clear blue sky. It was as if I could hear her giggling faintly in the distance.

The seesaw stood in the shadow of a large oak tree at the center of the playground. I remembered how Lenny and I had played on the seesaw, me holding Kelly, and Lenny balancing both our weights at the other end. And for the first time since we separated, I was conscious of how deeply I had loved this man whom my imagination now placed on the end of that seesaw. As I floated on the crest of the past I heard laughter, female and male, and then the slamming of car doors. I walked over to the park's old wrought iron fence and stood among the bushes watching as a merry foursome left a limousine and walked across the street to the fourth brownstone on the block. The Dragon was in there. Errol had told me. The foursome didn't go up the steps to the front door, but down a few steps and into an entrance beneath the stoop.

I stood there for a long time watching the silent block and the empty stoop across the street. I stood there, remembering when Lenny and I were first married and how we hoped to live on this block someday. I was caught halfway between hatred and longing, and the sandstone stoop across the street became another stoop that was old and chipped and cracked, a stoop on East Eighth Street, where mom, dad, and Brian and I had lived.

I was sitting shivering with my knees around my ears, and I had stopped crying a long time ago. Inside the first floor apartment I could still hear mom and dad shouting. Every once in a while I'd hear something break. They had been fighting for hours and even though it was January, I had climbed out the window onto the stoop just to get away. I was thinking that there ought to be someplace I could go, but it was dark and I was afraid. So I just sat there listening to them rip each other up, hoping that nobody would really get hurt. I had stuffed cotton in my kid brother's ears and left him sleeping in his bed. I was twelve and he was nine and we shared a room that faced the street. Brian was a very deep sleeper and could sleep through the worst. I figured he had trained himself to be deaf. But after the big fights, he would bolt up in bed and repeat the arguments almost word for word. Or he would wake up crying and squeeze into bed next to me, shivering from head to toe, saying that the devil had tried to get him again. I was hoping that the neighbors wouldn't call the cops when I saw two feet on the stoop below. I studied the shoes for a while, thinking they were imaginary, but then I looked up. It was Lenny, our upstairs neighbor. I admired him. He was twenty-two and had his own apartment.

"What are you doing out here?" he asked as if he didn't hear the screaming inside. I didn't know what to say, so I just sat there sniffing and saying nothing. He sat down next to me, took my chin in his hand, and made me look at him. "What happened to your cheek?"

I touched my cheek to find out what he was talking about. Even though it was freezing outside, my right cheek was burning and swollen. I could feel the dried blood. "I dunno," I lied.

He put his arm around me. "C'mon, you can tell old Lenny. I ain't gonna tell nobody."

So I started to tell Lenny about the fight. My mom didn't believe that my dad couldn't find a job. My dad was pissed that my mom had found a job as a barmaid. I told Lenny how I tried to stop mom from slugging dad and how she had hit me instead. I told him it was an accident. She had this ring the shape of a heart, and the heart had cut right into my cheek.

"They're gonna quiet down soon," Lenny said. "C'mon upstairs for a while. I'll put some ice on your face and make you some hot chocolate. Then you can sneak back in through the window."

A shadow crossed the window on the top floor of the brownstone across the street from the park. Then the light went out. I was wondering if Lenny lived up there when a hand touched my shoulder. My heart turned over. I was expecting a mugger, but it was Lenny. "Where's your uniform?"

I stepped through the shrubs away from the fence to one of the tall oaks. "I'm on my way home."

Soledad Santiago

A smile played on his lips. "You're living in the park? Or did you get lost?" He stepped in front of me, blocking my exit.

"Get out of my way, Lenny." I walked around the tree, getting ready to split in the other direction.

He followed me. "I've always been on your side," he was saying. "You seem to have forgotten that."

We were headed back toward the playground. As the seesaw appeared in the blue haze of streetlamps, I stopped and so did he. For a moment we were both staring into the same past. Then I turned to his enormous black eyes. He seemed to be waiting for me to say something. I was lost in his eyes, feeling twelve again, feeling as if he were my savior. There was a sadness etched on his face I hadn't seen before. Even though we were a few feet apart, I felt his touch. Then I heard him say, "I still love you, you know."

As he spoke, the door to the Dragon must have opened—I heard a moment of music and laughter. Then I remembered everything else that had happened between us. "I hate you," I said.

"What are you telling me?"

I hit the seesaw with my hand and the balance slowly shifted, the upside went down and the downside came up. I smiled sweet as poison. "Payback is a bitch," I said. "You taught me that." I thought I saw the shadow of fear cross his pupils, but he just looked down at our feet opposite each other on the sparkling pavement. A few more musical notes escaped from the Dragon's door. Then he returned his eyes to mine.

"I made my share of mistakes," he said. "But nobody's ever gonna love you more than I do."

He looked suddenly ruined and much too old for his age. The skin seemed thinly stretched over his beautiful face. He trembled as he raised his hand and pointed an angry finger at me. "Your mistake was leaving me in the first place."

UNDERCOVER

In that instant the yearning that had filled me was gone and I was consumed by so much hatred that the air left my lungs. When I tried to speak my throat was closed. Finally I said, "What did you mean when you said I was gonna pay for leaving you?" I was thinking about his threats back then when I left. In the neighborhood it wasn't uncommon for a guy to show his love by scaring the shit out of his woman. I said, "Maybe a little garbage fire that got out of hand? Maybe you expected Brian to notice but Brian was too high."

He groaned and his eyes clouded with pity. He reached his arms toward me as if I could return to them for comfort and whispered, "Sweet Jesus, I may be possessive but I'm not a lunatic."

I couldn't yield and he pulled his arms back. I gave one of the swings a push. It went to and fro, creaking and empty. I nodded my head in the direction of the Dragon. "What about that?" I was thinking how much I hated him for having survived so well.

He became young again. "You'd love it," he said. "It's very classy inside. The top two floors are my home, just like you always dreamed."

I was going to ask him about the drugs. Was he dealing now? Who had he become? But I decided not to show him all my cards. I needed to know more before I could ask more. So I just started to walk away. He called after me, "You've done pretty well for yourself, young lady."

I was going to tell him that I was a grown woman now. But by the time I turned around we were separated by the whole playground, and I thought I'd play on old times instead. I said, "Thanks for keeping your mouth shut."

He shrugged, "What goes around comes around."

After that I just kept walking. This time he didn't follow.

Even darkness had not lifted the summer heat. My

limbs felt heavy, my legs weak. I thought of the sadness around Lenny's eyes and wondered if I had hated him so much just because I had loved him so much.

When I got to St. Marks Place, I stopped in front of a small bookstore and stared at the titles in the window. Because the streetlamps were behind me, I could see my own haunted reflection there. I recalled the day I surprised Lenny with my letter of admission to City College. Kelly was two then and I was nineteen. I could still hear Lenny's angry words, "What the fuck are you doing? You have a husband and a baby to take care of. You're not some teenager with no responsibilities."

The letter trembled in my hand as I stepped back toward the cold refrigerator. "I thought you'd be proud of me, Lenny."

He grabbed the letter and ripped it to confetti. I started crying then and so did Kelly. He took me in his arms. "I am proud of you, honey." He stroked the damp hair back from my forehead. "But I don't want you going up there. That damn school's in Harlem. It's too dangerous."

I looked at the many books in the little bookstore window, remembering how passionately I had wanted to go to college. Then I started walking again. As I crossed Astor Place, which divides the East Village from the West, I recalled defying Lenny and how he had paid me back.

The apartment was dark. I stepped in quietly, thinking Kelly might be asleep. I didn't even turn on the light. It was a railroad flat, and her crib was in the kitchen where I entered. The crib was empty. As I stood there wondering where she could be, I heard a long fitful moan from down the hall. I turned to see a monstrous shadow bobbing on the living room wall. A candle flickered on the coffee table. Then I saw them. A woman was on her knees, and Lenny stood before her. Her head was in Lenny's hands. I couldn't see her face.

"That's good," he said. "That's good, don't stop."

I knew I shouldn't stand there watching, but my feet wouldn't move. It seemed forever, then Lenny pushed her to the floor and climbed between her legs. Now he was on his knees. I could see his ass in the candle light, her hands cupped around his cheeks, pulling him in. By her moans I could feel his movements. In the candle glow, I saw the blissful set of his beautiful face.

"That's right," he said, "give it to me. Don't hold back." The same words he said to me. I steadied myself against the crib.

They went on that way for a long time, pushing, grinding, her legs wrapped around his back. Finally, her breathing quickened and became more shallow. I heard him moan that familiar moan, and I knew he was getting ready to come. Then, he called my name as he came into the woman whose face I couldn't see. My name. Once. My name, twice. Three times. I slipped out the door.

When I came back several hours later the kitchen light was lit and Kelly was sleeping in her crib. I was very drunk, so I didn't get too close, I just dimly wondered where she had been during Lenny's escapade. I was standing there by the crib when I heard him call, "Where the fuck have you been?"

I turned. He was in his jeans, bare-chested. "I'm leaving you," I said calmly. "I'm gonna take Kelly and leave you." Then I stumbled toward the living room. He stepped in front of me. It was winter and I was wearing my fake fur. He grabbed at it. "Take this fucking thing off and calm down."

I saw his nostrils flare. "You've been drinking," he said.

"So . . . you've been fucking."

"You're drunk, you say you're going to school and then you come home drunk. What the fuck is wrong with you?"

31

I tried again for the hallway to the living room. I wanted to take a look at the rug. He pulled on my sleeve trying to get the coat off me. I resisted. We danced in that tug of war until I told him to take his paws off me. Then I felt the back of his hand across my cheek. I just stopped. My cheek was hot, red hot, and when I touched it I remembered another time when he was my protector. "I'm leaving you," I repeated, "that's all." And then I heard Kelly crying behind me. I turned.

"Don't touch her," he hissed. "Don't touch my kid, you goddamn drunken cunt."

He went to take Kelly from the crib. Cuddly and wrapped in sleep, she nestled against his chest. "You're gonna pay for this," he said. "You're gonna pay big. Nobody leaves Lenny da Rosa. You never shoulda crossed me."

"I didn't cross you Lenny, I just went to school."

After that I couldn't stand up anymore. I went quietly to the couch and slept there. The next day, when he had left for his numbers run, I packed my things and Kelly's and left. I went to a building on East Fourth Street where I knew one of the supers and he gave me an apartment. Later that week, I got a job at the greasy spoon on Avenue A. I was determined to start over. But Lenny was determined not to let me. On my first day home from work, I found him there, huddled in the darkened hallway, crying.

"What are you doing here?" I whispered. Kelly was in my arms.

"Come home," he said. "Come home, I miss you. I miss you both."

Kelly reached for him. "I can't," I said. "I don't want to."

"Please," he whispered, "please."

But all I could remember was the way his face looked that night in the candle light. "Forget it, Lenny. I don't love you anymore."

He reached out and slapped the side of my head. Kelly screamed. A neighbor on the flight below opened her door and peeked up the stairwell.

"Get the fuck out of here before somebody calls the cops," I told him.

He stopped crying, his face now hard with rage. Silently, he headed for the stairway. As I watched him descend, I heard his words. "This is your last chance. You'll regret this. You'll pay big."

He looked back at me, and his angry eyes were the last thing I saw—the eyes I remembered that night of the fire. Had he been speaking prophecy or was it something else?

Even though it was almost two in the morning, the West Village was alive with people. As I walked toward my apartment on Twelfth Street, I became aware of how alien all these people felt to me. I didn't belong like I had on the Lower East Side. I searched for the differences in these two sides of the city. In the Village, everyone was rushing somewhere. On the Lower East Side people lived their lives right there in the street. They laughed, cried, danced, fought, and by default everything was shared. That was the difference.

Inside my apartment it was dark and quiet. Mary was sound asleep. I undressed and slipped under my sheets. I lay staring up into the darkness, thinking about Lenny and mom and dad and Brian. For some reason I kept seeing Brian playing stickball. After a while he started to look like Kelly.

The kettle was whistling when I opened my eyes. Mary, in her Snoopy T-shirt, was standing by the stove. I sat up. My bed, like hers, was a mattress on a boxspring on the floor. Before I was really awake my mouth was already talking.

"Do you have to let that thing scream like that? It's giving me nightmares."

"Some tea?" she said, pouring hot water into a mug. Mary's way of fighting was never to fight back. It was fine when we were partners at the Academy, but now, living together, it made me nuts. She bobbed a tea bag up and down in the hot water.

"No, thanks," I said.

For a while the whir of the air conditioner filled the silence between us. I wanted her to be gone, but we were still on the same schedule. I couldn't pretend I was going back to sleep so I got up. I walked over to the window. "I made a collar yesterday," she announced after a long silence.

Relieved that she was talking, I figured it was good news, so I turned to her and politely replied, "That's great."

"Yeah, it is," she retorted, her hazel eyes squinting against the sunlight, looking older than she actually was. "Yeah, it was great. The girl turned out to be fourteen, a fourteen-year-old junkie. The boyfriend was eighteen. Sevinsky broke his jaw before he cuffed him. I hate to think what he did to her the couple of times he got her alone."

I walked into the bathroom. She followed. I started brushing my teeth so furiously that I drew blood. She just stood there staring at me in the mirror. I was waiting for her to accuse me of everything that was wrong with the department. My mouth full of toothpaste, I shrugged. "Did I create this stinking world?"

That made her snap. She lost her considerable cool and screamed at me. "I'm not talking about the world, I'm just talking about our Precinct."

"I didn't create that either." I calmly rinsed my mouth.

"But you chose it," she hissed. Mary was very fair. When she got mad, all the blood that rushed to her head showed right through her skin. Mary's whole head turned purple—except for two parentheses, one on either side of her nostrils. She looked so funny that I took pity.

"It's not forever," I said. "Besides, I didn't have anything to do with your being there."

The purple color drained from her face. She became her orange self again.

"Look," she said with some effort, "I know it's not your fault. But it's doing something to me, something bad."

I stepped away from the mirror so she could take a turn.

"How's your partner?" she asked.

"Too early to tell. But he's definitely weird."

"Mine's a bona fide sadist," she said, sounding as if I were to blame. "He used to be a narc before they shot him back down."

"I wonder what he did."

As I pulled back the shower curtain, Mary turned to me with a sad little smile. "It's what he's gonna do that worries me."

CHAPTER THREE

It was eight-thirty. Daylight was fading fast, but in the distance, images were still distorted by the oppressive heat. We were taking a coffee break on East Fourth Street, and our air conditioner was still broken. I was sitting in the car sweating, watching the steam from our containers rise, embrace, and disappear. Across the street the stoops were empty now. Errol and I had developed a routine. As soon as we got on shift, whatever the shift, we took our coffee on the run and headed straight for East Fourth Street. Then we'd stagger the hours, but we'd keep coming back. He'd use his bullhorn. I'd play with the siren—just pop up out of the darkness and scare the fuck out of a congregation of junkies hugging a corner. They all had such bad nerves it was easy to scare them. In just three shifts, the character of Fourth Street had changed. It had become a jumping block where children and teenagers gathered in the school yards, their laughter punctuated by the steady slap of a ball against a concrete wall.

Errol took a sip of his coffee. "I love watching those junkies hightail it out of here."

I tore two sugar bags, and dropped the contents into my Styrofoam cup. "We should be picking these guys up. How do you expect to find out who the suppliers are without arresting these fucks so you can talk to them?"

He began unwrapping his cruller. "The block is cleaning up pretty good. It's working, why do we have to pretend we're detectives?"

He shoved his cruller my way. "Want a bite?"

I shook my head. "No, thanks. You didn't answer my question."

He was licking powdered sugar from his fingers when he leaned toward me intently. "I wanna get the dealers too, but not if I have to turn into an animal to do it."

I was looking at him but I was seeing Lenny. That might be why I was getting mad faster than I should have. I forced myself to be nice. I reached for his beard and shook loose some of the soft white powder that had gathered there. "What kind of a cop are you anyway?"

"The kind that's human," he said. "I see a little more than you give me credit for, and I'm not going to let you manipulate me into throwing the book out the window to play Wyatt Earp."

He swallowed the last bite of his cruller and he looked like he was swallowing a whole lot more, so I decided to back off. The truth is, I was learning a lot just by spending so much time on the block. I got to know the dope fiends' faces, and I filed them in my head for future reference. Some of those faces had gotten high with Brian. One of them had gotten him started in the first place. And I was going to make them all pay.

I sat there blowing on my coffee, trying to figure a way around this guy. In the rear view mirror a young mother pushed a stroller while a little boy clung to her skirt. He looked like he had just learned to walk. His small round face was a mirror of wonder and expectation.

As they came up alongside the squad car, the mother leaned down to talk to Errol.

"You guys are doing a great job," she said. "And just to show you we wanna help, we're gonna turn that into a garden." She pointed across the street at a rubble-strewn empty lot.

Errol pulled his upper lip over his teeth and pushed his cap back. "It was my partner's idea."

The woman leaned down farther to get a better look at me. She smiled broadly. "How's it going, Officer?"

"Pretty good." I smiled too and asked, "How old are your kids?"

"The baby's three months, and Jamie is just over a year."

Jamie's pudgy hand examined the side view mirror where he saw himself. I was watching him reach up and bite the mirror when she asked me if I had any children.

Her eyes looked into mine, and I was afraid I was going to fall apart. My heart hammered at my throat and my eyes began to burn. I turned from her gaze and said no. I managed to shake my head too.

"Thanks again," she said and started off down the block.

"C'mon, Stutz, this break is over." I tossed the remainder of my coffee out the window and placed the empty cup under my seat. As we pulled out to return to patrolling our sector, I asked, "Do you really think the guy in the Caddy is a dealer?"

"Lenny da Rosa?"

I tried to sound nonchalant. "Do you really think he deals?" I repeated.

"I think that club of his is a front, a fancy front."

"What makes you think that?"

"He's too cocky, he's too slick. Everytime the squad goes over there on a routine raid the place is cleaner than the Metropolitan Museum, not one patron packing so much as a joint. That's unreal for an after-hours."

"Maybe you're wrong about him. Maybe he's on the up and up."

I said that because I wanted to believe it. Errol squinted one eye and looked at me like people do when they're looking dead into sunlight. I didn't know him well enough to interpret the weird look on his face. Finally he said, "Maybe somebody's tipping him off."

"Then let's crack heads till we get him." I said.

Errol didn't bother to answer. I listened to the steady crackling beat of the police band. We cruised uneventfully, yet unable to resurrect our conversation. As the evening claimed the day, a peaceful languor seemed to settle over the sector. It was as if the people had agreed to suspend their daytime struggles. Until tomorrow, nothing more could be done, no more trucks loaded and unloaded, no more telephone poles climbed, no more jobs hunted and no more welfare workers fought. In the cafe on East Sixth Street Puerto Rican poets recited their yearning for a tropical homeland. In pocket parks the *congeros* drummed a song of human longing more ancient than words. The dispatcher's monotone recited the violence that surrounded us. We circled our sector, passing the same spots over and over again. Dusk faded into darkness, and I felt the night begin.

We were crossing Sixth Street and Avenue B when we spotted a crowd. From it emerged a balding man in gray slacks and a T-shirt, frantically flailing his arms. We stopped. His head came in through Errol's window. Beads of sweat quivered on his upper lip, his ashen, unshaven face was a mask of rage.

"Goddamn it, where were you guys when I needed you? Those motherfucking dope fiends robbed me again." Errol called in the burglary. We got out and followed the man to his small Italian grocery store. The crowd followed too.

"They made me empty my cash register and they

took the meat too. I'm gonna have a heart attack. It's gonna kill me. Can't you do something?"

"I think they went into that building," a young kid said, pointing to an abandoned building across the street. The windows were boarded up.

"Yeah, that's right, officers, I seen 'em," another kid confirmed.

"All right, sir." Errol put a soothing arm on the storekeeper's jumpy body. "Just try to calm down."

I pulled out my pad, "What did these guys look like?"

"Two black motherfuckers," he said, wiping sweat from his upper lip. "I know them. They're from the neighborhood." His T-shirt was gray with sweat and clung to his sagging body. His defeated eyes followed the trail of his own fingers through the empty compartments of the cash register.

Errol said, "All right, look, we're gonna check the building in case the kid is right. Then we'll come back for the paperwork."

I slammed my pad shut and followed Errol out the door. The kids were oohing and aahing. "Wow, a lady cop. She's tough. See her . . ."

Once inside the abandoned building, I didn't feel so tough. Darkness engulfed us and I couldn't see anything. When my eyes adjusted, I saw a bannisterless stairway that led into a black hole above. We drew our guns and quietly began to climb. Beneath us the wooden steps were worn, cracked, and damp. From above, water dripped down on us like heavy raindrops. A drop fell on my lips and I tasted the rust. A moldy, putrid smell crawled into my nostrils. There was only one apartment on the first floor. We stood in its doorless doorway silently peering inside. "Stay here," Errol whispered. I heard his feet crunching the old newspapers that covered the floor. A few minutes later he came back. There was nothing and no one inside.

UNDERCOVER

We began climbing again, my heart hammering so loudly that its echo seemed to reverberate throughout the tenement. The higher we climbed, the greater my fear. I began thinking of all the people the storekeeper had cheated or sent away hungry because they didn't have any money. Suddenly, I didn't want to risk my life for him and I became angry. Just then, we turned a corner, and I tripped on something soft and wet. I slid across the floor and landed with my face in raw meat.

Errol helped me up, "These guys were gone before we got here," he said.

We continued upward through ten empty apartments. On each landing there was slightly more light, until we reached the open door to the roof. A trail of blood and steaks led to the roof's edge.

"They musta jumped onto the next building and cut out," Errol said as he wiped his damp brow in frustration.

In a semicircle at the center of the tar roof a few rusted old milk crates formed a makeshift patio. I was out of breath and panting, less from the climb than from my fear. Errol touched my arm and said, "Let's sit for a minute."

The two of us sat there catching our breath. Above, the sky was starless, beneath our feet, the tar sweltered. Somewhere nearby I heard pigeons cooing as I felt more than saw Errol's nearness. After a while, my breathing became regular again and my eyes adjusted to the glow of the streetlamps below us. Errol was sitting across from me when he suddenly emerged in clear focus. In the half-light the wave of his sandy hair and the blond stubble covering his chin conspired to cast him in a shimmering halo. Compared to Lenny's olive tan, his skin was very white and he almost glowed in the dark. He took a deep breath and ran his thumb and forefinger across the yellow lines that were his eyebrows. Then he just sat there and stared at me. I didn't know what to make of him. Was he waiting for me to speak?

"Do you think we should go back down?" I asked, my voice small and shaking just a little. Could he tell?

"You're very brave," he said. "I felt safe with you. I could tell you were right there with me." Then he fell silent again. Should I tell him how scared I really was? As if reading my thoughts he said, "It's places like this building that are the most dangerous. You never know what's coming." I agreed, reiterating an old Academy cliche—"A cornered rat will do anything."

"Exactly," he said.

I stood up and walked toward the edge of the roof. It was an incline, like climbing a slight hill, and my knees buckled and resisted. Below, I could see the tops of the streetlamps. Across the street a small group of children and adults waited for Errol and me to emerge, victorious or defeated. On East Sixth Street I saw the beginnings of the would-be Little Italy. Several huge vans were parked on the block and two buildings already had false fronts. A funeral parlor had become an Italian bakery. I was wondering how many stiffs were in there, when I heard Errol say, "Don't stand at the edge like that. It gives me the creeps. C'mon, let's go down and talk to the storekeeper."

I had barely nodded my agreement when a siren went off in the next sector a few blocks away. From the roof its hollow whine sounded high and thin, and it gave me goose bumps. In moments another siren went off somewhere to my right. It got louder as it got nearer. Then a 10-50 came over. We looked at each other, then he responded to the call. We were ordered to leave our sector and head for the river, where a group of demonstrators was getting rowdy. At least three more sirens went off around the neighborhood.

"Let's go," he said, and we ran through the blackness down the precarious steps back into the illuminated street, down to our car. We unlocked the doors and jumped in. The paperwork would have to wait.

"What's going on?" The distraught store owner and some of his customers, probably those he gave credit to, gathered around the squad car, making it difficult for us to get away.

"They weren't in there mister."

"We got an emergency now."

"We'll be back."

The projects are on the edge of the neighborhood. Beyond them lies the FDR Drive and the East River. Far from public transportation, public institutions, and public scrutiny, these nineteen buildings house about five thousand people. Taller than most in the surrounding area, they were built back in the 1940s, and in those days were inhabited by Eastern European immigrants. Now garbage is spread across the sidewalks, and carcasses of cars line streets with potholes the size of craters. Despite the thousands of people who live there, the area seems an unpopulated wilderness.

The crowd had many heads and many legs that thrust forward and away from us, focusing on something I couldn't see. There were no other bluecoats. I wondered with horror what was in front of the crowd. Just before Errol and I left our squad car, he grabbed the bullhorn. We took a long hard look at each other. "Stay close," he said, and the look on his face told me I wasn't scared for nothing.

"Where the hell is everybody?" I asked. "I heard at least half a dozen cars called into this sector."

He gave me a sorry shrug. "They must be on the other side of that mob."

No eyes were facing our way, and when we first stepped out we went unseen. A giant crane and four big Mack trucks surrounded both the crowd and us. The whole avenue had become a construction site. Somebody screamed, *"La hara. La hara.* The cops." But nobody else seemed to hear.

We made our way further up the avenue, where a squad car and ambulance were just pulling away. Their sirens mingled with the howls of a small chorus of women left behind. Five squad cars, lights flashing, four TV camera crews with their vans, and a long shiny black limousine were lined up in front of the large neighborhood supermarket. The red circling turret lights created a strobe effect over the heaving crowd, which sounded like an angry flock of birds.

Farther away, a group of demonstrators carried placards and chanted, "Hell no, we won't go. Hell no, we won't go. Hell no, we won't go."

Across from the demonstrators, the cops made their own crowd. They stood in a wide-legged stance warily watching—anxious but ready. The captain was talking to a very pretty television reporter, who pointed a microphone elegantly at his chin. A man in a three-piece pinstriped suit stepped out of the limousine into the floodlights. Television cameras rolled. Other reporters stuck microphones in his face. "What precipitated the crisis here tonight, Commissioner Mulwihill?"

"Well, Ruth," he began, as if he knew the reporter well, "these projects have been an administrative nightmare for over a decade. A few years ago the city decided to shut them down and the land was sold to a developer. The tenants were advised back then that eventually we would relocate them. Now the time is here and they refuse to go. Tonight vandals tampered with the elevators in building 14. That's why this terrible accident happened." He looked up from the microphone, directly into the camera. "The protest has to end. It's dangerous."

The reporter turned to face the camera. "This protest may have cost a life here tonight. When Mrs. Cruz and her three-year-old daughter entered the elevator in building 14, it began to move prematurely.

UNDERCOVER

The child was caught in the door as the elevator began to go up and was very seriously injured. While trying to pull her daughter from the elevator's grip, Mrs. Cruz was also hurt. Only moments ago both mother and child were rushed to Bellevue Hospital. The mood of area residents is grim. From Avenue D, this is Ruth Winslow."

As soon as the reporter signed off, the crowd began to engulf the commissioner and his limousine. The reporter was left outside the crush, and instructed her crew to keep shooting.

"You lying son of a bitch, the elevators in these buildings have always been fucked up!"

"It don't have nothing to do with the protest."

"Hang the fucking guy by his balls."

The crowd was crazy with anger. The commissioner rushed to his limo. He only made it back because Errol and I stood firm between him and the arms that reached out in rage. But the mob closed in on us and now I was being crushed against the limo. The crowd began to rock the limo, and I could just make out the commissioner's expression, somewhere between terror and disbelief. I wondered why he had come to this neighborhood in the first place.

Then Errol stuck that damn bullhorn of his into my hands. "Here." he said. "A woman's voice will be more soothing."

That's when I began to rap my ass off. I was in the middle of saying that violence would only defeat their cause when I heard a gun go off somewhere behind me. It sounded like the Fourth of July, and then the screaming began as the crowd began to stampede. People fell, tripped over each other and got up to run some more. In moments Errol and I were alone by the limo. The news crews had moved across the street to film the stampede. Behind us a cop returned his gun to his holster. He had ignored the prohibition against warning shots. Errol had a sickly look on his face as I sadly handed him the bullhorn. He wiped the sweat from his brow in a quick angry move. He avoided facing the captain and the mass of bluecoats behind us and tugged disdainfully on his jacket. "Sometimes I hate this uniform," he said.

I couldn't take my eyes off Errol's twisted face. For once we were in complete agreement. As the captain approached, I listened to the sound of running feet on gravel and heard the electronic whiz of the limo window as it opened. "Nice try, young lady," I heard the commisioner say.

"In a few hours this little show of power will percolate into guerrilla warfare," Errol said as anguish, his version of anger, clouded his usually sparkling eyes. I didn't know how to comfort him, so I said nothing.

In the distance a window shattered. Above us a huge crane held the waning moon in its teeth. Errol gave me an almost pleading look, as if I had the answer, and asked, "Don't these people know anything about human nature?"

"You have to show them you mean business," came the voice from the limo.

Errol kept looking at me, his face slightly green at the edges, as if he were wondering, "Where the fuck did they get this guy?"

The commissioner grabbed my arm and looked to me for confirmation. "There was no choice," he said with sinister satisfaction.

I was spared answering him by the captain's arrival. He patted me on the back. "Nice try, Officer. But you can't talk to these animals." Then he bent toward the limo window. "Close call, huh George. Maybe you better tell Hizzoner to get another trouble shooter."

"Just keep on watching my back, Harry." The commissioner and the captain shook hands. Then Mulwihill's expression soured as he studied the camera crews across the street. "Those bastards look like they're settling in for the night. How do you think this is gonna play?" he asked.

The captain leaned on the stretch and pushed his cap back. "Look, we're out here keeping the peace and we're gonna be out here for as long as it takes."

"Okay. I'm heading up to Bellevue now to see the people who were injured because of the vandals."

"Yeah, those vandals," the captain slapped the limo with a flat palm and shook his head. "They started this whole thing. We'll just have to do the best we can, George."

The two men shook hands. They had closed ranks and both felt better. Then in the blink of an eye, the commissioner's self-assurance returned as he ordered his driver to pull out.

The captain watched the limo drive off and cursed. "Goddamn these savages," he said. "You men are reassigned to this sector for the night."

Errol looked at his watch. "Captain, our shift's over in twenty minutes."

"There ain't no regular hours until this thing is over, son. You and your partner are gonna hafta stay."

He didn't wait for Errol's answer before heading off to talk to the other cops. "We're sitting ducks," Errol said, as if thinking out loud.

I followed his eyes to the rooftops and the many dark windows along the avenue. "What next?" I asked.

An eerie stillness was my answer. Nothing moved. The world seemed suddenly empty. It was almost midnight, and a fog of fatigue descended over me. I looked off toward the river and wondered where all the people had gone. The crane above held the paralyzed moon and seemed ready to devour us too. Errol broke the silence. "Let's get some coffee and cigarettes."

We headed for the all-night Chinese takeout on the corner. For some reason I was thinking about the garden that would grow on East Fourth Street and all the good stuff we had accomplished in just a few short weeks. I turned to Errol with sudden hope. "These people aren't gonna hurt you. They know you care about them."

He gave me a wistful, longing look. "You really believe that, Toni?"

I didn't actually answer him. I just shook my head because I knew like he did that the darkness held a rage that could not see past the uniform to the face.

We spent the rest of that night cruising Avenue D. At around two in the morning the all-news radio station reported the death of Nydia Cruz, the little girl in the elevator. She had never made it through surgery. Her skull had been too badly crushed. The mother, her hand amputated, was unconscious. As the report came over the air we passed the place where the first of the project buildings had already been demolished.

A huge pit signaled the beginning of the end of the projects. Hour after hour, we circled the sector, passing that pit over and over again. Though night gradually gave way to a gray dawn, the blackness in the pit didn't lift. It held on to itself like a darkness so deep that no dawn is possible. Errol and I were wrapped in stillness. Frozen in my mind was a picture of agony—mother and child.

When we finally returned, the station house was alive with morning activity, the sound of laughter and lollygagging laced with the smell of freshly brewed coffee. I grabbed a cup but my fingers could barely close on its handle. I switched hands and let Errol pour for me as he was doing for himself, but he was shaky too. Around us a dozen conversations blurred into one as cops mapped out their day. Untouched inside me, the stillness remained.

We descended the stairs toward the locker rooms. "Get some serious rest," Errol said.

At the foot of the stairs, in a small alcove, a locked

door caught my eye. I had never really noticed it before. "What's in there?"

"Dead files. They come in handy sometimes, whenever a new crime digs up an old one."

"Dead files?" I echoed.

He was already unbuttoning his shirt. We both stood there bleary-eyed, each ready to walk off in different directions.

"Not much use if you can't get in to study them, is it?"

Errol yawned. "Oh, you can get in. The sarge has the key, and you just sign out what you need." As he unbuckled his garrison belt, he seemed to wake up again just long enough to ask, "Why? What you got in mind?"

I watched that vee come and go in the center of his forehead and shrugged nonchalantly. "Nothing. Locked doors arouse my curiosity."

"Want a ride home?"

"No thanks."

He slouched toward the men's locker room slow as an old man. As soon as he disappeared from sight, my whole body tingled with a surge of adrenalin that shot through me like an electric charge just under my skin. I hurried back to the sarge's elevated desk, which looked like a longer version of a judge's bench. I stood looking up at the sarge. "I lost my women's room key. Have you got a pass key?"

He glowered down at me and then winked. "Is it an emergency?"

I did a little hop skip from one foot to the other, then reached my hand up to him. "It sure is, Joe."

He handed me a jagged wad of keys on a chain heavy enough to be a weapon. "It's on there. You'll have to find out which one."

As I descended the stairs again, my heart fell into the pit of my stomach. My head throbbed, my calves ached, there was a gulch in my chest where my lungs should have been. I was breathless, as if I were climbing instead of descending. I began trying the keys, one after the other. Some didn't fit at all. Some fit but didn't turn. Beads of sweat grew on my upper lip and my fingers trembled. Suddenly, I felt trapped in an unbearable heat, and time became long, slow, and anguished. I began to feel I would never find the right key. I was still trying when Errol put his hand on my shoulder.

"What are you doing?"

He seemed very different out of uniform. "I'm looking for a . . ." My voice caught in my throat and refused to finish the sentence. The truth is, I didn't know what I was doing.

He helped me. "Clue?" he said.

I began nodding my head like a broken doll. "Yeah, about past violence in the projects. Maybe we can find out who the vandals were."

His eyes widened in surprise, the rest of his face too tired for expression. Then he gave an exasperated sigh. "You really believe that shit about the vandals?"

"Don't you?"

His shoulders came up and fell back down, "It's a cover-up. Maintenance in those projects has been non-existent for years. Today's elevator accident wasn't the first. They want those people out, so they're not giving any services. Not even the minimum. I thought you knew that."

Just then I felt a key begin to turn in the lock. I pulled it out. Errol continued, "Besides, those files are organized by name and date. You have to know what you're searching for."

What was I searching for? Errol was looking at me with a distant kind of pity, and tears came to my eyes. His tired face softened, and he tried to fold me in his friendly arms. I flinched and he withdrew quickly into words. I heard a tenderness in him I had not heard before. "Don't feel bad," he said softly. "You're just overtired and frustrated. You wanna do good and you don't know how. This job will do that. It happens to the best."

I sniffed and smiled, recovering my composure. "I guess you're right." But he was being so kind I didn't know what to do. In my palm, separate from the others, I held the key.

"Let me drop you off? You don't have to be tough all the time."

"Thanks, but I need to walk. I'm too wound up to sleep and walking always helps."

"Okay then." He disappeared wearily up the stairs, tall and lean in his jeans. I returned to the women's locker room and removed the key from the chain. It took a while because I had to take a lot of other keys off first. Then I changed and returned the batch of keys, minus one, to the sarge. I put them in his hand. "Thanks, Joe, you saved my ass."

"Anytime." He laughed.

I went to Second Avenue and made a duplicate of the key to the dead files. Then I returned to the station house. "Hey Joe, I left my house keys in the john."

He shook his head. "Dames," he said as he handed me the keys a second time. I returned to the locker room, placed the original key in its original spot, and then returned the bunch to the sarge. The duplicate safely in my pocket, I returned home. Taking that key was a move I would soon regret.

CHAPTER FOUR

The portal was shaped like a key, and Kelly waited for me on the other side. When my feet didn't move, I looked down and saw the ball and chain. I pulled forward with all my might and moved slowly, my ankles bleeding, toward the gate. I saw her face. She reached out with beautiful hands. I strained toward her healing touch until a scream cut through me, once and then twice.

My hand picked up the telephone receiver, and the ringing stopped. I waited, halfway between dreaming and waking, until I heard "Toni? Toni, it's Errol."

I looked at the clock. It was two in the afternoon. In my clenched fist I held the key.

"What's up?"

"Things have calmed down in the precinct. No more double shifts for a while. In fact, we're changing tours. You don't have to report for work until eight tomorrow morning."

A gray semidarkness made the room seem small and very old. The venetian blinds were drawn, and the summer sun sliced around their edges, casting its rays like sharp prison bars. I was having trouble focusing on who and where I was. There was another long moment of silence while I tried to shake off the dream and find my voice.

"Are you all right?" he asked.

I nodded as if he could see me, then said, "Sure. See you in the morning."

He seemed to be waiting for me to say something more, but I didn't. "Okay then," he said, and the line went dead.

I lay there watching the dust swirl in shafts of sunlight, afraid to go back to sleep and afraid to fully wake up. I was thinking about the locked door to the dead files. Now I would have to wait another full shift before using my key. But it didn't really matter whether I got in today, tomorrow, or the next day. I remembered Lenny's sad face that night in the park and thought about Errol's words. It made no sense that the man I had once loved so much was now a dope dealer.

I slept through the day and the night. When I awoke the next morning, Mary was already sitting at the table with the *Daily News*. I knew she had felt me wake up but we both remained silent.

"Returning to the living?" she finally said.

"Reluctantly," I answered as I rose to totter toward the coffee.

I dropped a slice of bread into the toaster and poured some hot water over two spoonfuls of Savarin.

"I'm too old for double shifts," I mumbled.

She threw her head back and laughed, her long neck momentarily lost in red locks that crawled all around her shoulders.

"I'm not mad at you anymore," she said with a smile as she traced the ridge of her cup with a finger. "I realize you had nothing to do with me being assigned to the 166th. And if you choose to work in the asshole of the universe, well then . . ." She opened her palms and spread her hands. I went over to the window to crack the venetian blinds and peer at the morning.

"What about it?" I said, turning to meet her sparkling gaze.

"Then it's your prerogative."

As we made our truce, a truck belched its way toward Seventh Avenue, and a shopkeeper unlocked his many locks. At the fruit stand neat rows of apples, oranges, grapes, bananas, and watermelon offered the sweet taste of summer juices. The Korean owner negotiated with his first customer of the morning. I saw their lips move but heard no words. The air conditioner obliterated all sounds from the street with its incessant whir. I watched the shopkeeper remove the final padlock and push back the gate. Then I pulled up the blind.

Mary covered her eyes as if the sun had slapped her in the face. "Was that necessary?"

"Were you at the riot on Avenue D last night?"

She shook her head. "But I heard what happened, and I'll be stationed there today. That's why they changed our tour."

"How's Sevinsky?" I asked.

She got up and headed for the bathroom. "I'm gonna hop in the shower," she said, pulling her shirt over her head. And then, just before she stepped through the doorway, she turned to face me. "Why? You interested?"

I practically burned my tongue on my coffee. "Should I be?"

She puckered her whole face into a tight, lined little ball. "Only if you're into psychos."

"Then why ask if I'm interested?"

She raised her shoulders to her wrinkled face as if not quite knowing the whole intent behind her question.

"I dunno," she said. "It's just that you two are always asking about each other."

My arm twitched a little as I put my cup down, and

some coffee spilled on the table. Across the room I saw the key glisten on my pillow. By the time I managed, "You're kidding?" I heard the rush of the shower begin.

That morning Mary and I took the Fourteenth Street crosstown together. We were running late, so we both rushed to change. I hadn't finished getting into my uniform when a fist banged on the locker room door. At first neither of us answered. Then I heard, "Hey, Conroy, the captain wants to see you. Now!"

"Coming," I yelled, rough and loud like one of them.

"Animals, aren't they?" Mary smirked.

I put my hand in my pocket where the key lay cool and still. Inside me everything was going haywire. There was a hammer in my head and a lead weight in my gut. I was afraid that the fear would register on my face and speak through my eyes, so I tensed my muscles and tried to lock my face.

"Since when are you scared of these fucks?" Mary asked, as if she could see straight through me.

"I'm not," I said, trying to calm myself by concentrating on what I planned to accomplish as a cop.

"Well, get your ass up there and find out what he wants."

My knuckles hit the old wooden door in several short hard knocks.

"It's open," the captain grunted.

The worn door creaked as it swung back at the push of my hand. I closed it behind me then stood, waiting to be asked further into the room. The captain was shuffling some papers on his desk and didn't look up. Rotund, Irish, and ruddy, he sat behind his gray government-issue desk like a Buddha in uniform. He was chomping on a cigar, and its pungent smell filled my nostrils. I stood there studying the unwashed window behind his head. Raindrops had made rivulets through years of soot. The phone rang and he picked it up.

"Tell Hizzoner we're handling it. And I don't need Mulwihill down here again. That only stirs the shit, and next thing I know I have six camera crews looking over my shoulder. Can't you City Hall bigwigs get it through your heads that sometimes no PR is the best PR? . . . yeah . . . yeah. I'll keep you posted."

He threw the receiver onto the hook, and then from under two unruly eyebrows he looked at me. "Come in, Officer."

I took a few steps closer to the desk. He puffed long and hard on his cigar. "How long have you been with us?"

I looked at my watch as if it could tell me something. "Three weeks, sir."

"Alright, Conroy, let me level with you. When they first told us we were gonna hafta have women officers I was against it." He stood up and came toward me. "You wanna know why, Officer?"

What was I going to say? "No sir. I don't give a fuck, sir." I looked dead ahead and thought about what the uniform meant to me and answered, "Yes sir. I do, sir."

"Would you like me to demonstrate?"

I figured I might as well know his whole game now because I was a dead duck anyway. So I said, "Yes sir. I would, sir."

"Well, step over to this wall here."

When I had my back to the wall, the captain grabbed me by the throat and pushed up until my feet almost left the floor. I was on my toes; my eyes burned. His cigar smoke was like a cocoon around my head, and I couldn't cough. Anyway, I didn't want to. I wanted to stand there as if I didn't notice that he was choking me.

"Now, Officer, if somebody was choking you like I am now, think about this, who would you trust to rescue you? Somebody like you, or a man like me?"

It took me a few seconds to get it. I fantasized about decking him, kicking him in the balls, or just plain spitting in his dumb eye. But I whispered. "You sir. You're obviously stronger than I am. If I were in trouble I would want someone like you to rescue me. Not someone like me." I stopped short of saying "not a woman."

He let go. When my feet landed, I stepped around him and out of the circle of smoke. I was dimly wondering if the demonstration had any purpose beyond his fun. The captain headed back to his desk, his satisfied gut bouncing over his belt.

"Now Conroy," he began, "you're Irish, you're one of us. I wanna give you the benefit of the doubt. How do you explain your behavior?"

I rubbed my neck as he glared across the desk at me. In my pocket the key was burning a hole in my thigh. Was it all over? Did he know? I stalled my response with a coughing fit. I was grasping, unable to find an answer, when the door opened. There was Errol. He had never looked better. His hair was all shiny and golden.

"You sent for me, sir?" he asked the captain.

"That's right, you dumb Polack. You and that partner of yours are giving me a hotfoot."

"Sir?" Errol's jaw locked, his face got whiter. His long frame became rigid as a statue. His legs seemed to grow from the ground. He was as cold as a block of ice. This made the captain even more angry. After a short but brutal silence during which he found his next line of attack, the captain huffed and puffed around Errol like a dog looking for a spot to piss. I was halfway expecting him to raise his leg when he starting shaking his finger at Errol's face. He was a lot shorter than Errol, and it looked as if his finger might go right up one of Errol's nostrils. From across the room Errol's gaze locked with mine, and I tried hard to ignore the spark of laughter in his eyes. I was so relieved to be out of the spotlight that the scene did seem comic, except that Errol's dignity was getting a little bruised.

Finally, the captain turned crimson, grunted, wheeled around, and pointed at me. "Do you know why the mayor's office calls me three times a day?"

It was like the sixty-four thousand dollar question except that I didn't know the answer. "No sir, I don't, sir."

He turned back to Erroll. "Got a thing for bullhorns, son?"

Errol and I stared at each other, both realizing the captain's rage had something to do with our cleanup program on Fourth Street. But the explanation took us by surprise.

The captain started strutting like a Nazi on parade. "You both must know they're going to start shooting the Mafia movie any day now." He stopped and looked at Errol, then at me.

"Yes, sir!" we chimed.

"You know the mayor's office wants that area free of junkies and street vermin. You were told that."

"Yes sir."

"Well then, I only have a few more questions." He smiled sourly. "Would either of you happen to have any idea where the fifty junkies who just relocated on East Sixth Street came from?"

Errol looked at me and I looked at him, and then we both looked at the fat little captain, who flailed his arms helplessly, like a bird that can't fly. I controlled an hysterical attack of laughter while Errol's eyes twinkled suspiciously.

"All the goshdamn junkies from Fourth Street set up housekeeping on Sixth Street," the captain continued, his voice growing high and shrill. "You and that fucking bullhorn of yours."

"Sir, there's a school on Fourth Street. I felt that . . ."

"Fuck what you felt. Don't feel. You wanna feel, be a social worker. I told you that before, son. Now get rid of that damn bullhorn and start sweeping up. I wanna see collars and I want Sixth Street clean."

He dismissed us and we left quickly. We were already late to roll call, so there was no time to talk. But my heart pounded at the thought of my first collar.

Later in the car Errol was rigidly silent. I began to fidget. I was so anxious to begin sweeping junkies that I was afraid it showed. While I was shifting my weight in the seat, he turned to me. "I guess you're finally gonna make those junkie collars."

"I'm not happy about the way it happened."

He softened a little. "Don't get too excited. Nine times out of ten, for a bluecoat, a junkie collar just means a loitering collar. It's a lousy misdemeanor—loitering for the purpose of buying or using drugs. What else are you gonna get them for? You're not undercover, you can't investigate. You only get the obvious or a fluke that falls into your lap."

Because I planned to get around this monkey suit and be creative, I didn't argue with him. I just changed the subject and told him my story about the captain.

"The captain's a trip, ain't he?" Errol said.

"Sexist too."

"Son of a bitch really pinned you to the wall, huh?" he chuckled.

I stared out the window, unaccustomed to the morning rhythm, frustrated at the thought of trying to collar a junkie in broad daylight, and wondering if I should confront Errol now and ask him not to be so by-the-book. Instead I asked, "When do we go back on night tour?"

"Probably next week. Son of a bitch really pinned you to the wall, huh." Errol shook his head in disbelief.

"He doesn't know he's messing with a brown belt in tae kwon do."

"No shit!" Errol gave me a sideways look. "You never told me that."

"Masters aren't supposed to go around advertising their skills," I said as I examined my hands.

I saw a smile play on his lips. "Yeah, but I'm your leader. I should know these things."

"Partner," I corrected him. "We're equals—you've just been at it longer."

I felt a curious mixture of camaraderie and competition between us and suddenly found myself liking him more than before. I felt for the key in my pocket. The sky was a clear cloudless blue, and I felt hope open my heart in a way I had forgotten.

"Why don't you drive today? Take advantage of the day tour to get used to the wheel," Errol said as he pulled up to the curb.

"Are you sure?" I asked.

He opened the door on his side. "Yeah, I feel safer with those deadly hands of yours occupied."

As he walked around to my side of the car, I slid behind the wheel and moved the seat so that I could more comfortably reach the pedals. The truth is, I was a little nervous. Although I had my license, I had gotten it just before entering the Academy and had little driving experience. Errol slammed the door and smiled broadly at me. "Worried, sensei?"

"I ain't no sensei," I said sharply because I didn't want him to know that I was scared.

"All right." He pushed his cap back. "Just concentrate on the driving. It's still early, the junkies are still snoozing, people haven't been awake long enough to cook up any schemes or get really hostile."

"Yes sir, Dr. Freud."

It was a quiet morning, and I became gradually comfortable behind the wheel. Errol was feeling mellow too, and his small talk seemed to be getting more and more personal. I decided to cut him off by doing the asking.

"How are we supposed to make junkie collars in broad daylight? We can't come in without a few collars, can we?"

"I'm not going to invent a collar just to keep the captain happy," he said sourly. "But let's start making our presence felt on Sixth Street."

I turned right on Avenue A and headed for the make-believe Little Italy. Paramount had stationed twenty-four-hour security guards up and down the block. False fronts had been placed on most of the buildings, and Sixth Street genuinely looked like Little Italy in the twenties. I was cruising slowly, watching as workmen continued the transformation. I didn't see a single junkie, there was no loitering going on, and even the block's residents, rushing to work, politely avoided the Paramount crews. I wondered aloud, "What the fuck is the captain talking about? There's nothing happening on this block."

"We're on the wrong tour. The junkies are probably sleeping in there somewhere," Errol said, pointing to a building mid-block that had the facade of a mom-and-pop real estate operation.

"Why there?"

"That's an abandoned building that's connected to several other buildings by its basement. It would be the logical place for them to set up shop."

"You wanna go in?"

He shook his head no.

That was when I got mad. I parked the car. "Our orders are to sweep this block. If you don't go in there with me, I'm going in by myself."

"On what charge? On what charge are you gonna arrest a bunch of sleeping dope fiends?"

"Possession," I said sourly. But I knew that I was wrong.

"You'll get thrown out of court."

"I'll charge them with loitering."

"Indoors?"

"C'mon Stutz, cut the crap. This isn't a civil liberties course. We need these collars. We need to keep the captain happy."

"Where were you when they were teaching the basics at the Academy?" he questioned patronizingly.

I got out. He followed.

"C'mon," I said, "you know between the two of us we can come up with a way to make it stick. But we gotta get them first." I looked up and down the empty street, desperate for a way to convince him. "We could say we followed one guy in."

"Alter the facts?"

He squinted at me as if I were from Mars. And that made me madder because I knew that he was right. He played with his garrison belt, then snuck a peek at the rooftops before meeting my eyes. "Boy, I learned a lot about you today." He shook his head like a disappointed father. "You're out here looking for trouble and just because you want to kiss the captain's ass, you're willing to bend the law."

He was glowering at me, and I wasn't sure if he was pissed or amused. That, of course, made me even madder. But before I could launch into my next line of attack, I spotted a guy climbing out of a top floor window onto a fire escape. At first I thought he was a workman, but a second look told me he was too greasy, too sneaky to be legit. Errol and I stopped yelling at each other and watched the man decend from the sky like the answer to our argument.

"Right into your arms, baby," Errol smirked. "Lick your chops. He's all yours."

"Probable cause, counselor?" I asked Errol, and his eyes told me that the moment was mine.

We ran across the street to where the fire escape ended a few feet above the sidewalk, and when the guy landed I was ready. His feet hit the pavement not two feet from mine.

"Freeze," I said.

He froze.

"Whose apartment is that?"

"It's mine," he said. "I lost my keys so I hadda come out the window." He had the face of a boy, a boy so scared he didn't move a muscle. His big brown eyes popped froglike from his skinny face. His shirt was dirty and torn, his jeans full of holes. He seemed very young to be so down and out. But then I saw the tracks on his arms. My heart was pounding; I felt my face flush.

"What's your name?" Errol asked. His voice was very cold.

"Larry Baker."

"Let's go take a look." Errol said.

"Larry Baker," the junkie repeated as if to hold the moment still.

"Do you wanna tell us what we're gonna find when we get up there?" I asked. "It'd be better for you."

Baker remained silent.

As we began walking, I felt Errol change. It was like we switched parts. I'd been dying for a collar, but now I felt bad for Baker; and Errol, who had played the philosopher about right and wrong, became all cop. He was acting mean and ugly, but I had seen enough movies to figure he was playing good-cop, bad-cop. I tried to put Baker at ease so he would feel comfortable spilling his guts. I figured he must know about the abandoned building, which possibly housed a shooting gallery.

"It would be better for you if you talk now," I said.

Errol growled at me. "Don't bother with this fuck. I wanna see him put away and put away good."

As we entered the building and climbed the stairs, Baker was so quiet he seemed to be holding his breath.

"Maybe it's his first offense and I can help him out," I tried. But the junkie didn't say anything. There was a raw terror in his eyes that made me pity him despite myself. Errol's face was locked like a steel door, his eyes narrow and icy. He shoved the junkie up the stairs.

Baker started to cry.

"I didn't kill her. I swear to God I didn't touch her." Errol and I looked at each other. The apartment was only one flight away.

"I used to carry her groceries and stuff upstairs for her. When I didn't see her for a few days, I climbed in through the window. She's dead in there. She was dead when I walked in."

Errol kicked open the door, and a terrifying smell enveloped us. The apartment was a neat little railroad flat. We passed through the kitchen first. A loaf of bread soaking in a dish of milk had turned a moldy green. I covered my nose and mouth with my hand and followed the hall to the bedroom.

She lay on the bed very white and very still. She was covered by a quilt, and the sun cast the pattern of the old lace curtains across her bed, covering her in phantom roses, roses with no stems, roses with no thorns, just blossoms scattered over the quilt, over her face, and over her thin, pale hands.

I kept one of my hands tightly over my nose, with the other I held my prisoner by the arm. Errol held him too, and it was a good thing because Baker was shaking from head to toe. I was so busy trying to figure out how she could look so peaceful and smell so bad that I almost forgot why I was there. The three of us stood there hypnotized, like worshipers before an alter, when Errol broke the silence. "Mirandize him, you got a possible homicide."

Baker got heavier on my arm. I felt his knees

buckle. I didn't see how it was a possible homicide because the old woman looked so peaceful. Still, I knew it would be stupid to question Errol now. I let my prisoner go and took my hand off my nose while I pulled my wallet from my back pocket. I thought the stench was going to knock me out. I fumbled around with dollar bills for a while before finding the card. The letters swam before my eyes, but I read Baker his rights. The words droned one into the other. I listened to the tremor in my voice and watched Baker shake. After I asked him if he had understood, he whispered yes and started crying again, quietly this time.

I went through Baker's pockets and came up with two antique-looking rings and sixty dollars. Errol radioed the sergeant on patrol. Baker shook his head back and forth.

"Oh shit," he moaned. "Oh shit, you gotta believe me. She was already dead."

"Where'd you get this stuff?" I asked, pulling out my pad to take notes.

"Over there." He pointed to a dish on the bureau by her bed. The dish was shaped like a chicken sitting on an egg. She was there too, reflected in the bureau mirror, serene as a portrait. A chill went up my spine. Baker kept crying and moaning. His nose was beginning to run. I took my cuffs off my belt. He didn't even wait for me to tell him anything. He just put his hands behind his back. His hands were dirty, the fingernails bitten to the quick. The cuffs clicked loudly and then it was quiet.

I was getting nauseous and hoped Errol didn't notice. It seemed like the three of us had been standing there forever, when I heard the sarge bounding heavily up the stairs.

"Holy shit," he said as he stood in the open doorway. "That's some smell." He walked right past the suspect to the stiff's bedside. "She must be rotting under there." Then he turned to Errol. "You're right, possible homicide. I'm gonna get forensic over here. You can take the suspect back to the precinct."

As we went back down the stairs, I started to breathe again. But I didn't feel good. All these weeks I had been wanting to collar a junkie so I could make him pay for messing up the neighborhood by being a lousy dope fiend. And now that I had one, I was sick about it and I didn't know why. Maybe it was because he was so scared. When we left the tenement Baker flinched, as if the sun had slapped him in the face, and at that moment I remembered Brian. I remembered his suffering, how greasy he had become when at just fifteen he had started messing with skag. I remembered how many times he had tried to come clean. How it had never worked. And I remembered finally locking him into my apartment and refusing to let him out until he had kicked. But drug addicts are so sneaky that he had gone back on the needle without so much as a hint. When I remembered that, my hate came back to me and I felt a lot tougher. By the time we got back to the station house, I was ready to use the collar for all the information I could get.

We took him upstairs to the squad room, but all the detectives were out. I told him to sit down and put a UF 61 into the rickety old typewriter on one of the detective's desks. As I started filling out the arrest report, Errol called me aside.

"Listen, I don't want him to hear me, so I'm going downstairs to talk to the DA and call BCI for his priors. You're doing good. Once I leave he might really open up to you."

I wondered what, if anything, the Bureau of Criminal Investigations would have on this kid.

"You don't really think he killed the old lady, do you?" I asked.

I saw Errol's face soften for the first time that morning. "What's the difference? You got your first collar."

"It just doesn't seem likely," I said. "Did you smell that stink? She's been dead a couple of days. Why would he return to the scene of the crime?" I felt like my uniform was suffocating me. My discomfort brought a twinkle to his eyes.

"That's the DA's decision, not yours. Besides, you got a much better chance of grilling him as long as he's scared shitless." He winked and turned to leave, so that there was nothing else I could say.

I turned back to Baker. He was leaking like a faucet now and he was shivering. It began to dawn on me that he was sick for the cure. I sat down behind the typewriter and asked the routine questions. He had no home address and no matter what I asked him, he punctuated his answer with, "I'm a burglar, I ain't no murderer."

Finally, he told me he had been arrested for burglary three times before and that he had done eighteen months on Rikers Island.

"Well, you ain't gonna get no eighteen months on this charge," I told him. I took the cuffs off him so he could blow his nose. When he was through, I cuffed one of his hands to the heating pipe near his chair.

"What do you know about that shooting gallery down the block from you?"

"Nothing," he sniffed.

"Don't hand me that. You're a dope fiend and you're gonna sit there and tell me you don't know what's happening on your own block?"

He rubbed his cuffed wrist with his free hand. "That group just started hanging out there a couple of weeks ago. It's just a place where down-and-outers can shoot up and fall out. It ain't a factory or nothing."

"You know a guy named Cobra?"

He buried his face in a bunch of tissues, blew his nose hard, and shook his head. But his whole body tensed. It tensed so much he stopped shaking.

I asked him again. He blew his nose once more and wouldn't meet my eyes. I knew I was on to something.

"Yes, you do," I said softly. "There isn't a junkie in this neighborhood who doesn't know about Cobra."

"I heard of him like everybody else but I never seen him. He don't let nobody see him."

"Cigarette?"

His eyes were watering. He nodded his head. I lit two cigarettes and handed him one. He sucked long and desperately, then coughed as if he had a coal mine in his young lungs. Then, I played a hunch. Maybe he could lead me to Brian's pusher—the one who sold that last dose that had caused Kelly's death.

"If you tell me what I wanna know, I'll talk to the DA. I'll tell him it looks like a burglary to me."

His face brightened then clouded. "I ain't gonna be no stoolie."

"I'm not asking you to be a stoolie. I just need a little info for another case I'm working on."

"Stoolies die young," he whispered.

"You know a kid named Brian Conroy?"

He bit his cigarette so hard I thought it was going to snap in two. "He's been dead a long time."

My heart hammered. I felt it throb in my neck and twitch in the corner of my eye. "How did he die?"

"I dunno. The grapevine had it he caught an overdose."

"C'mon," I said crushing my cigarette underfoot. "You gotta give on something, or I can't help you."

He wiped the dripping snot from his nose with a finger. "Brian had a girlfriend called Sunny. She was a real pretty girl until he got her going on skag."

His words were like a knife in my chest. "He got her on the stuff?"

"Yeah," he nodded. A tear ran down the side of his nose, not because he was crying but because his sickness was getting worse. "She's up in Harlem now hustling her ass. She hangs out on 103rd Street at a joint called Robert's Place."

"What do you know about Lenny da Rosa?"

"Nothing. I ain't never heard of him."

"He runs the Dragon."

"Guys like me don't get into places like that."

I was going to get a description of Sunny, but I heard Errol's footsteps on the stairs. He came in huffing.

"BCI says this kid's got a yellow sheet as long as my arm, three prior arrests for burglary."

"Yeah," I said. "He told me that. But he's not a killer."

Errol was annoyed. "The DA will decide that. Let's go, buddy. We're going down to Central Booking."

CHAPTER FIVE

It was after midnight when I got back to the station house. After walking me through my first booking at 100 Centre Street, Errol had left me waiting to get my prisoner before the judge. Six hours later Baker had been charged with burglary and given $100,000 bail, pending the autopsy report. I finally had my first collar. I headed down the stairs to the dead files as if I were still working on my case.

I inserted my key, and the door creaked slowly open. Inside it was dark, and a musty smell grabbed me by the throat. I fumbled for a light switch and found none. Searching blindly with my hands, I took a couple of steps into the room until a string touched my face. I grabbed it and pulled. Above, the naked lightbulb clicked on and swung to and fro. File cabinets surrounded me. I closed the door.

I didn't have to look far to find a drawer labeled C, and in fact, there were several cabinets of C's. I assumed the case would be filed under Conroy. The drawer screeched on rusty hinges as I pulled it open. It was stacked tight. I fingered through the files until I found a bunch of Conroys. Then I found it. It read *Conroy, Kelly and Brian*, and was at least half an inch thick. I took it out, shut the drawer, yanked the string killing the overhead light, and made my way out of the dank and dusty room. I went to the women's locker room, changed, then stuffed the file into the extralarge pocketbook I had brought for the occasion and took a cab home.

Mary was sound asleep. I tiptoed to the bathroom, where I could turn on the light without bothering her, and closed the door behind me. The bathroom, one of my favorite rooms in the apartment, had gray walls, hot pink tiles, and a toilet from the forties that flushed with a chain that hung from the water tank. I unzipped my jeans and sat on the floor at the tub's edge. Before actually opening the file, I lit a cigarette, just for something to do. Then, with trembling fingers, I rested the file on my knees. Finally, I opened the folder.

An index inside the front flap listed the file's contents—no arrest report but plenty of DD5's—the detective's reports—along with two autopsy reports, two protocols, forensic, the fire marshall's report, a couple of reports from the narcotics division, and half a dozen photographs.

I stared at the index for a long time. Over and over again, I ran my finger down the list, as if some secret braille would tell me what to do next. I felt the cold tile under me and the hard tub at my back. My own breathing echoed like crashing waves in my ears. The slight rush of water in the old toilet tank echoed loudly and the silence deepened. I felt myself entombed in the grief I held in the file between my hands. Suddenly, I knew I should close that file, put it back in its dusty place, and leave the past in the past. But I could not. I could not escape the compulsion to see for myself what was in there.

With clammy palms and thundering heart, I began

to leaf through the contents. Brian's toxicology report was first. It confirmed what Detective Vogel, the cop assigned to the case, had told me—that Brian had been on a speedball. The toxicology report showed both heroin and cocaine in Brian's system. I read it several times, then turned the page and found myself face to face with Kelly's charred remains. My fingers turned to ice, and I froze staring at the eight-by-ten glossy photograph of an unrecognizably burned child. I don't know how long I stayed that way before I rose on my knees, clutched the toilet bowl, and began to vomit as if I could escape my horror by throwing it up. I retched until I passed out.

When I opened my eyes, I was looking at two naked feet. At first I didn't remember anything. Then I smelled the bile and felt the hard tile against my cheek and the tight pain of a locked larynx. I sat up. Everything ached. I looked up at Mary. She stood there like a saint in a pink nightgown, the faint light of dawn drawing her face in soft ambiguous lines. Under her arm, she held the file. I got up quickly and grabbed for it. She took a step back. Tottering weakly on legs that wouldn't move, I tried again. A deep ache started up my calves, pins and needles raced in my feet.

"Don't," she said.

"I need that, it's mine." I heard a hoarse whisper rise from my throat. She shook her head in a sad compassion that made my realize how pitiful I really was.

"Take a shower," she said. "I'm gonna make us some tea. Then we'll talk."

My eyes were glued to the file under her arm. I searched the amber flecks in her hazel eyes and lost all will to resist. So I went to wash. But even the gentle whisper of the falling water did not purge that evil picture from my mind.

Later, I sat at our small round kitchen table while

Mary served me tea and toast. She sat down across from me. I didn't know where she had put the file. I didn't ask. She waited for me to say something, but I could not find my voice or any words. I brought the tea to my lips and drank. It warmed me from the inside. Finally, I met her waiting eyes and saw there that no explanations were necessary.

"I read the names on the file and looked at the toxicology report and the pictures," she began. "I didn't need to see more . . . I had no idea . . ."

My throat constricted, and my heart seemed to stop beating as one solitary tear rose and fell. I just shook my head as if to say it didn't matter anyway.

"You should have told me a long time ago," she continued softly. "I wouldn't have been so cruel. I wouldn't have treated you the way I did. I didn't know you lost your kid because of your brother's habit. No wonder you wanted to come back and wage war on dope."

I found my voice then. "I couldn't talk about it."

She leaned toward me, the loose strawberry blond hair falling to obscure her face, and her sorry smile said she understood.

"Let's talk now," she said, straightening in her chair and showing the full width of her defiant shoulders. My eyes hurt, my whole body ached.

"Talking will help," she pressed.

I placed my clammy palms on the table between us. I didn't really want to talk. I wanted to look at the DD5's. But I couldn't seem to say the words. Finally, I spoke. "Let's just take a look at what the rest of the file says."

Without taking her eyes off me, Mary got up and went to her bed. The file was right there, under her pillow. She placed it on the table between us and put her hands on top of it. I studied her long thin fingers, the perfect nails, the pattern of her veins glistening blue through the alabaster skin. Then, I raised my eyes to hers. They were fractured by a kind of pain that I had not seen there before.

I wanted her to open the file but at the same time I was afraid. I remembered my favorite instructor at the Academy telling us about a cop who was killed by his own fear. Sergeant Nardelli was a decorated World War II veteran who had been on the job for twenty years and had the awards to prove it. One day he had crawled into a huge old piece of piping as he was searching for a missing child. The pipe was full of rats. Nardelli had faced bombs, grenades, muggers, and murderers. But he had never faced his own fear. He never knew it was rats. When the rats began crawling on him, he screamed for mercy. He tried to turn back, but the route back was longer. When he finally got out, he realized that a rat was still biting deep into his wrist. A rat has more than two thousand pounds of pressure in its bite, and Nardelli's men had to chop its neck off before they could pry open its jaw. After that the sarge was never himself again. A few months later he died trying to stop a robbery. He was killed by his own gun. He let someone take it from him.

I was thinking about him as I studied Mary's eyes for a clue. Was I broken too?

Then Mary said, "I'm with you. You're not alone," and a surge of hope rose in me like the light in the darkness.

"Go ahead," I heard myself say, "open it."

"And will this help you accept what happened?"

I didn't know the answer to that, but I explained that once I knew the file existed I had to read it. That's why I had taken it. I couldn't just put it back unopened.

"All right then," she said, pulling her chair close to mine so we could look at the file together. She flipped it open and we started with the toxicology report.

Then there were a few pieces of bureaucratic bullshit and then the fire marshall's report. At least that's what the index said. But the fire marshall's report was missing. The bulk of the file consisted of reports filed by Detective Vogel. I remembered him well. He had never given me any useful information. But the file showed he had been trying. He must have interviewed the whole damn block, but no one knew anything. Or, at least, no one told him anything. But every time he interviewed someone, he submitted a report. And there were plenty of them, plenty of minute details that people on the block remembered about that night. Things like who was hanging out. Who had fought. Who was wearing what. Some remembered what they had bought at the bodega, others what they ate or drank. Everybody remembered the cold.

The index also showed that a narcotics detective had worked on the case but his name and his DD5's were missing.

"So there was a narc on this case," Mary said.

There was also an interesting interview with a woman named Bianca Navarez. One of the neighbors had once heard Lenny threatening that I couldn't leave him without paying, so Vogel had checked out Lenny's activities the night of the fire. He had gone all the way to Atlantic City to trace Lenny's steps. The DD5 said that Lenny had spent the night with Navarez. She remembered because they were fucking each other's brains out.

The pictures were next. I covered my face with my hands. "Put them away, please. I can't see them again." With my eyes closed, I heard Mary flip past the pictures. Then came Brian's autopsy report.

It was called an Autopsy Work Sheet. At first glance it looked no different than a job application, an application for credit or college, or any one of a dozen applications I had filled out in my life. But this application was a little different.

* * *

The first box read:

NAME OF DECEASED: Conroy, Brian.

The next box read:

CAUSE OF DEATH: Fracture of left
temporal bone and right third rib.
Cerebral contusions, left cerebral
and right cerebral hemispheres.
Body severely charred. No smoke in
lungs.

MANNER OF DEATH was a multiple choice question:
Natural, homicide, suicide, undetermined, unclassified, pending
further study, pending fire marshall investigation, circumstances
undetermined pending police
investigation.

The final choice was circled.

It was as if an iron fist had grabbed me by the throat.
I couldn't breathe, the letters on the page began to swim
before my eyes. I wasn't sure if I was seeing what I
thought I was seeing. The room was so quiet I could hear
Mary's breath quicken.

"Do you know what this means?" she said finally.

I couldn't even nod my head. My hands trembled
on the table, and something monstrous was biting at my
heart.

Very softly she said, "No smoke in the lungs means
the fire didn't kill him. He was dead before the fire
started."

I clung to my denial. "Maybe he died of an
overdose."

"But he had a broken rib and a crushed skull." She
stopped short of saying he was beaten to death.
Murdered.

I heard a lone car horn on the street below.

"Go on," I said. I was wrapped in a stone cold terror.

She turned the page and I heard the papers rustle. My child's autopsy report; I touched it. I touched the nervous scrawl in which her name was written. I touched the date. Then I looked at the text. The letters jumped from the page. The report read:

```
Cardiac arrest, ischemic cerebral
necrosis, third degree burns. No
smoke in lungs.
```

The Cause of Death (like Brian's) read: circumstances undetermined pending police investigation.

"Cardiac arrest," I said dumbly. "I know what that means but what's the other thing, ischemic . . ."

Mary stiffened and looked at me as if the last thing on earth she wanted to do was answer my question.

"It means . . ." and she stopped. My heart throbbed in my ears.

I tugged on her arm pleadingly. But nothing could have prepared me for the answer that I got.

"It means broken blood vessels in the eyes. . . . That's what happens when . . . you're strangled."

"Oh my God, no. . . ." I clawed at the paper, tortured by the horror of Kelly's last moments. I saw Kelly's face, her pretty face, and then the whole world stopped around me as I felt the tears sneak from my eyes. But that was all. When I finally raised my head, Mary was still sitting there.

"Are you all right?" she whispered.

I rose on shaky legs to wash my face at the kitchen sink. The pain was so profound I could hardly walk. It was as if the last two years had never happened, and I had just lost Kelly all over again. After I washed, I walked to the window. Outside, the night had passed and the city was coming to life.

I ran my fingers down the pane and formulated a plan. I would do my own investigation. Obviously what had happened to Kelly happened because she was with Brian. That hadn't changed. But now my revenge took on a face. It had a very specific focus. And my hatred had a target too. I would retrace Brian's last night, find that face, and make it pay.

I turned to Mary. "Vogel lied to me. Why would a cop on the force lie like that?"

Mary just kept shaking her head and looking at the file. "They sure covered their asses with paper."

"But there's one paper missing."

I knew she and Sevinsky were on the bodega arson that had been a live case ever since we came to the precinct. In a low tone I hit my first mark. "You could get your hands on the fire marshall's report if you wanted to."

"I'd have to start asking questions. What if my partner notices?"

"He won't if you're careful."

She didn't say yes. But she didn't say no either.

CHAPTER SIX

As that summer deepened, so did my obsession. Brian's last day, that last night—I didn't care about anything else.

Errol and I were fighting all the time. He had been right—it was almost impossible for a bluecoat to make an arrest that would lead to a conviction, and I was pissed just looking at his face. The captain just wanted Sixth Street clean for the filming. When he said "sweep the junkies," he only meant pick them up for loitering, hold on to them for the night, and then send them back to the street. Any street but Sixth Street. Once in a while a dope fiend would be holding and then you had him on possession. But chances were that he would walk, unless . . . maybe . . . if . . . he had a long yellow sheet or if he was violating parole. It was frustrating as shit. Still, I tried my best.

Night shift or day shift, I was locking them up. One conniving junkie after another playing that sympathy game, thinking that because there was a woman under the uniform they'd get a play.

But they were wrong. My need was greater than

theirs. I worked my ass off to get every one of those junkies, no matter how sleazy, no matter how crazed. I got each one alone in the squad room, under the stairs, in any corner available, and I grilled him as best I could. Even though many of them remembered Brian, nobody had any facts about his last night. Two years is a long time for a dope fiend's mind to stay clear, and I couldn't even get a lead on Brian's pusher.

I always threw in a few questions about Lenny and Cobra to see what I would come up with. Then they'd really freeze. If they knew anything, they didn't talk. Nobody admitted that they had ever even heard of Cobra. The fiends who knew Lenny just knew him as a home boy who had once run numbers but who now was out of their league. In any case, they all knew they'd walk or get ninety days tops, so the junkies had no motivation to talk.

The more frustrated I became, the meaner I got. After a couple of weeks, the evidence of my frustration began to appear on any junkie Errol left alone, even momentarily, with me. I cracked a lot of heads and made a lot of sick junkies sicker.

One night I was kicking a dope fiend up the stairs to the precinct house, when Errol's patience snapped. He grabbed me by the arm, and his fingers dug into my flesh.

"What the fuck are you doing?" I tried to pull my arm away but couldn't. "I'm not having another scene in the squad room."

"This asshole deals to school children."

Errol grabbed the door handle and hissed, "This asshole is a school kid."

My hand was twitching on my nightstick. "He's probably lying about his age. He's over twenty-one."

I wanted the perp to be an adult because if he was a juvenile he'd cop out to Daytop Village or some other halfway house and have no motivation to tell me anything about anything.

Errol opened the door. I followed the two of them inside. The kid was over twenty-one. But Errol gave me no time with him.

The kid was just one of six guys we had swept off a stoop for loitering. The other five were old-timers. Half of them weren't even dope fiends, they were winos. Usually, Errol and I would book the perps together but only one of us would actually sit through night court at 100 Centre Street.

When it was time for one of us to cut out, he adjusted his garrison belt. "I'm gonna stay tonight," he said.

"Good, I'll see you mañana."

I felt him tense up and saw his face change. He looked down at his belt with all its bullets. "No, I want you to hang tight tonight."

I tried to hide my anger by studying the way the wall met the wall in the far corner of the room. I was still catching my breath, trying to adjust to his pulling rank, when I looked back at him. He was hiding his face in some paperwork. Now I knew that something serious was up. I switched gears, the adrenaline went up, then down, all through my body, but I managed to stay cool. "Okay, no problem."

We were both bitter, fighting all the time now. I kept wanting to bend the rules so I could reconstruct Brian's last days, but Errol just wouldn't cooperate. He didn't know what was at stake, and I couldn't tell him. Besides, I was pretty sure that even if he knew, he would go by the book. Sometimes I hated him. I sat looking around that crazy night courtroom, wondering which of these people had my answer. I figured the more of them I could run through, the faster I would know. But Errol was always in the way.

As we sat in the night court hustle and bustle—

waiting wives, waiting mothers, waiting girlfriends, hungry children—Errol took his cap off his head and fondled it in his large hands. His eyes grew bigger and seemed to swallow the room. And then he asked me, "Have you ever lost anyone to skag?"

The other voices in the room blended into a flock of sound that fluttered in the background. His satisfied face said he knew me better than I thought. Then, his expression changed again as it mirrored my horror. My eyes were suddenly brimming, and he lost both his satisfaction and his desire for confirmation. Instead, he took the weight off me by answering himself. "I get it now. I finally get it."

Right about then we hit the docket. Time to get our prisoners from the bullpen into the courtroom. Errol went inside and left me alone. The night's cadre of hookers were lined up against the wall.

"Is your name Sunny?" I asked a blond.

She didn't answer. Her eyes went down to the floor, up to the ceiling, between her tits, any way but my way.

"Hey, I'm talking to you. Are you Sunny?"

"Do I look sunny to you? Goddamn, how can you be sunny in hell?" She adjusted her wares. The other hookers cackled.

After a while, Errol emerged from the bullpen and we went through the bizarre charade of night court in Manhattan—which for once had been quick and dirty. We left Centre Street and walked toward the Municipal Parking Lot. Except for the few stragglers emerging from court, Lower Manhattan was a giant graveyard. We were standing on a curb watching a rat rise from a gutter when Errol picked up the topic again.

"You want to get one of Lenny da Rosa's runners, don't you, someone whose trail you can follow to the Cobra. You want that more than anything worth wanting in life."

It felt weird to hear him talk about Lenny like that.

Fortunately, he didn't know as much as he thought he did. I didn't see much point in responding. The rat disappeared like an ugly shadow.

"You're trying to even some sort of score, aren't you?"

I stepped down into the gutter. "Look," I said, "you're gonna think what you're gonna think."

We entered the lot, found the car, and were moving before he continued. "You think that cracking junkies' heads will lead you somewhere, don't you? You think it will lead you to Cobra and that way you can a-venge . . ." He took both hands off the wheel as if to say "whatever." There was a long silence.

He was close but not really on target. "It's not really your business," I told him.

His foot jerked the accelerator ever so slightly. "You're my partner, so it is my business."

We both knew he was taking the partnership concept a little further than he had to.

"Meaning?" I said.

"Meaning I'm gonna give you a hand. I'm gonna go along with your program for a while and see what we come up with. Maybe then you'll get this mania out of your system and settle into the job."

I was trying to stay cool and keep my eyes on the beam our headlights cast on the empty street ahead, but the muscle in my chest was going rat-tat-tat. "Why?" I asked. "Why the change of heart?"

His eyes were strangely hot when he turned to face me. "I'm not sure I can answer that honestly."

I looked away and stared out at the night.

"You have to promise me one thing though," he said, his voice low.

I held my breath for the punch line. "When and if we get a runner, whether he's Cobra's or da Rosa's, we're gonna follow procedure and turn him over to the squad."

Though I was delighted that we were finally going to

get aggressive about rounding up the dope fiends, I couldn't help but ask, "What's the point? What's the point if we're gonna turn him over to the detectives?"

"The point is we're bluecoats, and we can't do our own narcotics investigation."

His body stiffened, as if he were trying to tell me, take what you can get. So I agreed. I agreed because I had to. I told myself I'd change the rules later, change the rules to suit the moment, like Lenny used to do.

For the next few weeks Errol and I questioned everybody that crossed our path, everybody. We watched each other's backs. I saw him in a new way. His gentle tenacity fascinated me. When he thought he could get an answer, he didn't let go until he got it. He was smooth on the tightrope, that fine line between scaring a guy into talking and actually doing him damage. Errol could be scary as shit but he never became abusive. He was looking for leads to the Cobra. I was looking for something smaller but more elusive. Two years was an eon in a doper's world. A lot of leads could grow cold. For me the stakes were so high that it was hard to play fair. Still, neither of us came up with anything.

One night I took about twenty bags of skag from a junkie and I just kept them. They were tied together by a rubber band. The junkie kept quiet because to him it meant loitering, not possession. After that, I always had the bundle on me when we were on tour. Whenever I got a dope fiend alone, I'd show him the bundle and tell him to talk—otherwise his loitering charge might mysteriously grow into possession. More than one man fell for it. But one night the technique backfired.

I was alone in the squad room with this old-timer when I tried to run my number on him. He started screaming and hollering in Spanish. I couldn't shut him up. Every once in a while he'd throw in some English. Some very incriminating English. He screamed like a six-year-old having a tantrum.

UNDERCOVER

"No yo no aguanto eso . . . I haff no drugs. I haff no drugs."

He was so loud and went on for so long that a couple of the men came upstairs. One of them was the sarge. I shoved the bundle under some paperwork.

"This man giving you a hard time, Conroy?" The sarge fingered his holster.

I was about to give him the "everything under control" routine when the junkie opened up in perfect English, "She is trying to plant some heroin on me. *Mira. Mira.*" He pointed to the stack of papers that hid the bundle. Nobody moved. The junkie pulled the bundle into view. The sarge and the men looked at the bundle, at me, and then at each other.

"He had it on him," I said firmly.

"I deed not. I deed not," the junkie whined.

I gave him my coldest stare. "I guess because I'm a woman he thinks he can play games."

The junkie's voice went up an octave. "She ees lie. She ees lie."

The sarge scratched his bald spot looking for an approach to the dilemma. Who to believe? A woman in uniform or a junkie? His loyalties were torn. He hated women cops but he loved the uniform. What if the junkie were telling the truth? It might be his chance to get rid of a woman in uniform. It was a tough one, so the sarge took his time.

"I found that bundle on him when we first picked him up," a familiar voice said. I couldn't take my eyes off Errol as he lied for me. I hadn't even seen him come in.

"Shit, why didn't you say so," the sarge said, before he and the other men backed off toward the stairs. "And don't leave her alone with this asshole—lock him up."

We put the junkie in the cage together and then just stood there. It was about nine-thirty and the squad room was unusually quiet. Errol walked over to one of the filthy windows as if he could see out. I followed him over and whispered, "Thanks."

"It's not over yet," he said. "We're gonna have to stick to this stupid lie all through night court, and who knows where it will end."

We had to talk low to make sure they couldn't hear us in the cage. As I repeated my thanks, I realized just how far he had gone for me—he had risked his badge.

"Why did you do it?" I whispered guiltily.

His blue eyes churned violet and silver and opened like a book. "I care about you."

I looked away.

All through the night court the junkie protested his innocence. But because he was like a thousand others, no one listened. We brought him before the judge on possession, and he pleaded innocent. He couldn't make bail, so kicking and screaming, they dragged him away.

When it was over, neither of us said much of anything. I knew it was time for some answers. He was out on a limb for me, and I couldn't just let him hang there. As we drove back to the precinct house, I didn't beat around the bush. I just talked straight.

"You're right about something," I began. "My kid brother was a junkie. He's dead now."

"It figures."

Then I was quiet for a while because I didn't really want to go on. But after what he had done for me, I knew I owed him the truth. I braced myself. "I had a kid, a beautiful five-year-old girl. She died with my brother. The cops said he was high on a speedball and set his mattress on fire with a cigarette."

"I've seen that a few times."

I paused for the bottom line that was stuck somewhere in my throat. "But the autopsy reports in the dead files say they were murdered."

At first he didn't register any surprise. "So now you're doing your own investigation?"

"I want to nail whoever's responsible."

We were both quiet for a long time. I felt something gnaw at my guts, a pain with teeth.

"You were married?" he said finally.

I studied his profile before answering. "Yes . . . to Lenny da Rosa."

He jerked his head toward me, and the car came to a dead halt. We sat there for a moment, then he pulled over to the curb. He put his head in his hands like a child about to cry, then rubbed his hands around his face as if trying to wash. He took a long look out the car window.

"You were married to Lenny da Rosa," he said, his voice was slow and very low.

I didn't say anything.

"Did you know he was a dope dealer when you married him?"

I heard the accusation hidden in his question.

"When I married him he was a numbers runner. In the neighborhood we didn't think that was a crime." Weakly, I added, "I was fifteen."

He looked at me for a long quiet time. He even reached over and touched my cheek as if he needed to reassure himself. Then, he cupped my face in his hands. "You're so full of hate you can't see straight. You can't even tell right from wrong any more."

I shook free of him. "It's not for me, it's for my kid."

He put his hands solidly back on the steering wheel, then stared out at the Houston Street traffic debating with himself. Would he decide to turn me in? I said nothing. I had no cards left to play. The vee came and went on his forehead.

"It all falls into place," he said finally. "I picked it up that first day in the restaurant, the way he looked at you. The way you froze."

I was feeling guilty that I had ever loved somebody like Lenny but was unable to say so.

"I always hated that fuck," he went on, "always hated him. Now I know why."

"What are you gonna do?" I whispered.

For a very long time we were silent in the parked car. I watched an occasional nighttime straggler amble up toward Allen Street. The air was full of a terrible tension, and I thought if Errol didn't say something soon, I'd explode. The radio crackled a message about a homicide in Manhattan South. Errol started the engine.

"Now that I know what you're really looking for, I guess I'll keep my word and help you find that lead," he said.

I could hardly believe it, so I just touched his face like he had touched mine.

Between the two of us, we finally got some dope fiends to talk. But when it came to Brian, there were no leads. He was just a fiend like the other fiends. After a couple of days, it became clear to me that Errol was going for something else. He wanted to get Lenny. He seemed to hate Lenny in a more personal way now. I thought it was a little strange but as long as we were rounding up the fiends, I didn't really care what his motivation was. In any case, Errol didn't find anything on Lenny. But we did piece together some real leads about how dope came into the neighborhood. Half a dozen runners served the Lower East Side. One guy came into the area every Thursday night via Avenue D and made a drop somewhere in the projects. We had a target and we started our hunt. Thursday nights, whether on duty or off, we were on Avenue D.

One night I was at the wheel after chasing a couple of purse-snatching teenagers when I saw a man in a three-piece suit come up the block. With his big cheap briefcase, he looked like somebody's Legal Aid lawyer. But the look in his eyes said different. My gut told me who he was.

"Watch this," I said to Errol, steering the squad car toward the sidewalk. The guy tried to cut across the

street, but I aimed for his ass. He ran into an alley. I
swerved to follow and pinned him between the car and
the wall of a building. We jumped out. My hand was on
my holster.

"Where you going, buddy?"

"You tried to run me over!"

"Aw-w-w not at all, you're paranoid."

He made the mistake of clutching his briefcase to
his chest. I smacked my lips. "You wanna show me what's
in there?"

"You can't," he said. "You can't do that. You got no
reason to search me."

"Look, anybody who sees a cop car and starts
running, I got reason."

His eyes darted back and forth from Errol's face to
mine. Then he tried to crawl over the car. I pulled my
piece. He slid back down to the sidewalk quietly. Errol
grabbed the briefcase and placed it on the hood of the
car. "Open it," he said.

The runner snapped the case open. I gasped. It was
neatly packaged with that brown Mexican skag the
junkies were calling black tar. I wanted to throw the
runner in the back seat and grill him, grill him to death,
grill him till he told me where the factory was—the
factory where all that heroin was going to get cut.

But Errol wouldn't let me. He reminded me of my
promise and ignored my pleas. Short of pulling out my
gun and shooting the fuck, I had to ride back to the
station house and watch as Errol turned my best clue yet
over to the squad.

"You creep! You fucking creep!" I screamed at him
on the street afterwards. "I could have broken him—I
know I could have. Who knows what I could have
gotten?"

"Whatever he knows, the squad will get."

"Fuck you! You complacent motherfucker. Fuck
you!"

"You made a promise," he said with a sad smile, then headed for his car.

I grabbed his arm. "Why don't you help me? Help me all the way, not this half-ass shit."

He unlocked his car, climbed in, and rolled the window down. I stood there powerless. He inserted the key in the ignition. "Want a ride?"

"Are you fucking nuts? What I want is to talk to that runner."

Slow to burn, his face was finally going red. "Listen," he said. "Listen, if you want to be a real cop you should think about giving up this insane revenge. Look around you, it's a new life."

As he pulled out, I gave the car a couple of good shots with my foot.

Later, I would learn that while I was at home with my foot hurting like hell, the squad cracked the runner. He told all he knew. He led the detectives to an apartment in an abandoned building where six naked women in doctor's masks cut and packaged smack. The air around them was smoky with dujie—horse—skag—smack—whatever name you choose. The women's eyes were glassy with it. Uzis hung over the backs of their chairs. When the squad broke down the door, it was war. There was blood, guts, skag, and broken, naked women everywhere. But not one cop got hurt and that was good.

Errol and I got a lot of stroking on that one. The precinct house buzzed for days. But whoever ran that shop regrouped overnight and all the runner's other leads were dead ends. I was no closer to the truth of Brian's last night than before. My morale was washed up.

I slid into another route. I forgot that I owed Errol some loyalty or even some honesty. I went undercover to reconstruct those last twenty-four hours and find Brian's girlfriend Sunny, the one Baker had told me about. I figured the uniform was holding me back. So I went as myself, by myself, without the badge, to blend and let the answer come to me.

I still didn't get it. I didn't understand that you can't touch some things without them touching you. Some things change you, and you can't change back.

CHAPTER SEVEN

The street was empty. I was alone. My spikes clicked on the pavement and echoed in the hollow night. It was the day after my falling out with Errol and I was going undercover for the first time. I had waited for the scene at Robert's Place to mellow out before coming uptown. Now that it was after eleven, everybody would be nice on whatever combination of drugs they were doing with their alcohol. It was early enough for me to blend into the action and late enough so that I would not be particularly noticed.

The bar was on 103rd Street between Second and Third avenues, mid-block. As I opened the door, the juke box embraced me with Latin funk. There were tables along the wall, and the bar was deep in people. I decided to walk all the way to the back as if I knew the place. First I would go to the ladies' room, check myself out, and then elbow up to the bar as if I had been there a hundred times before and were waiting for someone. I got a few looks as I passed the bar. I didn't realize until I got to the end of the bar that there was another room with black walls, fluorescent grafitti, tables, and another bar. People intent in conversation gathered in small groups. There were very few women. I stood in the arched entrance way, uncertain of my next move.

"Looking for someone, sugar?" a stranger asked.

I checked my watch to delay answering, and as I did I realized that the wall across from me was a mirror, because the young woman standing opposite me in skin tight jeans, spike heels, and a tank top was me. My eyes wandered the room, which seemed to be L-shaped. Mirrors covered the walls and several square pillars. I couldn't distinguish real people from reflected people. At a table in a corner two men were deep in conversation. I saw the face of one and the back of the other. The one I could see was doing the listening. I saw the talker in reflection and only the back of his head. He wore a funny fisherman's cap. His bulk and the way he moved his hands reminded me of Sevinsky. I looked across at my own reflection. Even if I could explain my presence to another cop from my precinct, how could I rationalize my outfit? I decided to move.

"The ladies' room is downstairs behind you," the guy in front of me said. He must have been reacting to the expression on my face, which said I was looking for something. I turned on my heels and wiggled quickly to the bathroom, knowing that I was going to stay there for a while to give Sevinsky, assuming it was Sevinsky, time to leave.

There were no windows in the underground bathroom. The walls inside the stalls were painted a hellish red enamel, and the acidic smell of stale urine nipped my nostrils worse than the cold in winter. I opened the stall nearest the wall. I was acutely aware of every move, as if I'd been smoking reefer. I peeled out of my blue jeans, sat down on the bowl, and waited. Music vibrated through the floorboards. As I sat there listening, I became pretty certain that the reflection was Sevinsky.

I heard the door open. Someone staggered into the

stall next to me and sat down. I flushed, got up, put
myself back together and exited the stall. Four songs had
passed upstairs. I heard another toilet flush, and a
buxom young woman dressed just like me came out of
the other stall. I pulled out my makeup and played with
it in front of the mirror. I put on several layers of lipstick.
She washed her hands, dried them, and then pulled out
a lipstick of her own. I stepped back, giving her access to
the small mirror that hung over the sink.

"Seen Sunny tonight?" I asked, as if she and I had
been friends for years.

She dabbed her lipstick on a paper towel and shook
her head. "Where've you been, girl? Sunny ain't hung
out here since last summer. She's on the corner now,"
she said as she pointed upstairs. "She hates these barra-
cudas."

"So do I," I said. "Where's she hanging, Lenox? Or
by the park?" I mentioned two well-known hooker spots
in that part of Harlem. I knew about them because the
grapevine travels from ghetto to ghetto. Lower East Side
types would often party uptown to avoid getting caught
by their old ladies.

She shook her head. "I don't know. She could be
anywhere. Last time I saw her she was working the
tunnel traffic. She never used to hustle but when . . ."

"Brian died."

"Yeah," she dabbed her lips with a paper towel and
pulled her jeans loose from the crack in her butt. "She
changed and her habit got the best of her."

"How did he die, anyway?" I pushed.

She pulled back from the mirror, tilted her weight
onto her right hip and cocked her head quizzically,
stopping to look at me for the first time. By the way her
head tottered on her shoulders I knew that she was
stoned. "Why you askin' so many questions?" she
slurred.

I leaned up to the mirror, as if my lips were the most

important thing in the world. "Hey, don't get smart with me. You started talking about the bitch. Her and I happen to go way back, so I got sucked in."

She tottered a little, then pointed a finger at me. "You brung her up, not me."

I blotted my lips and dropped the lipstick back in my bag. "Yeah, but you're out here telling her life story, not me."

After that I went back upstairs. Sevinsky was gone. For a split second I wondered what the hell he was doing hanging out in East Harlem, but because I had an agenda of my own I didn't give him a lot of thought. I didn't even bother to go to the bar for a drink. I just cut out and hopped a cab to the diner on Forty-third and Eleventh, a few blocks from the Lincoln Tunnel. The diner lit up half the block and was centrally located to about half a dozen hooker corners. I had decided to give myself a coffee break before trying to find Sunny. I went inside. Truck drivers and cab drivers were busy eating and talking shop. I grabbed a seat at the counter. The waitress gave me a nasty look. "Do you wanna see a menu?" she snapped.

I shook my head. "Just a Coke, please."

"Large or small?"

"Large."

I sipped my soda at the almost empty counter, then turned to stare out the window, which ran the whole length of the diner and even went around the corners. The diner's neon glare contrasted with the darkness outside. Eleventh Avenue is so close to the Hudson that it's like a highway, and cars go faster than anywhere inside the city. There are no stoops, no people, few stores—just warehouses, parking lots, and motels for out-of-towners who come and go by car. I sat there wondering how I was going to find Sunny without getting myself raped or killed. I wasn't afraid of the streets because I had grown up on them. But this was different. It was not a neighborhood. There were no rules here. As rough as the Lower East Side looked from the outside, the locals tended not to mess with each other, at least not arbitrarily. I had never gotten ripped off or been attacked, because people knew me, my father, my brother, and later Lenny. There was some accountability. But not here. Here everything was anonymous, especially sex and death. I finished my soda and stepped out into the night before giving my fears any more time to grow.

I walked down Eleventh Avenue from Forty-third to Thirty-eighth street. There were clusters of hookers on almost every corner. They came in all sizes, shapes, and colors. Most were young, very young. Many had beautiful parts. If a girl had beautiful legs, she would wear shorts and high heels. If she had a great ass she'd wear skin tight jeans. If her tits were something special, she'd wear a tight T-shirt or a blouse halfway open. And if her face was striking, she would push her hair back and expose the bone structure. Whatever was saleable was displayed. What went on inside these women was a sad mystery.

Pimps in Cadillacs guarded the female merchandise. They wore flashy, wide-lapelled suits, often white, often with a matching wide-brimmed hat. Most of the pimps were black. Every time I saw a blond hooker, I'd stop for a few minutes and try to blend in. But it wasn't working. Even though I was dressed like one of them, they knew I wasn't. In the Academy we had learned that hookers could smell cops but that they rarely messed with them. To a hooker an undercover cop was bad for business but not really dangerous, because the undercovers were after the johns. If word got out that an undercover was on the scene, the johns wouldn't come around. A car stopped for me. There were three other girls on the corner, one was blond and the reason I had stopped there.

"How much?" asked the driver as he leaned out the window.

My heart jumped into my throat. "A hundred," I said quickly.

"For a blow job?" He looked incredulous. "You gotta be kiddin'."

"I'm not." He screeched off into the tunnel.

"Whattaya writing a book or something?" the blond asked me.

"What do you mean?" I said, but I was really dying to ask her her name. "I'm Toni," I added.

"When you first got here, we thought you was undercover, but if you was you wouldda nailed that guy. So what are you doin' here?"

"I'm trying to make a few bucks like everybody else. What's your name?"

She ignored my question.

"You look scared," she said, even though she was several years younger than I. Another car stopped. One of the other girls got in.

"So why'd you tell the guy so much money. You got something special in your throat?" She laughed. "Or don't you know the rates?"

I didn't have to come up with an answer, because just then a caddy came sliding across the avenue and stopped in front of us. The window rolled down and the head of a black man in a yellow suit appeared. He locked eyes with the little hooker and showed her his teeth. "Is this bitch payin' you to stand here gabbin'?"

Her eyes opened wide with fright. She rubbed a spot on her upper arm where a bruise was turning from blue to purple. "I ain't doin' nothin', Jack." Then she turned back to me. "I was just tellin' her to get the fuck off this corner."

She moved a step closer and yelled into my nose as if it were a microphone. Her face was contorted in rage, but a sharp fear hid in her eyes. As much to spare her as myself, I backed off. The pimp raised an arrogant eyebrow that dispatched me down the avenue.

That night I went home early, but in those next few weeks the world of pimps and whores and the cure claimed me. The slide started easily enough that next Saturday. It was just before dawn when I joined the gathering community of working girls at the mouth of the Lincoln Tunnel. The girls kept disappearing into cars, and that camouflaged the fact that I was just standing there bullshitting. It was still dark. The descending cars were preceded by their headlights. Traffic was slow in the silence of the ending night. Across from me a brief negotiation took place. A girl climbed into a car. I heard the sharp metallic slam of the door shutting. Tires echoed on the damp cement. I looked back into that tile tunnel and imagined the filthy river above. Trucks from Jersey climbed out of the tunnel into the city, which was belching to life.

The girls drifted to the front of Edison Park at Forty-second and Eleventh Avenue. It was a moist night, and we could smell the rotting river as it pushed up from the shore less than half a mile away. There were four of us—me in my short white shorts, a Latina who looked about fourteen, a white girl in a halter top and the shortest miniskirt I had ever seen. Everytime she moved, her pink underwear flashed. Then there was an African beauty in a white jersey that clung to her shapely body with every move. I had been around every night that week and hadn't brought the man or cut into anybody's business, so the girls were letting me hang. One of the girls had a small portable radio, another had some bad smoke. Reefer was the only drug I had ever tried so when the joint was passed to me I didn't hesitate.

A bottle of spiced rum was making its way from hand to hand. For me, it had been a lousy week on the job. No good collars, lots of bullshit arrests, and lots of paper shoving—an old lady shoplifting for food, a teenager trying to lift a leather jacket to wear on the block, a domestic dispute when a city marshall put a family of nine on the street. No progress in my search for Sunny. So that night I wasn't feeling very good about myself.

But the smoke made the little radio sound sweet. I had forgotten how it could do that. The cheap rum lit a furnace in the pit of my stomach that warmed my limbs, and I began to chill out. We were listening to a swinging samba. The Latina took me in her arms, and we just started to dance. She was trying to teach me some complicated moves but I kept stepping on her toes. She'd giggle and try again until we doubled over in laughter. She shoved the little bottle into my hand.

"Everybody can't lead," she said.

I took a swig. We both laughed again.

"I don't know, girl," she said, "you're gonna hafta get your toes out from under my feet."

Just as we were going to give it another try, a truck came to the mouth of the parking lot. The driver looked down on us. "Twenty bucks," he said.

My laughter died. "He's all yours."

He shook his head. "I'm talking to you."

"Catch you later," my laughing partner said.

I reached for the bottle one more time, just to stretch the moment. But I knew I was about to climb into that truck and drive off with this asshole. I took a long swig then caught him in the corner of my eye. He looked about thirty-five, thick, chunky, muscular, red-haired, and ruddy. He didn't look like a guy who needed to buy it.

The truck cab was high off the ground. I put a foot on the running board, and he grabbed my hand. I was in. He hit the gas and we slid up Forty-second Street, across Eleventh Avenue toward Times Square and the strip.

"I've never seen you on that corner before."

"You need glasses."

I was sweating, sweating his next move. How was I going to get away from him? Maybe traffic on the strip would be slow. I'd hop out of the truck and keep stepping. But when we got there the street was wide open. He pulled through at thirty miles per hour.

"I hate this lit-up shit house," he said as he studied the junkies, pill poppers, acid heads, the uppers, the down-and-outers, the sleeze ball hustlers that populated the night outside. I watched him.

Neon flashed all around us. Red, white, blue, orange, aqua. At the corner of Broadway he turned downtown and doubled back to the river. I fumbled with the door handle. It was no go.

"Whatareya, a claustrophobic whore? That's funny, a claustrophobic whore. I had that door fixed. It don't open unless I open it from my side."

He pulled into a corner parking lot and backed his truck against the back wall. Then he killed the lights and cut the engine. Everything was quiet. He looked at me blankly.

"My wife is pregnant, and I'm a horny kind of a guy."

"That's why you're out here? Because your wife is pregnant?"

"The back of the truck is okay," he said.

"Not for me. Look, this is a scene I don't dig. Let me out."

He raised an eyebrow slightly. His upper lip twitched, and his eyes were agate cold. "I call the shots. I'm paying so I call the shots."

"You haven't paid me yet. Let me out. Just let me out."

He stroked the lower half of the steering wheel then ran his finger over the horn in the center. He slouched back in the seat and plunged a hand into a pocket and extracted a wad of bills. He peeled off a twenty and a ten. "Here." He shoved the bills into my halter. "That's twice what you usually get. Now climb into the back. I ain't got all night."

I sat there cursing myself for not packing.

I poked my head through the curtain. The back of the truck was empty. It had floorboards like a room but nothing I could use as an equalizer. His hand was on my ass. He shoved me over the seat. I complied and scrambled quickly to my knees. He was right with me. I jumped to my feet. The truck was big enough for me to stand in but he was too tall. He hunched in half, and that was my moment. I offered a kick to the groin. He went down on his knees. I kicked him in the stomach a couple of times and tried to scramble back over the seat. He grabbed my calf and pulled me down.

"You stupid bitch." He tried pinning my arm behind me to bring me to my knees. I took an ear between my teeth and bit, bit till my teeth went all the way through. It took a few seconds for the pain to hit home. Then he bucked like a steer and his grip on my arm loosened. I kicked his gut, and the air shot out of him in a long, deep groan. I scrambled over the seat, opened the door on his side, and fled down the avenue in the direction of the players and the hustlers and the cops who spelled safety.

CHAPTER EIGHT

After that, I started packing my .22. I bought a bellyband that fit snugly around my tummy and kept my piece right over my pelvis. Hanging in the streets was like a tour of duty—you never knew what you'd find. Some days it was more dangerous to be packing than to be unarmed. It was impossible to plan ahead, so I played the odds. Some days I packed. Some days I didn't.

About a week later, I was packing when I shouldn't have been. I tagged along to a hooker's birthday party. Her name was Tiny. We had become friendly on the corner. She was half Irish and half Puerto Rican. Although she hadn't told me herself, the grapevine had it that Tiny once ran with Sunny. So I was into staying close to Tiny. I had dropped a hint that Sunny was my cousin.

This particular Saturday one of the girls had rented a room at the Motor Inn on Tenth Avenue and Forty-second Street. One by one, we straggled in, all six of us. Tiny, myself, a washed-out white girl named Laura, China, the brunette I had danced with the week before, and two other Latinas I didn't know. Everybody was carrying a paper bag of something. I had two six packs,

Heinekens, not the cheap stuff. Once inside, we broke out the paper plates and spread a buffet of cold cuts, slaw, potato chips, and dip. We even had cupcakes with candles.

Tiny had her blaster and some tapes. She wore a leather mini, a studded T-shirt, and a leather bracelet with spikes. Her short hair was orange and purple.

"How old?" I said, pulling the beer from its cheap paper hull.

"Nineteen."

"Like Sunny," I said.

Tiny studied her reflection in the mirror. She played with her purple sideburns. They were short and sleek. Her little mouth was heartshaped, her wide ass high, her skin cafe-au-lait. "You're obsessed with Sunny," she said. "Are you in love with her?"

I cracked a can of beer. It fizzled onto my thigh. Tiny grabbed the can from my hand and brought it to her lips. She threw her head back and took a swig.

The beer frothed on my thigh. She reached down and wiped the foam with deft fingers. "That shit is ugly," she said. "It looks like scum."

"What you got against scum?" one of the girls asked as she unfolded a packet of cocaine. "Scum paid for this, and this is a party."

Everybody laughed.

"Mercedes, you know Sunny's cousin Toni?" Tiny formally introduced me to the small Dominican hooker with the body of a woman and the face of a child.

Mercedes laughed. "How you doin'?"

"So, so," I said.

"Mercedes makes the big bucks," Tiny said. "A lot of these sickos like to look at her face and think they're fucking a kid."

Mercedes tenderly emptied the packet of coke onto a hand mirror. With a razor blade she made some lines and offered the birthday girl a straw. Tiny leaned over the mirror. She sucked the coke in fast and hard like a pro. No hesitation. Then she wiggled her nostril with a practiced finger and waited for the quinine aftertaste. The bitterness slid down the back of her throat. She hit another line. When she looked up, the room came to a standstill. Everybody waited for her reaction. What would the pecking order be? Who would get the next line? She picked me.

Since I had never done coke, I got nervous, but I was sure I didn't show it. I took the staw in my hand. After Kelly died, I had hated any kind of drugs. To me they were all the same. Bad. But tonight it was join or be left out. So I did like Tiny had done and didn't fumble. The effect of the coke was fast. To my surprise, I lifted from within myself and felt the party spirit. I was suddenly very up, certain that Tiny would give me the lead I hungered for.

Tiny took the mirror in her hand and one by one the girls snorted a line, then a second.

"It ain't about sex at all. Sex is just a tool to power," Tiny said, creating a new set of lines. The razor scratched the mirror.

"What about all that scum out there? What about all that scum willing to pay for a blow job, what do you call that?" China asked. Her voice was low and mellow.

"Capitalism," Tiny said. "They call it free enterprise."

The white girl, Laura, spoke in a plaintive wail. "I'm sick of this street shit. I wanna have my own steady clients."

"You must be kidding! You're not call girl material. You can't be a dope fiend and keep a schedule. You're on the corner for a reason. You're a dope fiend first and a hooker second. Shit, you're not even a professional hooker."

The room laughed. The would-be call girl retreated to a corner.

"Sunny was call girl material. Sunny had a snapper." Tiny cracked another beer can. The air conditioning unit whirred like a DC-10, and the room was icy. I was frozen in a spectator's reverie until Sunny's name hit the air.

"What's a snapper?" I asked.

The girls looked at me dumbly. "You don't know?" Tiny asked.

I knew I'd better know, so I covered up with humor. "It's some kind of fish." The room laughed dirty. I had gotten away with something. Sounded like I fit.

"Sunny's pussy used to work overtime. She could make herself come by contracting her muscles. She could make the johns howl."

"She had mucha labia," China said, "choca loca. . . . Me I don't feel anything unless I'm in love."

"In love!" everyone groaned.

"I have to feel it in my heart." She tapped on her chest and offered a smile that concealed a secret.

"That ain't no heart," Tiny said, "it's just another muscle."

I laughed, but I thought about it. I thought about how many things sex could be—about its power and magic. I remembered how Lenny had made my body feel and how sure I was that meant he loved me. I thought about how he took that love away when I started to go to school. I would lie there aching for that love that wasn't really love at all. I laughed with the others. Tiny was right—lots of hearts were just muscle.

Conversations were slowing and slurring. Somebody turned the air conditioning off. I nodded out. Musk filled the empty air and slid down the back of my throat. Raspy breathing and an orchestra of deep sighs played around my ears. I opened my eyes. On the bed a molten mass bucked and rose. Three naked women were intertwined, hands, breasts, tongues in secret places. I killed the overhead and sat back down. China pulled a perfume vial from between her breasts. But there was no perfume in it, just some small beige rocks. I closed my eyes. Then, somebody handed me something. When I looked, I saw a glass pipe which held one of the small rocks on a net. I was scared shitless. Crack was the latest high on the street and like everybody else, I knew it was the worst. It made addicts and killers out of children. I felt the abyss open below me. Still, I didn't step back. There was no stopping me. Whatever it took to unlock the door to Brian's last night, I would do it. I placed the pipe to my lips and pulled.

"Gently," Tiny whispered hoarsely. "Gently."

A milky white smoke swirled in the pipe's glass bowl. I inhaled. Inside my head, I turned a merry somersault. My fuzzy lips went numb, my skin dissolved, I was soft, a soft yearning cloud.

Tiny leaned over me. "C'mon and gap those legs, I'll take you the rest of the way."

I touched the piece over my pelvis—that drew the line for me. I gave Tiny a half smile. "I'm on the rag," I lied, and watched her turn away.

A gossamer veil fell over my eyes as Tiny stripped from her leather garb and strapped on a generous dildo. She gave me a wink and spread China's creamy thighs.

"All right," somebody whispered loudly like a wind from the window. "Show her that you know what no man knows."

China bucked up from the bed. Tiny grabbed her ass, cupping the cheeks in both hands, and drove herself all the way home. China rocked the cradle of her hips from side to side and shuddered, whispering "Hit the walls, baby, hit those sugar walls."

They caught a rhythm that entwined them as together they climbed a long invisible ladder. When they reached the top China dissolved in a wrenching scream.

Then Tiny turned to me. "See that—that's power." She offered me her dick. "Here take anybody you want."

But I didn't want. I was beginning to crash, my pulse fluttered in my throat like something that was dying. I stood on shaky legs. "Look, I gotta go out there and find my cousin."

Tiny shrugged. "Try the flophouse on Forty-ninth and Ninth, but you're missing out on a party."

As I wandered toward the flophouse, I realized that I was very high and for the first time since Kelly's death I was conscious of being horny. Every cell in my body tingled with the cocaine high and I yearned for some warm arms around me. I rubbed the soft skin of my upper arms with my fingertips, cradling myself as I walked. The long blocks from Eleventh to Tenth to Ninth were empty, except for an occasional working girl, an occasional pimp. The cars passed by as if I didn't exist. I watched my feet moving on the pavement, my long naked legs looking like they belonged to someone else. The glass in the pavement twinkled like starlight, and my yearning took me backwards. Backwards to the memory of something warm—long before sex.

I thought about my mother's chubby short arms and the way she felt when I was still small enough to sit on her lap and fit completely into her embrace. I remembered her deep laugh and her round face when she was happy, before dad's accident when he was still bringing home the bacon, before everybody started hating themselves and each other too. I remembered watching her in the kitchen and the sweet smells of her baking, muffins and soda bread. My mom's family was from the Old Country—Ireland. On the Lower East Side everybody was from the Old Country, lots of different Old Countries.

I was in front of the Port Authority building. A mobile soup kitchen with a flat tire stood there unmanned. Up against the building, surrounded by shopping bags, were the garbage people. Tonight they were all women. Even though it was July, they wore lots of clothes, dresses, sweaters, coats, hats, rubber band bracelets. Everything was crusted in grime; even the naked skin, in the few places that it showed, was lacquered in grime. I could smell them too. I wondered whether the human animal was the only one to snap this way—to abandon nature and self—to destruct.

I asked myself why I had never crossed that line to the other side. Their side. I knew that I had come close after Kelly died. For weeks I lay in Zelda's apartment and wouldn't move. I lost my job at the greasy spoon. Finally, Zelda threw me out to go job hunting. I remembered long subway rides to nowhere. I would answer a want ad and forget my destination, forget to look up at the stops and just sit there lost inside myself, seeing those flames cruise to the sky over and over and over again. Finally, I got a job in a hamburger joint on Forty-second Street where junkies would come to eat. That was where I formulated my revenge against dope, and it was from there that I took the police exam. All that time I thought of myself as sane. I didn't realize the line is so thin you don't feel the crossover.

I saw the flophouse coming up ahead. A man in a black suit with a black hat and brown ringlets shot out of a lit hole in the building, feet barely touching the ground. He brushed past me as if I weren't there and disappeared into the night. I stood at the mouth of the flophouse wondering what the chances were that Sunny was in there. I walked up the short steps and pressed my face to the glass door. A buzzer sounded and I pushed the door open. Inside, a young Italian with a Mastroianni mustache sat behind a desk that, like everything else, was old and sleazy.

"What can I do you for?" he asked.

I tottered on my heels, and my ass went left and right. I let my voice come out breathy, in the higher registers. "I'm looking for my cousin Sunny." I grabbed my ass. "She's about my size." I flipped a piece of my hair forward, "but blond."

He shook his head like I was a waste of time. "Look," he said, "I ain't nobody's baby-sitter. You wanna do business, the rates are on the board." He pointed up. "If not, I got things to do."

He returned his attention to a paperback in his hands. I was dismissed. I tottered back down the stairs unwilling to call it a night, unwilling to go home. But the block was dead. Half an hour later, I gave in to exhaustion and went home.

For the next three nights, I hovered at the mouth of that flophouse, waiting for Sunny to show. Once in a while I'd go upstairs with a john. Once I had him in the room, I'd flash my piece and ask my questions. The johns would answer willingly. Anything to get out of there. They'd leave peacefully, never to return. With them, I knew I had no worries because these guys had no one to complain to but the mirror.

On the third night, a john who looked like a computer salesman gave me the nod. Figuring he might know something, I followed him in. We climbed the crooked stairs together. The room was old with grime. His pallid skin sweated fear and the sickly smell of guilt. Rancid water seeped from the pores of the damp plaster. On the concave bed, the yellow sheet was thin as paper. His shaking eyes darted around the room. I was going for my piece to scare him into answering some questions when he opened the briefcase he carried and pulled out a whip.

My heart skipped a beat and I froze.

"Whip me," he said.

Right then I should have flashed my piece, but I didn't. I looked into his eyes and wanted to wipe out the sickness that hovered just under his fleshy lids. Then, as he handed me the whip, I said, "It's gonna cost you more."

He handed me a C-note which I buried in my back pocket. I took the leather handle. Suddenly it was as if I could smell Lenny all around me. It was a smell laced in violet, sugary like the candy on a child's birthday cake. Violet like the breath mints he sucked. Violet like the taste of his kisses. And as the john took off his clothes, his ugly flab faded and he became Lenny, young, virile, and treacherous. I was mesmerized seeing him but not him. Superimposed on a thousand memories, I watched him take off his clothes. Fat fingers scurried over buttons like frightened rats. I heard the scraping of fingernails at the quick, and he offered me his naked back. I just stood there. He peered impatiently over his shoulder, his jaw suddenly again Lenny's. Inside me something cracked like a faultline opening. The whip broke the brittle air. He folded down onto his knees. A hot red welt scarred his back.

"The ass," he groaned, "the ass," and crawled away from me. The whip snapped back and forth, shattering the room like a kaleidoscope. From him came a sound I didn't recognize, a crazy twisted blend of pleasure and pain. The venetian blind over the room's one crooked window was slightly cracked. Between us pulsated the multicolored neon from the strip below. The leather gripped my hand like burning ice. I was cold, very cold. Again, he peered over a shoulder. A gleam of red neon caught in his pupils, flashing like the nocturnal soul of a reptile. I stopped dead.

"What are you waiting for?" he demanded.

Outside a siren screamed. I hit him once.

His head dropped limply forward and he groaned. "Yeah, like that."

My arm wouldn't move. He turned to me again. I felt his hunger, his impatience. That devilish light flashed in his eyes.

"C'mon bitch, do it."

The whip cracked and cracked; the corners of the

110

room slid closer and closer. A crazy, sick, ecstatic pain growled in his throat, and, as a maze of welts appeared on his skin, he got hard. All the mercy drained from me, and my arm moved faster and faster. Shuddering and crying, he spilled onto the slimy linoleum where his translucent seed glistened in the pulse of neon.

The emptiness between us was filled by a long deep silence, and then the rush of sound from the street poured in. I loosened my arthritic fingers from their rigid grip on the damp whip. I touched my piece safe in its spot. I expected him to turn for revenge. Instead, he thanked me and quietly began to dress.

As he sat putting socks on his feet, I asked about Sunny. He put a foot into a shoe. "Don't know her," he said.

He leaned forward like a boy to tie a shoelace. A wave of remorse washed over me. I pulled out his C-note. "Here, take this back."

He went onto the next lace.

"Take it, please."

He circled his neck with his tie.

"Take it."

"Are you nuts?" he said.

On the street below someone cried for help. Shifting neon sliced the room. The money in my hand went orange, then deep green. He walked out the door and I followed. It was three in the morning.

A bunch of dope fiends had gathered at the mouth of the flophouse selling beat. They tried to get my attention. "Jays, bags, smoke, coke, I got crack. Crack it up."

Every cheap hustler had a ten-dollar cure for the soul. I ignored them, but that night as I walked down the avenue, the john's money in my pocket, I knew that no investigation in the world could justify what I had done. I couldn't go home. I couldn't face Mary. I lingered on the corner of Forty-second Street and Eleventh Avenue. The girls were still hard at work. I joined a crowd.

"Anything happening?" I asked.

"I gots mine," a brunette pulled a wad of bills from her cleavage.

"Stop showing off, bitch." A young blond madonna's laugh chimed like a high bell. "We know who's gettin' most of that when you leave here." She nodded her head in the direction of a maroon Cadillac across the avenue.

"What makes you so tough?" the brunette questioned. Her voice was deep and gravelly. "You think you can keep it all. But one of these days one of these johns is gonna show you different."

"Not me, baby. I'm free-lance now and I'll be free-lance tomorrow. I like my independence. And if you think that wise-ass punk can protect you from these johns, you even stupider than you look. That shit may work in the neighborhood, but it ain't foolproof around here. When you climb into one of them cars, ain't nobody following you. If that john wants to break your neck while his cock is in your mouth . . . shi-i-t." She spread her hands as if to say that's the way it is.

I took the opening to jump in and say, "I'm free-lance too. Can I hang out?"

"Oh yeah, how long you been in bidness? Ten minutes?" Everybody laughed.

"I'm from the Lower East Side, and my old man just got locked up. I'm sick but I can't hustle in my own neighborhood cuz my father'll find out."

Just then the light turned red and four cars stopped. The girls went up to the cars offering their wares. One unbuttoned her blouse, revealing her beautiful breasts. Only the blond madonna and I stayed rooted to our spots. She was wearing tight jeans with a denim jacket and nothing underneath.

"Get any money yet?" she asked.

"Yeah, I got bucks."

"I know a guy on Thirty-ninth Street and Ninth

Avenue. We could put our money together, cop, get off, and then come back."

For a moment I didn't say anything. Then I asked, "What's your name?"

"I can handle the johns better when I'm stoned," she said with a wistful smile and without answering my question.

"Me too," I said, and followed her across the street.

"Hey, where the fuck are you goin', you lazy bums," one of the girls called after us.

"To get nice," she yelled without turning back.

"Later," I chimed in.

We walked across Ninth Avenue making small talk. Her name was Sheri. She was a sixteen-year-old runaway from Plainfield, New Jersey, and she loved skag.

"How did you get started?"

"In school," she said matter-of-factly.

"My old man started me. I never even copped for myself. I don't know how to hit myself either," I volunteered.

"That's bullshit," she said. "You shouldn't let no guy control you like that. I got good veins, I can always hit myself. What are you doin' now that he ain't around?"

"Popping."

She shrugged, "That'll cure you, but you don't get no rush, and the rush is the best part."

The cop man lived over a meat market that took up most of the block. We entered through a door in the side of the building that also led to the back of the market. As soon as we stepped in, the smell of blood and raw meat enveloped us. We climbed the flight of stairs to his door. It had three locks, a police insignia, and a sign that read BEWARE OF DOG. She knocked loud and hard and yelled. "Joe! Joe, it's me, Sheri. Open up."

Inside I heard some barking, yapping, and growling. Then the locks opened one by one. A sleepy-eyed, thin, long-haired old dope fiend in boxer shorts stood in the dark threshold. I couldn't see inside, but the smell of dogs and their excrement jammed itself down my throat.

"Who's she?"

Sheri shifted the weight of her pretty body onto one leg. "Don't worry about her. She's nobody. We know each other from the old neighborhood."

He opened the door a little wider and I followed Sheri in. It was a big unfurnished space that looked like it might once have been a warehouse. There were two rooms connected by a large window frame with no glass in it. In the far corner a mattress lay on the floor.

Dogs in all shapes and sizes filled the room. Several started sniffing and licking me. I didn't know where to move because the floors were covered with newspapers and excrement. My eyes escaped through the windows along the back wall. Over the rooftops, I saw the night-blackened river.

I tried to discourage the dogs from sniffing and licking without making it obvious, because I didn't want to make Joe angry. Sheri sat on the ledge of the empty window frame and began rummaging in her pocketbook.

"What's your friend's name?" Joe asked, staring at my crotch, which one of his dogs was sniffing. I had never seen such an old dope fiend. His shoulder-length hair was white. Was he somebody's grandfather or did he just look that way?

"Ask her yourself. She's got a mouth."

"Toni," I offered and felt my face twitch.

I made my way over yesterday's headlines and dog shit to sit gingerly on the ledge next to Sheri. I looked hopefully at the real windows. None of them were open.

"Gimme what you got," Sheri said. I pulled some money out of my back pocket.

She took it and smiled happily at Joe, who stood there in his gray boxer shorts that had once been white and scratched his balls.

"I got twenty-eight bucks. Gimme three dimes."

"I told you I don't take no shorts from nobody. Not even you."

"Aw-w c'mon, Joe. I'll give you the cotton." She twisted her head coquettishly. "But you gotta let us use your works."

He pushed his hair out of his eyes and raised his hands in a gesture of frustration. "You gotta be kiddin' me. You don't have no works, you show up with this bitch I ain't never seen before, and then you wanna cop short."

"How about the cotton?"

"I don't want no cotton. I want a real taste. Take it or leave it."

"He can have some of mine." I offered, my voice practically a whimper.

Sheri looked at me as if I were crazy. "Okay," she said. "but I go first."

She handed Joe the money. Even though we had both watched her count it three times, he counted it again.

I could hardly breathe from the stench and my heart was hammering in my throat. I was thinking that I should just get up, walk out the door, and forget the whole thing. Joe disappeared behind a black curtain and came back carrying several glassine bags, a bottle cap, and a small black box shaped like a coffin. A skull and crossbones were delicately etched into the wood. One of the dogs jumped up trying to lick Joe's face. He kissed him on the mouth then slapped him down.

"Let's go into the bathroom," Sheri said, grabbing the bags from his hand. "I don't want these dogs making me spill this shit."

Joe led the way. We followed. Sheri gave my hand a happy little squeeze.

"This shit is nice," she whispered. "You'll see. Soon you're gonna feel good."

She opened the palm of her hand for me to get a

look at the bags. I saw that each was sealed with a small piece of green tape.

The bathroom was tiny. It had no tub and no sink, just a toilet and a naked lightbulb swinging overhead. A German shepherd tried to follow us in. He yelped as Joe shut the door on his nose. Joe handed Sheri the little coffin, and she opened it tenderly. It contained a needle and syringe, which she gave to me. I thought of Brian. I remembered the way he used to hide his works in his bed springs and how I would find them and destroy them.

"What the fuck are you doing?" I remembered him screaming at me, tears streaming down his face, "You think you're making it better, but you're making it worse. Don't you know that? As long as I have my works, I'll never be sick. I can always get a taste from somebody who needs works. Otherwise, if I'm sick I gotta go out and mug somebody. Why don't you leave me the fuck alone."

Then he collapsed on his bed and cried like a little boy. I would try to take him in my arms and comfort him, but he never let me. He was my baby brother, but I couldn't touch him. Who was I going to tell? Mom and her bottle? Finally, after we were married, I told Lenny. He shook his head, seeming sorry but not surprised.

"Your brother's a sponge," he said. "He's got no backbone. He can't even steal for himself. He just hangs out on the corner waiting for the guys from Jersey who need to borrow works. They give him the cotton and that way he stays high, a little at a time."

I pictured Brian standing on Delancey Street, waiting for his cure, playing flunkie for the Jersey crowd, leading them to cop in exchange for his taste, and I started to cry.

"He's not like you," Lenny said. "You're strong, he's weak. I can't make him strong."

Lenny folded his arms around me and I whispered

to his chest. "He's my brother. There must be a way to help him."

Lenny stroked my hair. "Brian's not the only one, honey. That's just the way life is. Everybody's always waiting for the cure, not just your brother."

When he said that, I thought of mom and dad and the bottle.

"When Brian gets his cure, he's happy. You should know that. A junkie's happiest moment is when the cure is just around the corner. He'll lie, cheat, steal, even kill for that moment. Nothing else matters." Lenny raised my face gently. Our eyes met. "Honey, don't suffer so much. You're probably suffering more than he is. He's doing what he wants to do."

He wiped the tears from my cheeks and helped me blow my nose into the clean white handkerchief he always kept in his back pocket. "C'mon, honey, smile. You gotta accept life the way it is, that's all. None of us are different from Brian. We're all waiting for our own version of the cure."

"Not you, Lenny," I said. "You're strong and you know what you want. You don't need a cure."

He shook his head. "What I want is bigger and better, that's the only difference. I like rolling the dice. I'm shooting crap for the big time and I'm taking you with me."

I thought about his passion for gambling. He was always making bets with anyone who would take his odds. I remembered Lenny shooting craps on the hot summer streets, telling me to blow on the dice for luck. Sometimes he would win big and sometimes he would lose big. I loved to watch him play, face flushed, black eyes flashing, his energy electric. But it made me mad when he didn't quit while he was ahead. So Lenny and I had worked out a deal. Every time he won, he would give me a portion of his winnings. That way, even if he lost, he never lost it all. When the game was over, he'd ask, "How'd you make out, kid?" I'd proudly show him my dollars and quarters.

"Yeah, you and me are waitin' on the big time." His lips touched the shadow of my mother's anger on my cheek.

"What about me, Lenny? What's my cure?"

He kissed me on the lips and held my face in his hands. "Don't you know kitten?" He winked at me the way he had when I was twelve. "You're a love junkie, hooked on love. That's your cure. The most dangerous of them all."

"Can you help Brian?"

Lenny shrugged. "I don't know what I can do, but I'll talk to him."

I was pulled back to the present as Sheri took the syringe from my hand and dipped it into the toilet tank. She pulled a bobby pin from her hair and made an ingenious handle for the bottle cap, then pulled the green tape off the bags, her tongue darting hungrily on her lips.

"I need a cotton," she said.

Joe handed her a cigarette. She broke off the filter and dropped a little piece into the bottle cap.

"See that green tape, Toni. That means this is Cobra's thing, so you know it's good."

Right then the action stopped for me. Joe watched Sheri's hands, his eyes as cold as glass, as hard as marbles.

"You got that from the Cobra?" I whispered hoarsely.

"Of course not, but it's his thing."

The white powder fell very slowly down into the bottle-cap cooker and she added a little bit of water. The empty glassine bag wafted to the filthy bathroom floor, carrying its green tape with it. *Cobra*, I thought. *Cobra. I'm very close now.*

"Gimme a match," Sheri said, without looking up,

reaching her hand to me. I didn't have any matches. Joe put a book in her hand. She lit several matches at the same time, picked the cooker up by its bobby pin handle, and placed it over the flame. The powder melted. She killed the flame with a quick flick of her wrist. Joe's eyes never left the cooker.

When all that was done, she got off the toilet seat, unbuckled her belt and tied it around her arm just above the elbow. Her arm, blue with bruises, reminded me of Brian's arm. The many needle marks formed hideous scars. She clenched her fist the way people do when they are about to get a blood test and slapped her arm. She slapped it so hard that it turned red and one big blue vein appeared inside the crook of her elbow. She massaged the arm to make the vein stand out more. Using the cotton as a filter, she filled the syringe from the cooker. Then she sat back down on the toilet, poked the needle into her arm, found a vein, and loosened the belt. A drop of blood popped up into the syringe, where it elongated into a thin red line.

"It's a hit!" Joe said. "She got a hit on the first try!" He rubbed his hands together happily. It meant his turn would come sooner. Sheri never took her eyes off her arm. She squeezed the syringe, and the liquid went down into her. Then she let go of the syringe and blood came up into it.

"Aw-w c'mon now, you're gonna make us stand here while you boot," Joe whined.

I was mesmerized by the blood coming and going in the syringe. Everytime she squeezed it, there was less clear liquid and more blood. It seemed to take a very long time before the syringe was empty. She pulled the needle out, licked the rivulet of blood that was descending on her arm and handed the syringe to Joe.

"Don't beat her," Sheri warned, but the slur in her voice told me she was too stoned to keep an eye on him. I was hoping he did beat me so I wouldn't OD.

He took her belt and tied up as she had done. He rinsed the syringe in the toilet tank. Then he searched for a vein. It wasn't as easy for him. He couldn't seem to get one. He kept pushing the needle in, then pulling the needle out, then trying again. His arm began to swell.

"They're rolling," he said. "I got lousy veins. They keep slipping away from me."

Finally, he found a vein in his hand. I watched as his blood came and went. In all the years Brian had battled his addiction, I had never seen him shoot up. Now, as I watched them, I saw Brian, nothing but Brian.

It seemed like a long time before Joe was finally finished. Then it was my turn. Sheri took the belt from his wrist and handed it to me. I shook my head. "That's okay, I'll pop it."

"Don't be stupid," she said. "Joe'll help you."

I heard the German shepherd whining at the door, scratching, calling his master. The smell of raw meat, blood, and excrement was all around. By that time, I was half hoping I'd catch an OD and die.

I sat down on the toilet while Joe rinsed his blood from the syringe by dipping it into the toilet tank. I tied the belt around my arm as they had done. Joe pulled it tight for me. So tight that it hurt. No vein came up.

"Make a fist," he said. I did. I opened and closed it a few times. Two big veins popped out, one in the crook of my arm and one just below the elbow, along the side of my arm.

Joe kneeled in front of me and began massaging my arm to make the veins stand out more.

"Where are your tracks?" he questioned suspiciously.

"She's used to poppin'," Sheri answered as she sucked the rest of the solution from the cooker. "Goddamit, you cocksucker. You beat her. There's nothing here," she accused him angrily.

He gave her a violent glance that silenced her

immediately. Then I watched as he inserted the needle into my vein. It was quick and fast and didn't hurt much. A thin sliver of blood rose into the dropper, and Joe squeezed the syringe. Blood dripped onto my thigh. I looked into his dead eyes, seeing Brian. Then, as the blood and the clear liquid disappeared into my vein, a gentle wave of peaceful acceptance washed through me, from my heart to my head. The knot of pain in my chest unraveled. I began to breathe slow and easy. My eyes turned inward on a rose of many petals. A sweet, deep red rose and my whole being curled into its center. I felt Joe pull the needle out. I licked my blood from my arm and thought I tasted good. Then my stomach turned over.

"Please," I heard my distant voice. "Please, I need to throw up."

They left me alone. I retched over the bowl as I had after seeing Kelly's charred body. But this time I enjoyed it. There was nothing but bile in me. When it was over, I stood up and wiped my mouth with some toilet paper. When I stepped out of the bathroom, the dogs were waiting with huge loving eyes. I patted their warm bodies and felt them push against my hands. The stench was gone. I waded nonchalantly over the excrement to Sheri and Joe, who were lying next to each other on the mattress.

"What kindda junkie are you anyway?" Sheri questioned. "How come you got sick? Were you puttin' me on? Is this your first time or something?"

I offered them both a cigarette. "Or something." Then, just to be cool, I added, "Nice stuff."

She took the cigarette. "Lady, you got balls. What's with you anyway?"

I said that the part about my old man going to jail was true, and I had the blues, so I figured I'd do what he used to do.

"Let's get outta here," she said, not seeming to care

that I had changed my story. "But," she said, "you
shouldda told me the truth. You couldda caught an OD."

I sat down next to her on the mattress, then lay back
like she was doing. I felt the dogs sniffing but I didn't
care. My eyes rolled away and I saw Kelly. We played in
Tompkins Square Park. When the flames came, I was
there and I pulled Kelly to safety. We laughed in the cool
water of the open hydrant.

"C'mon, we gotta get the fuck outta here," said
Sheri. Her voice sounded as if it were coming from far
away. She stood over me, offering her hand. Joe was
deep in a nod, and we just left.

I followed her down the stairs. Just before we got to
the door, she turned to face me. In her hands she held
the small coffin. It had a swastika on it I hadn't noticed
before.

"Here, babe," she offered. "Take this so you can
always get a taste."

I studied the hand-carved coffin in her pretty hands.
It seemed a long time before I took it into my own
hands.

"You're gonna need it," she said.

On the street in front of the meat market several
men unloaded sides of beef that looked like cows peeled
and cut in half. A young boy rinsed blood from the street
into the gutter with a hose. In the rising dawn, I took my
coffin home.

CHAPTER NINE

Errol and I were pounding the beat. We had just changed from day shift to night shift, so I had a whole extra day to recover from my encounter with Cobra's thing. I was weary and sad—my double life was taking its toll.

It was the first day of filming and we were on Sixth Street on foot. There was a reason for that—on foot we were more visible and that was crucial to the mayor's office. City Hall was watching Sixth Street because the mayor—always looking for ways to boost the city's economy—had just created the Office of Film Development, and it was important to him that shooting in New York City be a pleasant experience for the crews, the director, and, particularly, the stars of the movie. And this movie had a lot of stars.

I had trouble staying focused; my mind kept going back to yesterday. After leaving the loft above the meat market, I had gone home and slept so hard I thought I died. When I finally got up, the apartment was dark and empty. My uniform was hanging on a hanger hooked over the top of the bathroom door. A small tube of neon over the bathroom sink was the only light in the apartment. It took a while before I began to hear the noises of the street again. Horns, voices, sirens, trucks—everything seemed as though it were very, very far away.

As I struggled to wake up, I realized I hadn't even bothered to take my street clothes off—even my spiked heels—though at some point, I had unzipped my shorts. I looked at my right arm with its big purple bruise. I studied that bruise the same way I used to study my bruises after fights with Lenny, calculating how long it would take it to disappear. Then, in the play of light and shadow, I thought I saw the uniform move.

I looked up at the uniform and suddenly it didn't seem like just cloth hanging on a hanger. In the eerie neon glow of the bathroom light, the uniform took on a life of its own. It towered over me as I sat on the edge of my bed, like a big stern father pointing an incriminating finger my way. Behind the uniform, the white porcelain of the toilet reminded me of yesterday—the dogs, the stench, and Cobra's thing. I couldn't stop thinking that last night I had changed. When I put that needle in my arm, the thing I despised most had become a part of me. Now I understood something that only hours before I had been blind to. I understood that heroin made the world stop, and I understood why a person would want that.

Then Errol's voice brought me back to Sixth Street.

"These people have created a whole imaginary world," he said, "just like you're doing inside your head."

I looked down and saw his feet next to my own. We were wearing the same kind of shoes and the same pants. He was my leader, but I wasn't exactly following in his footsteps. I was ashamed to look up into his eyes because I thought he might see too much in mine.

He rattled on. "You see this, these guys didn't like

the real world so they created another. Another time and place."

"Yeah, and here we are in our monkey suits protecting their dream."

Errol laughed. "Who stands guard over our dreams?"

As he spoke, I glanced around and realized it was morning. Dawn on the Lower East Side is always sneaky. It rises over the rooftops in one move, as if somebody had turned on a big dirty light bulb. The cast and crew were getting ready for work. Lights were coming on in the trailers. Electricians were moving coils as big as boa constrictors.

"The stars will be coming out soon," I said. "We should enjoy that."

"Look, you have no idea how sorry I am that the runner we caught produced a dead end. But it would have been no different if we had kept him to ourselves. Except that we might have wound up on the street with no jobs and no badges."

I stepped over a huge coil and lied to his face. "I don't care about that anymore."

"You're letting go?"

I pointed to the middle of the street where the director was making his first appearance. I knew him from his picture in the paper. "That's Francis Ford Coppola."

He grabbed my arm. "You wouldn't kid a guy would you?" We weren't talking about the movies, this shit was real.

There was a look on his face that said he desperately wanted to believe me. I knew my whole face said that I was lying, and when I talked, my voice said so too. I couldn't help that. Still, he missed it; he sighed and said, "I'm relieved. You don't know how relieved I am."

We were stepping through the space between two very fancy trailer trucks when a door opened. A flood of bright, white light hit Errol's face dead on. He squinted, his eyes went liquid, and with his hand, he tried to shelter his face from the light. At that precise moment, I knew why he didn't see my lies. He had a gigantic blind spot—like the blind spot I once had toward Lenny. Then I understood why he had stepped out on a limb to cover for me that day with the bundle. Errol was in love. When the realization hit me, I just froze.

Finally, Errol called after me. "Coming, Conroy?"

"Bet." My legs started to move again.

Luckily there was plenty happening on that shift so we didn't do much talking. We watched the stars come out and huddle with the director and shoot take after take. Everything was backwards. They were filming a gangster-style shoot-out in a sidewalk cafe. First the killers came down the block in their 1920s sedans and machine-gunned everybody down. They did that about six times. Then, all the dead people got up, went to their trailers for make-up, and came back to eat dinner at the cafe.

Errol and I laughed as always when we were together. But every time I recalled what he had done for me and why, I felt lousy. I wondered if he knew he was in love with me. He must know. Could I count on him to keep his feelings to himself? What if he didn't? What would I do? I wasn't like those people in the movies who could die and live again. My feelings were dead. Besides, he wasn't my type. It was lousy.

I guess maybe a part of Errol felt that it was lousy too, because he got sick that week. He was the kind of cop who never missed work, so when he called in to say that he was sick, I knew that he was really sick.

"What's wrong?" I asked.

"I don't know." His voice came through very weak. "Some kind of bug, I guess."

I told him how sorry I was and hung up. That night

Mary came down with a virus. So that next week, Sevinsky and I were partners.

On our first shift together he never spoke to me. Not once. He pretended he was alone in the car. His eyes never met mine. When he stopped to eat, I just stayed in the car and napped. I didn't give him the satisfaction of knowing that he upset me. But something about him made my skin crawl.

By the third day, he had me catching stiffs. When someone dies alone and there is no doctor to sign the death certificate, a cop has to stay with the stiff until the assistant coroner arrives. It's an assignment they give to rookies they want to break. I don't know what strings Sevinsky pulled, but I was certain he was responsible for my new assignment.

In New York City so many people die alone that the wait for the coroner can be six to eight hours. Before they made their trip to Potter's Field, several lonely people waited with me. Each time the scene was quietly similar. A long railroad flat, well-kept, poor, and simple. One died at the table over a last solitary meal of cat food, one in the bathroom after a slip in the tub, and one on the floor reaching for the phone. They waited right where they had died, covered with a sheet as if that would hide the sad truth of their lives.

Hour after hour, we waited for the coroner to arrive. I always kept the door to the apartment open and stayed near it, just to try to escape the smell. I kept cigarette filters in my nostrils but there was no escaping that odor. And something always compelled me to return for just one more look. I would pull the sheet back and take another glance. The faces seemed to be waiting—waiting for someone to arrive before they made their final exit— someone who had known and loved them. But nobody ever showed up.

I had covered the pain of Kelly's death like an oyster makes a pearl, with a hard surface of hate. But those endless hours with death cut away that protection, and I was again left with a mouthful of sand.

Each day I longed for the end of the shift and the beginning of night. Compared to the quiet face of death, the hookers were alive, funny, and warm. They began to accept that I had my own reasons for being out there. I hung with Tiny and her crowd at the tunnel, and I copped several times to prove that I belonged—or was that why I copped?

By the time Errol came back to work, my nerves were so raw I was hanging onto the job by my fingernails. Another week catching stiffs, and I think I would have crossed that thin line to the safety of insanity.

"Damn, I'm glad you're back," I told him, as we headed for our car.

"I guess Sevinsky lived up to his reputation."

It was a statement that required no answer. The sun was burning down on the block and the handle of the car door burned my hand. "It's locked," I said.

He slid in on his side and opened my door from the inside. I got in. We both just sat there for a moment. He was studying me like a mother studies a child she is worried about. "You look awful. Was it that bad?"

He inserted the key in the ignition, the engine turned.

"I spent most of the week catching stiffs. I'm sick to my stomach. The smell never leaves me now."

He drove out of the block and around the corner, then pulled over. I could tell he just wanted to give me a comforting hug, but uniform to uniform it was impossible. Still, his compassion was so deep I felt it holding me gently.

"I'm so sorry," he said. "It must have been sheer hell. Especially for you."

I looked out at a pile of rotting garbage on the

sidewalk. "I'm glad you're back. I didn't think I was gonna make it."

He shrugged sadly. "Some of these sexists can really take the heart out of you. I apologize for him. He's an asshole. Not all cops are like him."

I wanted to say that there seemed to be something more wrong with Sevinsky, that he wasn't an ordinary sexist, but I couldn't put my finger on it. Instead I said, "I know that. After all, there are a few cops like you."

Again, he pulled out into the early morning traffic. "Are you sure that's all it is, nothing else is wrong?"

"Yeah, that's all," I said, without even missing a beat. Then I just sat there thinking that even sitting with stiffs was better than lying to Errol. But what was I supposed to do, tell him I was leading a double life now? That at night I dressed like a whore and copped dope.

"How did it make you feel?" he asked.

A light steady buzz went off in my head and then I sniffed my fingertips. "That smell is in my skin and my uniform now. Even after dry cleaning, I can't get rid of it."

"I know about that smell," he said quietly.

The buzzing got louder, more frantic, like something trying to escape.

"Christ, our windshield is dirty," I said, and I started to rub the inside with a cloth I kept in the glove compartment.

That was when I noticed the horsefly lying on its back on the dashboard. I tapped it with the cloth to help it turn over. It flew up, hit the windshield, and fell back down. It tried again and fell once more. Errol droned on. "In our culture we don't deal very well with death. We hide from it, pretend it doesn't exist."

I listened to the fly thumping vainly against the glass. "What are you saying?"

"I'm trying to share something with you. My first week on the job I held a dying kid in my arms. He was stabbed in a gang fight."

I was watching his oddly chiseled profile as he talked. The mouth was larger than it should have been, the chin wider, the ears bigger, but put together, I finally had to admit that he was a sexy guy. His voice was a soothing masculine rasp.

"By the time we got there the fight was over. All the other kids had run off except this one. He was hanging onto a chain-link fence clutching his guts in his hand. I took him into my car to run him to the hospital. Warm blood was everywhere. We looked at each other, really looked at each other, and we both realized he was going to die. I just held him in my arms. I watched a calm come over him. I watched him let go."

I didn't say anything. I was smelling my fingertips. Was it my fingertips or my jacket? Errol leaned in close. "I'm saying that I felt his spirit leave his body."

I swatted the fly, and it stopped buzzing. "You mean that reincarnation mumbo jumbo."

"I'm not calling it anything. I'm just saying I felt his spirit go. After that, his body was just a shell that turned cold. For a while it made me crazy."

"I'm awful sorry."

"I got help. I went some place. I went to this group called the Samaritans where people talk and when they talk they heal."

"Samaritans like the guy from the Bible?" I was sniffing my uniform at the shoulder.

He tried again. "Are you falling apart because you were catching stiffs all week or because you haven't come to terms with Brian and Kelly's deaths?"

"I'll come to terms when I get the fuck who did it."

He shook his head. "You're lying to yourself. That's not the answer. It's just a cover for your guilt. The one you really want to destroy is yourself."

I thought about my nights chasing that deadly cure. Was he right? Had chasing Sunny become just a cover? I didn't really want an answer, but I asked, "What kind of an asshole would do the shit that I do?"

"How many things are you blaming yourself for? For Brian, for Kelly, for loving the wrong man, or just for loving a man at all?"

He was getting under my skin, so I tried to start a fight about his turning the runner over to the squad. I pulled that routine every time he got too close. But this time, he didn't bite. He just kept on his own track.

"You're not God," he said. "You don't control events."

"I can't get rid of that smell."

"Another time a woman gave birth in my squad car, and I pulled the baby out. Its eyes were closed, it was in a glistening sheath—like a pod of some sort. That time I felt the spirit enter."

We turned a corner and reached the projects that were slated for demolition. I watched the pit that was going to become the new condo coming up ahead—it always gave me the creeps—and I wondered what planet this guy was from. Then I thanked my lucky stars that he was my partner.

CHAPTER TEN

The morning sun fell softly onto the precinct house floor, and the smell of freshly brewed coffee welcomed me. Even though I was running late, I had time to notice how much I had come to love this place. The precinct building had been built in 1912, and its age gave me a feeling of permanence I had never known before. The wood was old, the steps were worn. Several generations of cops had shared victory and defeat inside the safety of its walls. When I got to roll call, the sarge was already giving his rundown for the day.

"Filming started on Sixth Street last week. The cap says you men have done a good job cleaning the scum off the block, so let's just make sure we keep it that way for our Hollywood friends. Item two—the protesters on Avenue D, as you may have noticed, have turned into squatters, but the digging goes on. We've assigned two extra teams to that sector, but I want us all to keep an eye out for movement into the area. There's a rumor they're bringing people in from the East Harlem Community Council and we wanna stay on top of it."

The sarge droned on. I had a hard time listening. I

was tired and hollow, as if the skag I'd had again last night had made me forget who I was and what I was doing here. I thought if I could get safely into the squad car, I'd be able to pull myself together. The sarge's words grew fuzzy then, though I heard my name and Errol's too. A few minutes later we wandered to our still unair-conditioned car together.

"Wanna drive?" he offered. I declined. We went straight to the coffee shop. No conversation. When he pulled up he turned to me. "What's the matter? You look like your own shadow. Don't you feel well?"

"I didn't sleep well last night."

"Light and sweet?" he asked. I nodded.

"Okay, stay put. I'll handle it."

He got out and went into the bustling coffee shop. I sat there hoping a cup of coffee would wake me up. It was just eight o'clock, but I could feel the heat rising and wondered how I was going to make it through the day. We were parked on the corner of Seventh Street and Avenue A. Across the street the park was empty except for a few of the Polish old-timers playing chess on concrete tables. The few trees were thin and sickly looking. Spots of grass were already turning from green to brown. Several workers headed for the subway on Fourteenth Street, an occasional kid headed for day camp. It all seemed so very sad. I didn't even notice Errol come back until he tapped on the window. I let him in. He handed me coffee and a cheese Danish.

"I didn't ask for this."

He shrugged. "I thought you could use a little something extra."

I said thanks and opened the glove compartment to set my coffee and Danish down on its door. "Did the autopsy report on the old lady in the Baker case come in?" I asked, working the lid off the cup. Inside the coffee was steaming hot.

Errol nodded and took a sip of coffee. "Yeah, natural causes," he said. "But Baker copped a plea. Burglary first degree. He'll do a bullet." That meant a year in prison, and with good time he'd serve only six months.

"Where is he now?" I asked. My coffee was almost gone. I wasn't feeling any better, plus I was worried because I needed more to go on before finding Sunny. I needed to talk to Baker.

What's the difference?" Errol said. "You got your collar. You took a junkie off Sixth Street, and the cap's happy with you. Isn't that what you were looking for?"

I got out to throw my empty container into the corner garbage can and to get away from him.

"So I don't have to testify?" I asked him through the open window. I could see only half his face.

"That's right. You don't know how lucky you are. No testimony required."

"Where's Baker now?"

"On the Rock, where else?

I didn't say anything more after that because I was really too sad to talk. We drove wordlessly through our sector until a call came over the radio for us.

Errol picked up. "Yeah, I read you loud and clear. What's up?"

"You got a group in the projects, building three. Get over there quick and tell me if you need backup."

"Ten-four."

We sped off in the direction of the East River, rushing toward Alphabet City. We parked on Seventh Street because the avenue itself had become a campground. We locked up the squad car, and ran toward the projects. Twenty or more tents were pitched in the middle of Avenue D. Some women fed their families at card tables. Others ate on blankets spread over the cement. From above, the huge crane continued to bite at the earth. We ran toward building three and heard the shouts of the squatters. "Get the fuck outta here! We don't need you!"

An old Puerto Rican grandmother with a wrinkled face placed her fat little body in front of me and pointed an angry finger at me. In her thick accent she accused me. "A woman! A woman with these *puercos*, pe-e-egs? What about *los niños*?"

Just then a wild-eyed woman appeared in a third-floor window. She was screaming and throwing men's clothes down to the ground below. "Get your shit the fuck outta here you son of a bitch! I don't want you here! I don't want you in my life!"

Every sentence was punctuated by falling underwear, socks, or trousers. The crowd below began acting like spectators at a sports event.

"Yeah, baby, throw that skirt chaser out. C'mon, throw me some socks."

"Chill out, Karen! Chill out, the pigs are here."

Even from across the street, I saw the craziness in her swollen eyes, the anger on her swollen lips. Errol and I ran into the building, guns drawn, because in a domestic dispute, you never know what's coming. We ran up the three flights of stairs. I expected to kick down the door, but it was wide open. The woman stood in the hallway screaming at a closing elevator door.

"That's right, run, mothafucka. I'm gonna kill your scumbag ass."

"I'm going after him," Errol said.

That meant she was mine. I nodded to indicate I could handle her. Errol bolted for the stairs. She ran back inside the apartment with me on her tail. She returned to the window and busied herself throwing more clothes to the street below. I just stood there for a second. The crushed red velvet living room set was covered in plastic. Everything matched—couch, coffee table, end tables. Plaster statues of Greek gods and goddesses stood on the linoleum. On one wall a cluster of wedding pictures was surrounded by a host of smaller family pictures, a lot of them pictures of a baby girl. Where was the baby? The pile of clothes at the woman's feet whimpered. I moved toward the sound, and then I saw the arm—a tiny, tiny arm. I put my gun away. Before

I could get the baby, she had it. She still didn't bother about me. She just turned back to the window with the baby in her arms and demonstrated.

"See this, muthafucka?" She held the little girl up in the window. "Take this too."

"Hey," I whispered. "Hey, you forgot something." For a split second, she turned, bringing her arms back from the window. I lunged for her, hitting her in the jaw and in the stomach. She dropped the baby head first but I caught her by the legs. The mother was already back at the window, screaming, "I'll kill you. I'll kill that bitch too."

The baby looked awful, but I put her down on the sofa. Downstairs, Errol was wrestling with the husband. I told the mother to turn around and that she was under arrest, but she wouldn't listen to me. I told her twice, but she wouldn't stop screaming. So I took her arm and bent it behind her. She wheeled around and whacked me in the jaw. My teeth went into my cheek and I tasted blood. The baby started to make a gurgling sound as if she wanted to cough but couldn't. She made a soft, soft, painful sound and I started to lose it. The mother was clawing at my face, but she was no match for me. I hit her in the larynx, and as the air went out of her, I cuffed her.

I went over to the couch and picked up the baby. She was blue. One of her shoulders was lower than the other. The baby must have been about eight months old, chubby and well fed. She was trying to cry, the little mouth wide open, the face contorted; no sound came out. I cradled her to my chest, and she kept trying to cry. A thin trickle of blood flowed from her left ear. She clutched my uniform with miniature fingers and hiccupped for air.

Errol brought the cuffed husband into the apartment.

"You okay?" he asked me.

"She hit me. She's been hitting me," the mother wailed. The baby hiccupped. I nodded yes, that I was okay.

The husband looked at the baby. "Oh, my God! She used that baby like a goddamn weapon. She threw her at me. I tried to catch her but she hit the wall."

Errol's face was white with horror.

"He was fucking my neighbor right here in my apartment, right in front of the baby. He was supposed to be babysitting."

Errol and I stared at each other. In my arms the baby silently struggled to scream.

"Get an ambulance," I said, barely recognizing my own voice.

"Let's run the baby over to Beth Israel ourselves. We'll save time," Errol said. He turned to his prisoner. "Let's go, buddy."

I tried to make the wife move but she huddled over. "I ain't goin' no place. Why don't you hit me some more?"

Errol was already halfway out the door but he stopped and turned to me. "Don't do anything stupid."

"Take the baby," I said. "This bitch is giving me a hotfoot."

He took the child. "Are you okay?"

I shook my head. "We'll be right behind you."

I went back to get her. As soon she saw me coming, she lunged for me even though she was cuffed. I sidestepped her, reaching behind her back and yanking the cuffs up her spine. She yelped as the metal cut into her flesh. She went down on her knees.

"Get up," I barked. She wobbled to her feet, took one step toward the door, then refused to move any further. I gave her a shove that was harder than it should have been and she sprawled on her back. At the bottom of the steps, I saw Errol still holding the baby. I heard its anguished whimper and something in me snapped. I grabbed the mother by her ankles.

"What the fuck are you doing?" Errol's eyes caught mine. "Get her on her feet."

I saw him through a fog, the baby in his arms, his prisoner leaning against the wall, and I just stood there.

"Get her up," he screamed. Only then did I remember my duty to my uniform. Reluctantly, I pulled her up.

We put the couple in the back seat and sped toward Beth Israel. The siren screamed, and I held the baby as she fought for breath. Her lips and eyelids were swelling, and her little fingers curled around mine. I turned to the couple in the back seat. "Why didn't you animals kill each other? Why the baby?"

"I didn't meant it," said the mother. "They're gonna take our apartment. Luis was the super. Now he's out of a job and he makes up for it by screwing anything he can. Is the baby all right? I didn't mean it."

I watched the blood trickle from the baby's ear and felt her grip weaken on my fingers.

The mother kept repeating, "I didn't mean to . . . I didn't mean to."

I wanted to crawl over that seat, and slap her. Errol must have known because he turned to me. "Cool it," he said. "Just cool it."

When we got to Beth Israel I ran to the emergency room and handed the baby to a doctor with a quick explanation. She took the baby inside. We stayed to file our report. Then we went back to the precinct house for the paperwork.

By the time we got to the squad room the baby's parents were lovey-dovey and nobody wanted to press charges. But we were going downtown anyway. We were charging them both with plenty.

After we put them in the car, Errol said, "Let's step aside for a minute. I have to talk to you."

We stepped into an alley between two buildings by the precinct house. As soon as we were alone, he started screaming at me.

"Have you lost your fucking mind?"

I shrugged because I knew exactly what he meant, and I had no defense.

"They call it police brutality," he said. "You could have really hurt her. Then where would the case be? Doesn't your badge mean anything to you?"

I rubbed an ache on my cheek as I looked into his angry, concerned eyes and whispered, "I guess I wanted to hurt her the way she hurt the baby."

"You can't let it get to you that way," he said quietly.

"I saw what she did to that baby." When I remembered the infant's helplessness, I wanted to collapse and just cry. But I didn't.

"If she were a little hipper, she'd try to file charges against you. You're too good a cop to have that happen."

I clenched my teeth and tried to swallow my own bitterness. We were mostly in the shadow of the building, yet the sun bit brutally into my eyes.

"It won't happen again," I said.

Then he looked away and took a deep breath. "Listen, have dinner with me. I wanna talk to you off the job."

I just stared at him and wondered what the hell was happening between us. His face was cut in half by sun and shade, and I could see his pain. I figured I had caused it, so I said yes. I would have dinner with him, next week. We stared at each other, and then he cut me loose. He said he could handle downtown without me. I told him thanks, because I was really tired. Then I went home and after a short nap, I switched identities.

I went up to 110 Street and Lenox Avenue along Central Park thinking that I might find Sunny there. The park was a deep, dark shadow. I passed many large apartment buildings from the thirties and forties with fancy entrance ways and poetic names etched in stone above open doorways. Names like The Lausanne, The Manhattan, and The Champs-Elysees. Inside the remnants of human beings lay in drugged and drunken stupors, not caring whether it was day or night.

In a pool hall, I caught up with myself. I asked for Sunny in the routine way I always asked for her when staking out a joint. To my amazement I got an answer.

"She went over into the park. You missed her by one shot." The pool player pointed out into the night. "She just booked." He rubbed some chalk on the end of his cue.

Adrenaline shot through my veins. Her presence was still so fresh that I thought I could smell her. Central Park at 110th Street wasn't my idea of a stroll. But this was the shot I had been waiting for, and I was packing, so that made the night seem right.

In the park the walkway descended quickly into the pitch black underside of the full summer trees. A slight breeze rustled the leaves and devoured the last sounds of the street. I had my .22 over my pelvis. I was wearing jeans, and I could get in there pretty fast. But as I stood at the foot of the path that led deeper into the darkness, my heart echoed in my chest, begging me not to go. I touched my hand to my groin feeling steel shift over the soft flesh of my abdomen. I told myself that I had been trained for this stuff. My eyes adjusted to the lack of light, my ears listened for some sounds of life, coughing, moaning, laughter, words in the air. But I heard nothing. Only my pounding eardrums and the rustle of leaves. I walked in deeper. The arms of the trees closed around me. I followed a bend in the descending path. Twigs snapped low to the ground.

There were two of them. One was tall, lean, muscular, and purple black. I couldn't make out his face. Next to him stood a short, squat white guy.

"Looking for something, sweetheart?"

"My sister Sunny," I said. "I hear she just came in here."

They looked at each other. "Got any money?"

"I do, but I was gonna use it to cop. You fellas wanna cop with me?"

The black cat reached one long arm my way. "Just gimme the bread, and we'll leave you be."

"All right," I said, "but let's walk out of the park."

"The money," he said.

I reached into my pocket and handed him a twenty. "Is this all of it?"

"It is," I answered, like I expected to walk now.

"I want more than money," the white guy said and stepped onto a rock that made him much taller. "Take off those clothes."

"Aw-w-w c'mon, she gave us the bread. Let's get the fuck outta here."

"I want me a little piece first."

I started running. He jumped down from his rock and knocked me face first under him. He played with my right arm as if it were a chicken wing he was trying to wrench from the body. I squirmed, reaching into my crotch for the piece that was hard between me and the ground. I had just gotten my hand into my jeans when he flipped me over and went for his fly.

"That's right," he said, "open it up for me."

He unzipped me. The velcro that held the belly band snugly to my body ripped open. My piece bulged between my legs. I had my hand on it.

"Holy shit! Holy shit! She's a cop!"

I didn't have to do another thing. I just lay there and listened to them disappear right through the goddamn bushes.

I lay there aching all over, feeling Sunny's nearness, wondering if I would ever get that close again. I got up and dusted myself off wearily. I adjusted the holster and belly band to my body so that the piece was not visible in my pants. As I walked from the park, I decided on one more try. I'd walk to 105th off Lenox. It was a block like a drug supermarket. Maybe I'd find her copping there. And to do that, I figured I'd have to cop myself.

There were dope dealers on every other corner and in every other doorway. On one stoop a bunch of teenagers listened to a ghetto blaster, some danced on the street, others watched toddlers and babies in strollers. A little girl stepped in front of me. She wore a pink dress with a wide crinoline, and when she bumped into my knees I almost tripped over her. In order not to, I bent down and held her for a moment.

"What the fuck are you doing?" A young mother who looked no more than fourteen stepped up to me, a child herself. Her protective eyes shone from a blue black face, her compact body was African.

"Your kid?"

"What about it?"

I let the little girl go. "She's cute."

She picked her up and headed for the stoop. I called after her.

"Listen, maybe you can help me. I'm looking for Cobra's thing."

She turned to study me more carefully. Evidently she decided I was a safe bet, because she said, "How much are you looking for?"

"A couple of bags."

She shook her head. "I can get it for you, but you gotta cop at least eight bags, and only if you give me two bags for myself."

"Two bags. That's highway robbery."

She started walking again.

I took a few steps in her direction. "Okay, how much?"

"Seventy-five."

"What?"

"Look, you ain't from around here. Try somebody else and see what you get. It may sound cheaper, but there's nobody lookin' out for your white ass. You'll get beat and wind up empty-handed."

"Okay, but you gotta let me go with you."

She laughed. "And lose my connection? Forget it."

It was my turn to start walking away. "There's no way I'm gonna let you walk off with that kind of bread while I just sit here hoping that you'll come back."

She softened. "All right. Look, gimme the bread. You can hold the kid till I get back. But keep a serious eye on her. Last week they found a two-year-old boy in that dumpster. His hair was tied up in a pony tail, he had on nail polish and lipstick, and his little ass was tore up like a grapefruit."

My stomach lurched. I looked at the child in her arms and thought of my own daughter. The child I had failed. I hesitated, but finally I said, "The kid is safe with me," and she placed the child in my arms.

"Dee Dee get down," the little girl said.

I studied the roundness of her little legs. Two deep folds in her thighs reminded me of Kelly's baby fat, and my heart turned over. I put the little girl down. She toddled toward an open fire hydrant where the water ran like silver in the moonglow.

I took out some bills from my back pocket and counted seven tens and a five. The mother grabbed the bills from my hand. "Be back in a flash."

"What's your name?"

"Nancy."

"Is it all right if she gets wet?"

She looked at me blankly.

"The kid," I said.

She shrugged. "Whatever," she said, then split down the block.

Dee Dee was trying to drink from the hydrant. The water fell so fast and furiously that she couldn't manage it. After each try she giggled at me. Catercorner from the stoop, light spilled onto the street from a small bodega. I picked her up out of the gutter, where the water flowed like a river. "Want some soda?" I asked her.

She nodded and said, "Dee Dee down." She wanted to do her own walking, so I let her. Then, just to make sure none of the women on the stoop thought I was kidnapping her, I pointed to the bodega. "I'm going to buy the kid and me a soda."

One of the women nodded but didn't say anything. I took Dee Dee by the hand and matched my step to her waddle. Inside the bodega there was a candy stand. While I went to the refrigerator, Dee Dee fingered the different kinds of candy. She picked a cellophane bag of hard candy and pulled it off the rack. "For Dee Dee," she said.

I remembered how much Kelly had always enjoyed paying for her own candy, so I handed her three singles, one at a time. Her eyes opened wide. "For Dee Dee," I said.

"Dee Dee pay."

She rose to her tippy toes and shoved the money toward the old Puerto Rican behind the counter. "The sodas too," I told him.

He took the money, rang the register open, then offered me the change. I shook my head. "Give it to Dee Dee." She turned the pennies and nickles over in her hand, then offered them to me. "You can keep that," I said. "What do you say?"

"Thank you," she answered, and reached for my hand. Together we crossed the street. She sat next to me on the bottom step of the stoop. I opened her soda and mine. Then, while we drank, she opened the cellophane bag with her teeth, took the many-colored candies out, and arranged them in groups, according to color. She offered the other kids each a piece. Except red. She didn't let anyone pick red. Except me. I asked if I could give her a kiss. She offered me her cheek, then embraced me. "What's your name?" she asked.

I put her on my lap. "Toni, my name is Toni."

Across the street a little boy about Dee Dee's size broke free of his mother's hand and ran toward the street. The mother reached a fast hand to stop him. Then she pounded the little body and screamed, "You keep your black ass away from those cars. I want you safe."

A pair of teenagers came up the block, one brown, one white. They wore cut-off jeans and bopped up the block in their high-top sneakers. There was a lot of hand action too. The white boy was complaining.

"You always charge me twice the going rate."

"Going rate! Going rate! This ain't the Stock Exchange. You know you're a dumb white boy, just dumb. You know where the white man comes from, don't you? The albino gorilla, ain't you ever heard of the albino gorilla?"

"What about you, you rice and beans gorilla?"

"You make it hard for me in your world, I make it hard for you in mine."

"What are you talking about? It ain't my world, I'm a dope fiend like you."

"You're white, aren't you?"

"Yeah."

"Well, there's your answer. You're you and I'm me."

Dee Dee was still on my lap when her mother returned. I was playing with her tight curls, and we were talking about the colors of the candy. I told her she was much sweeter than the candy. She giggled, her whole body bouncing on my knee. Then she saw her mother.

"Mommy." Dee Dee offered her mother a red candy. Dee Dee jumped from my lap to hug her mother's knees.

"Step into the hallway with me," Nancy said as she brushed Dee Dee aside. We climbed the stoop and opened the first of two doors. In the space between the doors I asked, "Is it Cobra's thing?"

She opened her hand to reveal a small stack of cellophane bags, all marked with green tape. "You got works?"

"I'm going downtown," I said by way of answer. I took the eight bags, then gave her two. I glanced toward the street. Dee Dee was in the gutter. I pulled out another bag for Nancy.

"Thanks," she said, her eyes wide with surprise— nobody is generous with dope.

"Nice kid," I said as we stepped out into the night. I was wishing I could take Dee Dee with me when I remembered about Sunny. "Listen, I'm looking for a friend of mine from the Lower East Side. I heard she hangs around up here now. She does dope too. Her name is Sunny."

"Sunny," she wrinkled her nose. "Sunny who? That's a nickname. What she look like?"

It was then that I realized the absurdity of my search. Did I actually expect to find someone whose last name I didn't know and whose description I didn't have? "I don't know her last name, but she's a blond."

"There ain't too many blonds up here." Nancy flashed a wide smile. She was up the way Brian was up when the cure was a sure thing. Happy like Sheri, happy like I was now. Once again I realized how suspect my search for Sunny was.

I left Nancy and Dee Dee behind and listened to the tapping of my heels on the pavement. I tried to remember what it was that made me different from every other dope fiend out here—and I couldn't remember. I was hazy, tired, worn down from trying to be two people: one in uniform, striving to be perfect in every way, and one who stalked the nighttime streets searching for the cure, hiding behind an insane, impossible revenge—a search in which all the leads were cold and nothing I could dig up would matter anyway. I listened to the rhythm of my own steps and reflected on the sad truth that I was really no different from them—the junkies had their rationalizations too, but in the end we were the same.

CHAPTER ELEVEN

Mary had her back to me when I opened the door, and the apartment was dark except for a candle on the table. I was still locking the locks when I felt her turn toward me.

"Don't you want the light?" I whispered.

"It's up to you," she said, and I heard the tears in her raspy voice. Even in the half-light I saw the white gleam of papers in her hand. They rustled slightly in the air conditioner's artificial breeze. I knew what was coming so I just stood there, choosing not to move the moment forward.

"I got it," she said. "I got the fire marshall's report."

I hit the switch by the door, and fast, brutal light illuminated the room.

"What the hell are you wearing?" she asked as she took in my appearance. I thought about the dope in my pocket and the coffin hidden in the lining of my winter coat, tucked safely in the back of a closet. I shrugged. "I'm undercover."

"Undercover! Is that what you call the crazy shit you do?"

I just raised a shoulder and let it fall back down. She knew I slipped out at night, but so far she had chosen not to confront me and that was fine. We both continued to stand there. She was by the window and I still by the door. She turned from me again, her eyes searching the empty nighttime street below. She seemed whiter, more fragile. Her hair was pinned up and she rubbed the back of her neck. Even from across the room I saw that it was stiff with pain.

"I just can't figure it out," she finally said. I knew then that she had something more to say but couldn't. I crossed the room, took the several sheets of paper from her hand and read. The fire marshall's report left no doubt that the fire had been arson. I leaned my forehead on the window. My pulse crashed violently against the damp pane.

"I don't get it," she continued. "Why would Vogel lie and say the whole thing was an accident? Didn't he know you could have gotten your own copies of the autopsy reports? Damn, they could have been mailed to you."

"I had no address then and I was half crazy. I was no threat to anyone. Even a child could have run a game on me."

"But what was his motive in taking a chance like that? The fire marshall's report is conclusive—that means somebody killed this investigation."

"Why?" I asked. "Why did this case warrant a cover-up?"

I couldn't imagine Brian, sponger that he was, involved in anything really big. Brian was a little snake. He had crawled back into my good graces by pretending to be clean. I believed him because I loved him and he was my brother. I stood there looking at that fucking sheet of paper, cursing the word love. The report read "accelerated fire." I knew what that meant. It meant someone had gone through the trouble of dousing the apartment before striking the first match. Had someone come to the apartment intending to kill Brian and cover it up? That didn't make sense. If the killings were executions, they would have been cleaner. They would have taken Kelly and Brian upstate, out-of-town and away from a thousand eyes. I agreed with Mary. "It makes no sense."

With my fingertips I made circles on the glass. The air conditioner wasn't working right, and created the condensation I played with. Circles evaporated as fast as I drew them.

"Please turn around?" Mary whispered. But I didn't think I could face her without falling apart. I didn't want a friend, I wanted the cure.

"Please, you seem so far away."

When I did turn I saw my anguish mirrored in her face. There were deep lines on her forehead and around her eyes, lines that hadn't been there before. I broke free of her gaze to cross the room and blow the candle out. It died as soon as the wind of my breath touched it. Several drops of clear paraffin fell to the saucer the candle stood on.

"I need a witness," I said. "Somebody must know who went to my apartment that night. When I find out who, I'll know why."

I sat down wearily at the table in front of the extinguished candle, and Mary joined me. I played with the still hot paraffin, half wishing that she would just leave me alone now, but instead I continued to speak to her. "Thanks for getting the report. Was it difficult?"

She shook her head. "Not really. I just asked the fire marshall if he had this one in his files and he did. I don't think Sevinsky even noticed."

"How's it going with him?"

As soon as I said that I realized that she had been waiting for this question.

"That son of a bitch," she said. "I was hungry early

today, he let me stay hungry two hours because the car wasn't scheduled to eat yet."

"What? What schedule are you talking about?" I thought of how Errol and I always seemed to get hungry at the same time—although since I had begun dipping and dabbing I was never hungry anymore. But I knew that with Sevinsky, you ate when he ate or not at all. Hell, a lot of women lost their appetites that way. Endless eight-hour shifts. Dead air in the car. Not a kind word. I knew it was like that for Mary.

"Have you ever really looked into Sevinsky's eyes?" she asked me in a voice hoarse with anxiety.

"Yeah, I know," I said thinking about that week with Sevinsky.

Her face paled. "There's nothing there, nothing human, no feeling, no compassion. You know, the word around the precinct is that nobody wanted you and me as partners so they gave us to the two misfits."

"What's wrong with Errol?"

"They say he's too soft, cares too much. It makes him dangerous."

At her words, I felt a surge of anger awaken in me. But when I spoke my voice was surprisingly calm. "It makes him a better cop. Those fucks you're talking about have it all backwards."

"You know they say being partners is like being married?" She paused to make sure she had my attention. I nodded.

"Well, I want a divorce. I've asked the captain a few times but he just tells me he can't do it. Yesterday, we caught a burglar. Sevinsky locked me out of the building, then he put the guy face down at the edge of the steps and sat on his neck. But first he told him how much it would hurt and which of his bones would snap. The people stood there watching me bang on the door trying to get back in. I could see through the window in the door and I could hear Sevinsky laughing and the guy pleading. When they came out the guy's face was streaked with tears, he was covered in his own vomit, and his legs wouldn't hold up. Sevinsky dragged him along like a broken toy. And there was nothing I could do."

The fire marshall's report lay on the table between us. She turned it over. "Sometimes I think I'd rather die than stick with this guy. He makes me hate this job."

Her choice of words frightened me. For a split second I looked at her and saw Kelly, and I wanted to protect her from all the pain, the disappointment, the loneliness, and the terrible fear of poverty that had motivated her to seek a job for which she was not really suited. The lines on her face softened, and the sharp edge of her conflict blurred somewhat as my concern enveloped her. It slowly dawned on me that, despite my icy drive for revenge, I had found my first adult friend in Mary. When I was a kid I had lots of friends, at least the ones that my mother didn't scare off. But when I turned fifteen and moved in with Lenny, I stopped having friends. I hadn't really noticed until it was too late. I had been so caught up in being grown-up and being Lenny's woman. He hadn't wanted my friends around, and they had stopped coming.

As soon as I recognized Mary for the friend she had become, her nearness stifled me. Thank God she got around to leaving for her tour.

I pulled my coffin from its hiding place and opened it lovingly. I was meticulous. I had learned that the very act of cooking up, the preparation, the knowledge of the cure that was coming, were a high in themselves. Although getting my own vein was never easy, I happily punched half a dozen holes into my arm until I finally hit myself. The peace washed through me. High, with my eyes closed, I recreated the world just as I wanted it to be—I was with Kelly, mom, dad, Brian, and everything I had lost was mine again. Nothing was missing.

* * *

The next day was Sunday. I awoke with the same sensation that all memory and identity had been washed from me.

I had the day off. I hid the little coffin behind the commode as Brian had often done and then left for Rikers Island. Since I could find no new clues, I decided to try my best lead for something deeper. I needed to talk to Baker again. With me I had a large jar of instant coffee and two cartons of cigarettes.

Several buses left for Rikers Island from Queens, near LaGuardia Airport. Mothers, wives, children, girlfriends, brothers, and sisters—oddly I didn't see any fathers—were lined up and waiting. We had all taken a long subway ride to get to the starting point. Many mothers carried sandwich bags and cans of soda for the children, because the trip took the better part of the day. I had never made it before, but I knew from the neighborhood that the visit was short but the trip long.

I wondered if Baker had any other visitors. I stood by myself waiting for the bus, listening to the chatter of the others. I felt odd—I was one of them, but I wasn't.

"I told that son of a bitch to stop fooling around. I told him he better clean up or forget about me. Now he done gone and got hisself busted and expects me to wait two years, or else when he comes out he's gonna crack my skull."

"Mommy, will I be able to see daddy too?"

It was steaming hot. Most people acted like they were headed for a picnic on Coney Island and took off half their clothes when they got on the bus. A few solitary women looked like Juliets without Romeos. They looked pained and spoke to no one. I took a seat right behind the driver. On the outside chance that someone made me for a cop, it was the safest spot for me. We crossed over the bridge. I listened to many conversations merge into one and watched the beginning day reflect gray on the water below. I had been so tense about this trip that I had snorted half a bag of the stuff I had stashed at home. It had made me feel mellow, and nothing was bothering me. I felt I could handle everything smoothly but that I wasn't so high I'd be noticed. And I hadn't gone through the long and messy process of getting off. The slight high was like a cocoon that protected me from my own feelings. It also separated me from the others. Every time I closed my eyes, I could drift and go anywhere I wanted to go.

Behind me they were telling jokes and laughing. I guess because they were all there for the same reason they acted like a big family on an outing. One voice began laughing and the others chimed in, each in a different pitch, like instruments in an orchestra—the children's high shrill giggles like bells over the music of voices. The sound of their camaraderie opened me up, and I thought how much Errol and I laughed together. I closed my eyes and saw Kelly's laughing face, or Brian when we were kids and he and I would get stupid. Or Lenny when he won a big bet. I felt a sudden warmth for the strangers around me and wished that I could join in.

A deep male voice brought me back to the present. "This bridge wasn't always here. They used to bring the cons across on a ferry. They'd be locked in a van. One time a storm broke out, and the van slid off the back of the ferry. The pig drivers got out, but the prisoners drowned like rats. They were cuffed. They never stood a chance."

The laughter stopped. I felt their shared rage, their hatred for cops like me. My illusions of fitting in died quickly. Outside a soft summer drizzle had begun even though the sun was still shining.

Rikers was like a military command post. Even though we'd had our ID's checked before boarding the bus, we were checked again. The hacks treated the people on the bus as if they were criminals, not just friends and relatives visiting criminals. Finally, after sitting in the bus for another sweltering fifteen minutes, we were allowed off and herded into a large room in the main building. The room was divided in half by a thick plastic shield that was divided into cubby holes. In each cubby hole there was a telephone on either side of the clear pane. We were divided into two groups. I watched the first group sit down in the cubby holes. When the prisoners were allowed in, the crying began. I watched lovers kiss through the plastic and listened as they made promises I was certain they could not keep. Children were held so their fathers could see them better. Finally, it was my group's turn.

Baker came out. His head had been shaved, and he wore the same uniform they all wore—a loose-fitting gray shirt and pants that looked like pajamas. With his clean-shaven head he looked even younger than before. He gave me a long, leery look before sitting down. Then he just sat there without picking up the phone so I couldn't talk to him. I mouthed, "It's i-m-p-o-r-t-a-n-t," several times. I slapped the pane in frustration. Finally, he picked up.

I saw his lips move, his face contort, and the words emerged from the receiver in my hand. "What are you doing here?" he demanded angrily.

"I brought you coffee and cigarettes." I knew that in the can, coffee and cigarettes were like money. He could convert them into practically anything—extra meat, a better-fitting pair of pants, a high, or even a piece of ass. But he didn't fall for it.

"What for?" he asked suspiciously. "What do you want from me?"

I listened to the protestations of love and loyalty from the other booths and decided not to beat around the bush. "I can't find Sunny. I need her last name and a description plus her parents' address."

He put the phone down, terminating the conversation. I placed my two hands together as in prayer and mouthed, "Please, please, p-l-e-a-s-e."

He just sat there staring at me. His face began to soften, and even though he was the prisoner and I was supposedly free, he took pity on me. He picked up the phone once more. "You're Conroy's sister, aren't you?"

I nodded. "Yes, who told you?"

He shook his head. "Nobody. You look like him. I put two and two together. Why do you want Sunny? You gonna lock her up?"

It was my turn to shake my head. "I had a little girl—she died that night and I need to know what happened. Do you know?"

He shook his head no.

"Look, just give me a little more to go on so I can find Sunny. If you do, I promise I'll watch your back. I can try to get you out of here and into a drug program. If you help me I promise I won't forget you."

He rubbed his hand over his head as if the answer would pop out if he rubbed hard enough. He leaned forward and spoke into the telephone softly. "Sunny's real name is Susan Clark. I don't know nothing about her family. She's not from the neighborhood—I don't know where she's from. But I heard she's been on the run ever since Brian died. She probably doesn't even look the same anymore, maybe even changed her name."

Because I realized I wasn't about to get anything else out of him, I went for a long shot. "Why don't you tell me who this Cobra is?"

He clutched the phone so hard that his knuckles turned white as his hand turned red. Then he looked up at me as if to make sure I was getting each and every word. In a tense tight whisper he said, "Don't come back here. If you come back I ain't gonna talk to you. Don't ever come back."

He slammed the phone down and walked away. I watched him disappear through the door that led him back to his cell feeling that the whole world was an illusion, a house of mirrors where nothing was what it appeared to be. He had given me so little to go on. I wished that it was me walking back to that cell. At least I would be able to see the walls that confined me. I could neither touch nor see my torture chamber. My need for revenge began to feel like an endless sentence.

An odd thing happened then. I began thinking about the cure. I couldn't wait to get back to the apartment. All the way back to the city I looked forward to the cure, a tingling anticipation of something good, like looking forward to college, to coming home and hugging Kelly, to starting at the Academy, and to graduation. I yearned for the cure the way I had once yearned for Lenny's lovemaking. I was on a roller coaster from which few ever descend, and I had climbed on without so much as a second thought.

As soon as I got home, I snorted the other half of the bag. I showered and got dressed again. I decided to go down to the Lower East Side to try to find Sunny's old friends. Someone who might know why she was in flight and from whom. I was pretty certain that she was running because she knew too much. I was just about to walk out the door when I decided that I wasn't high enough. I locked myself back into the bathroom, this time with my little coffin, cooked up, and hit myself. It took four tries before I finally found the vein. My arm looked like a bruised pin cushion before it was over. Once my blood came up, I squeezed the syringe and let the dope flow into me.

A warm rush of satisfaction flowed through me, like a gentle lover or a homecoming. The high embraced me into the silence of its sterile womb, and everything I ever lost was returned to me. It didn't last long. After that a numbness set in, a numbness that made me oblivious to anger and pain. I looked at myself in the mirror. There was a glassiness to my gaze, but otherwise

I looked the same. Now I understood how Brian had used heroin for so long without any of us noticing.

My plan was to hang out in Tompkins Square Park and find out what I could about Sunny. It was the last week in July and the heat was oppressive. As I rode on an eastbound bus, I knew that even on a Sunday night the people would be out. Because I was high I drifted off, and I didn't come to until the bus was already on Avenue D. I got off and stepped into the dusk, which was just beginning to claim the day. The squatters on the avenue were preparing dinner on hibachis and barbecues. They had established a common kitchen and eating area and had even agreed on one ghetto blaster instead of ten. There were cops stationed all along the avenue, and I was careful to avoid them. I thought about these people's homes being razed and a luxury high rise built, while they were forced deeper into poverty—deeper into the ghetto, displaced by a gentrification process that would push them into Bedford Stuyvesant or Harlem, setting each family back a decade. Or the setback could become permanent, like when my dad never again found work. I ached for their futile struggle to hang on to the little they had. They had built one small bonfire in the center of the campground. Children gathered around it break dancing and rapping.

The two huge cranes stood silent now. I stared down into the huge pit. It looked like a grave for so many broken dreams. I thought of my own struggle. I had been on the job close to two months now and what did I really have? The case was closed. The only lead I had for sure was that some sort of cover-up was solidly in place—and the fire marshall's report told me that Vogel had lied. Had I been thinking two years ago, I would have looked at those autopsy reports when the facts were still hot. I thought about the 24/24 rule. It was a detective's rule of thumb—the crucial hours in any murder investigation are the victim's last 24 hours and the 24 hours after the body is discovered. The solution to the crime usually lies somewhere within those 48 hours. I had blown it. I was facing a cover-up that was two years old. I kicked some dirt into the pit and watched it fall, down and down to the wounded earth. The route was rocky and jagged. It took a long time before the dirt hit bottom. A lot of leads could grow cold in two years.

I started walking. Instead of going the direct route to Tompkins Square, I walked all the way to Fourth Street. When I reached the bottom of Fourth Street, I looked up. Night had not yet fallen but daylight was gone, and the sky sat on the tenements like a gray blanket. Fourth Street had become one of the most desolate blocks anywhere in the neighborhood. Cinder blocks sealed more than half the buildings—including the one where I had lived. The windows looked like uncarved gravestones. The whole street had died.

I walked slowly. Mid-block, a white neon cross glowed. As I passed it, I heard a chorus of voices singing "Rock of Ages" in Spanish. I recognized the tune, though I didn't understand the words. The lot next to the church was a garden now. The rubble and garbage had been cleared away and replaced by tomato plants, a lettuce patch, and flowers. The young shoots fought their way toward a crack of sky between two buildings. In the garden's green center a sign painted by a child's hand read: SAVE THE CHILDREN. I stood there for a long time savoring the hope and the common effort that had built that garden, reminding myself that by clearing the junkies off the block Errol and I had played a part in its creation. I left Fourth Street and headed for Tompkins Square Park.

Early evening was the most peaceful time in Tompkins Square. The sky was a hazy blue, the mood mellow. Dope dealers and mothers with small children mingled freely. I looked for Sunny, but not for long. I got paranoid. I kept thinking that even out of uniform, someone would recognize me and that would mess me up on the job. It was stupid to think I could go undercover in this neighborhood. But I was tired. Tired of doing it all alone. I took a step backwards.

I walked right through the cacophony of congas in the center of the park, out the exit on Avenue A, and to the foot of the Dragon's steps. There was only one chauffeured limousine on the block. It was early for an after-hours joint. Before going down the steps to the entrance under the stoop, I opened my purse, freshened my lipstick, and ran a brush through my hair. It frustrated me that in my jeans and T-shirt I was underdressed for the Dragon. I wanted to look good, to torture Lenny. My heart pounded. I descended the stairs to a large wooden door with a crystal window etched with a bouquet of roses. I touched the little golden button next to the door and pushed with my finger. The door opened a tiny bit and two eyes looked out.

"I'm here to see Lenny."

"Your name?" The voice was icy, British, male. For a second I wondered what the hell I was doing there. Then I showed my badge. "Officer Toni Conroy." The eyes opened wide.

"Just a moment, please." The door shut. I waited almost five minutes before it opened again, and then I stepped into a little foyer. "Follow me, please."

I followed the man's trim frame up the stairs. We passed a large room with a crystal chandelier and French provincial furniture. Several people sat talking quietly. Above I heard mellow laughter, soft music, and the tinkling of glasses. At the Dragon the evening had not really begun yet. My guide stopped for breath at the top of the stairs. There were at least four more rooms on this floor, their doors all shut. We continued up the last flight of stairs. The room at the top took my breath away. I felt that I had been there before, but I had not.

UNDERCOVER

I stood staring at a rug I had often admired but never touched. Deep, rich, and handwoven, it had for years hung in a local shop window. I had often lusted after its beauty. I remembered Lenny laughing, saying my taste matched his ambition and that someday I would have that rug. It was shaped like a lotus, the colors beginning with beige. From above, a delicate chandelier cast a mellow glow. I stepped onto the lotus, and it drew me in. I walked from beige to mauve to dusty rose, then stood in the soft blue center. In the far corner of the room, a pewter woman held a circle of light over a large teak rolltop desk. A small Modigliani hung on the wall. It looked real. All through my childhood, a print of that same Modigliani hung in the room I shared with Brian. I had bought it myself for a dollar at a street fair. Modigliani was my favorite painter because I didn't know there were any others. I loved correcting my friends when they would cozy up to the poster over my bed, read the caption, and mispronounce the name. And mostly I loved it because the long-necked girl in the picture looked the way I wished I felt. She had this expression as if she were watching a magic carnival. I never found the word that matched the look on her face until I heard Spanish kids say *chévere*. When things were just right, they would slap each other five and say "chay-ver-aye."

I didn't hear Lenny's approach, but I felt his nearness. When I turned he was standing in the doorway, casual in gray slacks and a loose-fitting summer sweater. He was tanned and his wavy blue-black hair was salt and pepper at the temples. There was still not a single ounce of fat on his body. I stared at him, inadvertently stroking the rolltop. A long moment passed while neither of us said anything. Then he stepped into the room.

"Like what you see?"

I didn't want to admit it but I said, "Yes, it's a beautiful room."

"Let me show you the rest of the place."

I shook my head. "That's okay. I just came to talk to you."

He stiffened slightly. I decided to play it his way, at least for a while.

"C'mon." He came over and put his arm on my shoulder. I stepped away to shake him off, but he grabbed me by the elbow. "This way."

First he took me to the kitchen. It was large and spacious, modern yet cozy. On an enormous pegboard hung every utensil imaginable as well as pots and pans in every shape and size. There were two ovens—regular and microwave—and a large butcher block for cutting things and a huge breakfast table. Small hand-painted Dutch tiles covered one wall, and the other walls were brick. There was even a fireplace. Lenny showed me everything as if the past had never happened and I were scheduled to move in tomorrow.

We stepped through French doors onto a terrace, which also led to the bedroom. A large black lacquer bed was covered with a white silk spread and white silk pillows. The bedroom was a carbon of a bedroom we had once admired in Macy's. Bouquets of gardenias filled the room with their scent. A crystal perfume atomizer on an art deco vanity seemed to be waiting for me. I stood there not knowing what to feel or say.

Lenny spoke in a low conspiratorial tone. "I always knew you'd come back."

I went to the French doors, pushed the lace curtain aside, and stared down at a lovely little garden with a running fountain. He came closer. The bed was just a few feet away. I felt his breath on my neck.

"Have you been faithful to me?" he asked as if he expected no less.

The sad truth was that I had had no lovers since

losing Kelly, but I didn't want to tell him that. I would have preferred saying I had been with a hundred guys better than him.

"Let's go back to the living room," I said.

"Okay, I'll let you go at your own pace, but there's one more room I have to show you." He took my hand and held it fast in his. We exited the bedroom, and I followed him down a long dark corridor to another door, which creaked as he pushed it open. He turned on a lamp. The lamp was a clown holding many balloons and cast a shallow light on a little girl's room. Stuffed teddies and bunnies and a panda sat on a white four-poster bed with a pink canopy. An empty rocking chair was poised for motion. The air seemed to leave my lungs. A chill rose from the pit of my stomach. I searched his beautiful black eyes for some kind of answer, and saw that they glistened with tears.

"What is this?" I heard myself whisper.

"Our daughter's room," he said, as if nothing at all were strange.

I took a deep breath. "Did you know the fire was arson?"

He pretended not to hear me, turned the clown lamp off, and pulled me from the room, shutting the door behind us. I followed him back to the living room, wondering which one of us was crazy.

"C'mon, sit down," he said as he pointed to the couch. "Let me get you a glass of wine." He picked up the receiver of a French phone. "Bring me two glasses and a bottle of . . . " He covered the phone with his hand. "Red or white?"

"Red," I answered. Inside I was dying.

"A bottle of the best red we have." Despite the surroundings he didn't know which wine to ask for. We both waited for the wine to arrive and to be served before resuming our conversation. Lenny raised his glass to mine. "Here's to a new beginning."

"I can't drink to that, Lenny. Our life together is over. We can't go back."

"Don't say that," he whispered, his voice husky with emotion. "Stay with me for a while before you decide. We can have a good life now. You don't have to work. I can give you anything you want."

I looked at the pretty objects around the room and remembered how much things had meant to me as a kid. I recalled being teased in school because Brian and I were always dirty, our clothes full of holes and missing buttons. By the time I entered junior high I took care of my own clothes and Brian's too. I would baby-sit and do odd jobs, anything to make a few bucks so that I could look good. After dad disappeared and mom started coming home drunk every night, we would always fight about my clothes. One night she cut my new winter wardrobe to shreds while I watched. When I tried to stop her, she stuck the scissors into my thigh. I could have knocked her out with one punch, but she was my mother so I didn't. After that I played hooky rather than go to school looking like a bum. When Lenny figured out what had happened, he took me shopping for a whole new wardrobe, even a fake fur coat. He was great. After that I was the best-dressed girl in Seward Park High. Just to be safe I kept my clothes at his house.

"I'm not a kid anymore, Lenny. You can't buy my love. Not now."

He swallowed his wine in a quick gulp as if it were a shot of whiskey. For a split second I saw the angry Lenny, the one I had learned to fear. "You're mine," he said, "whether you like it or not."

I stopped short of telling him that he was out of his fucking mind, or of punching him in that cool square jaw like I wanted to. I just said quietly, "I could never live here, Lenny. I'm my own person now. I'm on the force . . ."

He played it smooth too. But his eyes flashed with

contained rage and he filled his glass again. "What's wrong with this place. It may be an after-hours, but it ain't illegal. Do you think the kind of class that comes here would risk coming to an illegal joint?"

That was when I hit him. "They say you're dealing."

"They? Who's they? Not the cops. You think I'd be sitting here if the cops had anything on me. I'm not even into numbers anymore," he snapped. He stood up and started pacing back and forth. I had forgotten about his habit of pacing whenever he felt threatened. Dimly, I took satisfaction in the knowledge that I was the threat now. Still, he lied as smoothly as he always had.

I put the knife in another way. "Where'd you get the money for this place?"

He stopped and leaned toward me as if he were about to reveal a secret. But he didn't. Instead, he waved his hand in the air as if to say it was really nothing. "A gamble that paid off."

I was quiet for a while, thinking that he had opened up right after Kelly's death.

"I'm an upstanding citizen now," he said. "I'm on the board of the Boys Club. I'm a member of the Community Council and I make hefty donations to all the right causes."

I walked to the window and came back to my original point. "The fire was arson. Kelly was suffocated and Brian's skull was crushed. Our daughter was murdered, Lenny. Do you hear what I'm saying?"

He was silent for so long that I thought perhaps he had gone. I turned from the window back into the room. He seemed to have shrunk, his muscular frame just skin over bone, and he didn't seem to be breathing either. His eyes were fixed beyond the ball of light in the pewter woman's hands as if he were watching the murder happening right there in the room. Between us so much had died. He shook his head as if to clear it, then took a cigarette from a little golden box on the coffee table. With shaky hands, he lit it.

"Why are you always going back?" he asked. "We can't change what's already happened. We can change the future but not that. Not the past." He took a long hard drag. As he exhaled, the smoke flowered around his face like a sinister halo. "Why are you stuck in the past?"

Me stuck in the past? I recalled the room down the hall and wondered, was it a game or had he snapped?

"Look, Lenny, I need to know what happened that night. I need to see the killers punished. Then I'll be rid of the past."

"We never should have broken up," he whispered.

Why did he keep coming back to the breakup? I wanted to go beyond that to some truth. I tried again. "Lenny, the cops covered up the facts. What could Brian have been into that was big enough for a cover-up? You said yourself he was just a sponger."

For a minute I thought he looked confused. Then he shook his head as if shaking off a clinging memory. "How could you have left her with a dope fiend?"

"He swore to me that he was gonna keep his nose clean."

"Well, I guess he didn't, and we'll have to live with that."

"It's not enough for me," I said. "I have to know what happened. I have to for Kelly."

He crushed his cigarette in an ashtray. "What kind of love is that?"

I turned to the night outside. Streetlamps illuminated the playground of our past. "Somebody's gotta pay," I said.

"Let it go." He poured himself another glass of wine. "For the sake of our love, just let it go."

I thought about the dead file and Bianca Navarez. "Where were you that night?"

The glass was at his lips. "I was with a woman. We weren't together then, remember?"

I looked at his hand, the long gambler's fingers around the stem of the crystal. I felt that hand travel my body. A stab of jealousy cut from my abdomen through my heart, into my skull. "I'd better go now," I said.

He put the goblet down and crossed the room to stand behind me. I turned. He took my face into his hands. "You're the only woman I've ever really wanted. You're my little girl. Stay with me tonight."

"I can't."

"Why not?"

I lied. "I'm on twelve to eight." My mouth was still half open when he placed his mouth on mine. I pulled back but he wouldn't let go. His tongue was like a snake between my icy lips.

He stopped. "It's okay," he said. "I can wait just like I did before."

CHAPTER TWELVE

"What the fuck were you doing in the Dragon last night?" Errol said as soon as we sat down.

It was Monday, and we were having dinner at The Turtle, a vegetarian restaurant in the Village. He had picked the spot. It was the dinner I had been postponing since Errol had pulled me into the alley to tell me to cut the brutality. Several weeks had passed since that day when I couldn't control my rage at the mother who had used her baby as a weapon against her unfaithful husband. I was now deep into my double life and tired all the time.

I waited for the waitress to leave before I spoke. "What are you talking about?"

His face reddened and he seemed to be rising from his seat as he leaned over the table to get closer to me. "Don't fuck around. I know it was you."

I took a sip of water and studied him over the edge of my glass. "You went through the whole tour without mentioning a word?"

He took his eyes off mine and pushed his own glass

around the table. "I was afraid you'd get mad and cancel dinner," he said quietly.

He was right, of course, so I felt guilty. Nevertheless, I sat there and invented a lie. "I wanted to check the place out and see if they're dealing in there."

He continued to push his glass around, clutching it so tightly I thought it would shatter in his palm. "At eight o'clock? That place doesn't get rolling until after midnight. Do you know who saw you?"

Obviously I didn't, so I just shook my head. I thought about how much I hated Lenny for his lying ways. God, I didn't want to be like that.

"You went to see *him*, didn't you?" Errol said. "How could you risk your badge like that?" He paused. I didn't answer. When he spoke again he let the words sink in one by one. "Unless you still love him."

I managed a sound that was somewhere between a hiss and a whine because my throat wouldn't open up. "That's sick," I said, "that's sick. That's a sick thing to say. I hate him. I hate his guts. I just wanted to find out what I could find out."

Now that I'd blown all my fuses, he leaned back casually.

"Two sides of a coin," he said. "Why do you hate him so much if you don't love him?"

"You're being irrational," I told him, just to set him off.

"Me . . . me . . . it's me that's irrational? You're out there playing one woman posse and you think I'm being irrational?"

I didn't say anything.

"How's this for irrational. . . . Sevinsky saw you." He paused for effect. When he didn't get any reaction out of me he went on. "He was just leaving his tour. He told me this morning. He's giving me a chance to straighten you out. He said he wouldn't mention it to anyone else."

"I hate Sevinsky. He's a sadistic fuck, and I don't want his help."

"Don't be an asshole," Errol hissed.

Other people in the restaurant were starting to stare. It was obvious we were arguing though we weren't particularly loud. Errol opened his menu so that I could no longer see his face. "What did you find out?" he asked.

I opened my own menu. "Nothing."

His hand appeared on my menu. I ignored it until he pushed the menu down so our angry eyes could meet.

"Did you see Lenny?"

"No!"

"You're lying."

I reached for my water glass and our hands inadvertently touched. I felt a warm shock go through me. Then he cupped my hands in his, and his suddenly intense stare enveloped me like a cocoon. The rest of the world just stopped. I let him weave his fingers through mine as I studied the slight blue shadow under his fingernails, the little golden hairs on his arm, anything to avoid meeting those eyes. I knew what was happening, but I didn't want to admit it. Finally, he spoke. "This obsession of yours is dangerous."

"I know that, but I don't think I can stop now."

His face twisted as if he had tasted something bitter. The vee came and went from his brow. For some reason, I knew exactly what he would say next—and he said it as if it made him angry. "I'm in love with you. It took me a while to realize it."

He looked away at the strange assortment of health food cakes and pies in a chrome case by the window. I nibbled on my lower lip.

"And you're right," he said. "It's making me irrational. The worst part . . ." I could hear his voice sticking in his throat, and the words seemed to resist taking shape. "The worst part is . . . it's unprofessional. I'm your partner, your leader, I have no right."

I slipped a finger into my water glass and pushed the ice around while searching for something smooth to say. I didn't want to give him any hope. The ice cubes had little holes in the middle and I stuck my finger all the way through one before I could find words. "Don't worry about it," I said. "You're probably the most decent guy I've ever met. You've bent the rules for me. I have no complaints."

I guess he didn't know what to do with that, so he untangled his fingers from mine and picked up the menu again. "Wanna order?"

"Sure." I was tense and there wasn't a single thing on the menu I recognized. I laughed nervously.

"What is it?" he said.

I shifted back in my seat, and by mistake I kicked his leg under the table.

He smiled that crooked smile. "Don't know what to pick?"

"Let's eat family style," I suggested, "and that way we can choose together."

As we both studied our menus again, I thought how different he was from Lenny, how different our relationship was. We hardly knew each other. There was so little history between us, and yet when we argued it was real. Even though Lenny and I had so much more to fight over, it seemed that I was never able to stand up to him. Somehow the tide of the past would flood through me. I would turn twelve again and be unable to tell him what I really thought. With Lenny I always doubted his honesty, and with Errol there was no doubt that *I* was the liar. At first I had been so preoccupied with my own secret investigation that lying to him seemed not to matter. But I had made the mistake of letting him get close. And now it was different. I felt wrong. Still, I didn't know how to open up.

We picked three dishes—a spinach salad, an eggplant dish, and a brown rice dish. He signaled the waitress and ordered. After that we were quiet again. Then for some reason I thought that I should clear up my feelings for Lenny. I wanted Errol to know that it was not about love.

"I'm just curious about the Dragon," I began.

"But this investigation of yours is wearing you out," he said. "There are circles under your eyes, you've lost weight, and that quick laugh of yours has slowed down too."

I wanted to tell him that was because I was working double shifts, but I didn't dare. Fortunately, the food arrived.

"It looks weird," I said.

"These are acquired tastes but I'm confident you'll grow to like them," he said in his best pedantic style.

"Pine nuts?"

"Yeah. I guess so. What do you do with your nights?"

I shoved a fork into some brown rice and hid behind humor. "Is that a professional question?"

He ripped a piece of five grain bread into quarters. "Partly."

We laughed a little.

"This is good, real good," I said, busily occupying myself with the food.

"Answer me."

"I can't sleep, I don't sleep, I have nightmares." It was a half-truth. We ate for a while. When I sensed that he was about to start up again, I moved first. "Let's talk about you. I'm tired of my own problems."

"I don't want to fight you," he said. "But when I see you doing this self-destructive act, in the name of some harebrained investigation . . . it gets me so pissed."

He pulled on his beard. It was full now. His furrowed brow betrayed the depth of his concern. His eyes invited trust. I rubbed my arm, the arm that I had stuck so many needles into over the last few weeks, and thought about telling him everything before I got in any deeper. But the words just wouldn't come. Instead I asked, "Who do you think Cobra is?"

His expression folded in disappointment. He opened his hands in a gesture of futility. "I don't know. Does it matter? How does he fit into this conversation?"

"I wanna get him," I said, and pounded the table. I was going to pound it a few times more for emphasis but he stopped my hand by covering it with his.

"Every obsession is a cover. Let's talk about what's really happening with you."

"Let's talk about you," I repeated.

"You know all there is to know about me. I'm from Bay Shore. My dad's a cop and so are my two brothers."

"Are you the oldest?"

"Yeah. What about you?"

"Me too."

"And . . ."

"And there isn't much to tell. I had a brother who died, my dad abandoned us, and my mother never loved me. Is that what you want to hear?"

"Is it true?"

Oddly enough it was, so I just nodded my head and pushed the food around on my plate. "I guess she did love me in her own way," I added.

We ate in silence until he spoke. "My brother's getting married in two weeks. Will you come to the wedding with me?"

"Don't you have a girlfriend you could invite?"

He chuckled. "The answer to that is I did, but she left me. Didn't like cops, or the hours, or the fact that being a cop affected my moods. You could ask why she got involved with a cop from a family of cops. You could ask that. I did."

"And?"

"I didn't get an answer. Please say you'll come with me. I'll look stupid at a Polish–Chinese wedding with nobody on my arm. It isn't done."

"Yes," I laughed. Then I made a request of my own. It was linked to my search for Sunny, but he didn't know that. I told him that I wanted to buy a car, not new, just something decent to get around in. I knew from riding with him that he knew about cars and I figured he could help me find one. "Would you take me out to Reedman's in Pennsylvania next weekend?" I asked.

His whole face lit up as if I was doing him the favor. "You want me to?"

"Yeah. I think that's why I asked."

"Bet. How about Saturday? You want dessert?"

"Saturday's good . . . what do you recommend?" He ordered a nut cake made with no sugar, herb tea, and some goat cheese. For some crazy reason I enjoyed it, even though it was the strangest meal I had ever had. I had to admit to myself that I enjoyed sitting across the table from him too. But it didn't last long. I was drinking the green tea, eating the last crumbs of the sugarless cake, thinking how different he was from any man I had ever known when that vee appeared in the middle of his forehead. Then he grasped one of my hands and got very intense.

"I just can't do it," he said. "I've been waiting for us to have some time together off the job for so long that I didn't want it spoiled by anything. But if I wait until tomorrow you'll get pissed and shut me out again." His voice trailed off.

I felt my body getting anxious. "Don't stop now. What is it?"

He started talking fast, running the words into each other. "I found out before the end of the tour that the baby died—you're gonna hafta testify."

I didn't say anything. I just sat there thinking about the baby and Kelly and Brian and how I never was able to save anyone. For some stupid reason I thought about Lenny and his perfect apartment with its perfect rug. Outside some teenagers slapped each other five as they passed. Through the restaurant window, I saw their laughter but I couldn't hear it. Around me everything had become very still.

"Say something." At first I didn't hear Errol either, but when I did, the sounds of the people and the restaurant started again too. I heard the tinkling of silverware, the clattering of dishes, and the hum of other conversations blending one into the other.

"Where's the mother now?" I was surprised how the word "mother" bruised my throat.

"In custody," he answered. "She couldn't make bail."

I reached across the table and put my fingers between his eyebrows trying to make that stupid vee go away.

"It's open and shut, isn't it?" I said.

He shrugged. "Should be . . . unless she pleads insanity."

Outside the window the summer evening had turned a final deep blue. A blond crossed the street. I thought about Sunny and the hopelessness of my investigation.

"They should cement that bitch's legs together," I said as I rubbed my thigh where the scissors scar itched. "The baby's better off."

The waitress brought us the check. We hadn't asked for it. "There's one more thing. One more thing I gotta tell you," Errol said.

Hot and cold ran through me. I couldn't sit there any longer.

"Pay the check and let's get out of here," I said, thinking I couldn't listen to any more bad news. Then I tried to hand him my share, but he wouldn't take it.

I was worried because I was starting to think about

the cure. We left the restaurant and walked west to the river. The car was parked down by the pier. The Village was alive with couples of all kinds. The narrow sidewalks were crowded, and Errol grabbed my hand to avoid getting separated. Should I take my hand back? It would seem childish. We walked in silence. The warm, late summer evening was illuminated by brightly lit store windows with odd and varied contents. I felt the river nearing. Its smell reminded me of hot summer childhood nights, sneaking out of the neighborhood, diving into the river for a cool but dangerous swim. We reached Tenth Avenue. "Let's walk out there," I said, pointing to the pier.

Small waves lapped the rotting wood beneath our feet, the water black and inviting. Above, the moon lay heavily on its side. I don't know where the light came from but it reflected on the night waves like a moving neon sign. Nothing stood still. I said, "Hit me with the rest of the bad news." I was pretty sure he was going to tell me that I was in trouble on the job. Maybe Sevinsky had talked after all. He took my other hand in his and just looked at me.

I felt him search for words. "Baker committed suicide last night. He hung himself in his cell."

At first I had no reaction at all. Then I noticed there was a slight wind on the water. I couldn't feel the breeze, but the waves were churning in different directions. Errol seemed to be holding his breath waiting for something to happen. But nothing did. I took my hands back from him and turned to watch the other shore. It was very dark over there. I heard him say, "It wasn't your fault."

"Is there going to be an investigation?"

He stepped around me and looked curiously into my face. "What for? Why would there be?"

I looked up at the sky. It seemed to sit on us like a dome that was closing in. I was bursting from the inside.

I felt that I couldn't hold one more secret, not from him. He had been so straight with me, and now he stood there offering compassion. He probably thought I was feeling guilty. Actually, I was afraid someone would find out I visited Baker on the Rock. I started to walk.

Errol grabbed me by the elbow. I stopped. Beneath us the water continued to lap at the pier. "Look at me," he said, "and take a real look, forget the past. Listen to your heart. Trust your feelings."

His blond hair glowed like a halo against the evening light. And those blue eyes, I was beginning to be able to interpret them. Very gently I said, "I like you, but you're not my type." I said it because I believed it, because I wanted him to back off, but it came out sounding like a lie.

He shook his head and pulled me closer. "You don't trust your feelings, the last time you loved it cost you too much."

He put his hands on the small of my back. "You were a child then. You can't punish yourself forever."

A clear white light came from the black of his pupils as if his eyes had captured one star from the sky. I was watching that star twinkle, listening to my own breath quicken when his crooked mouth came down on mine. I was going to pull back but my tongue met his and the kiss took over. I grabbed his neck to pull him closer, and I was still nibbling on his lips when my foot slipped into a hole in the rotting wood. He caught me close and whispered, "Let me in."

I pulled away and started walking again. I wanted to tell him that I had been to see Baker and what he had told me. I didn't want to lie to Errol anymore. I wanted to be myself. But I had been lying for so long that I didn't know where to begin. One lie always led to another. My mind wandered to Sunny and how important she was to my investigation.

"Reedman's is open until ten," I said tonelessly. "Why don't we go when we get off duty tomorrow."

He looked puzzled and pulled on his beard. "Sure," he said, "but why the hasty change of subject? Why run from this?"

I wanted more than anything to get away from him—he was getting too close. I headed off the pier back to solid land, taking two steps to his every one.

"Slow down," he said. "Your nerves are shot. When a cop gets like that, mistakes happen."

I didn't answer and he took my hand in his. The electricity from the kiss was still cruising through me. I hadn't expected it to feel so good.

"Look, I'm going to walk you home and say just one more thing."

I licked my lips. I could have kissed him again and again, but it was a chance I couldn't take. So I just tried a hollow laugh and said, "I'm all ears."

"Forgive yourself," he said. "Until you do, I don't have a shot with you. No man does."

I didn't see how I could forget, and even though I didn't say so, I guess my face did. A big lump materialized in my throat and threatened to cut off my air. I rubbed my hands over my eyes as a snake of pain coiled up from my neck and settled in my skull. I was relieved to see my doorway. I took two steps up onto my stoop. Now, I was as tall as he. I took his face into my hands and tore into his mouth as if to wound. I didn't know if it was passion, or if I just wanted to shut him up. I kissed him till he moaned, then I pulled away and climbed the rest of the stairs.

"Still say I'm not your type?" he questioned before he turned to walk away.

Pretending I hadn't heard him, I continued on up the steps.

The apartment was dark except for a reading lamp over Mary's bed. She sat working on her sister's baby shower gift. For weeks now, she had been plodding away, color by color, at a needlepoint for her niece-to-be. Amniocentesis had told the family the baby was to be a female. I sat down at the edge of her bed. She was working with violet. "How'd it go?" she asked, inserting a needle into her pattern.

"He's a nice guy, different from anyone I've ever known."

"Not that you've known much," she said as she turned the needlepoint to make sure the stitch was neat. I watched her work for a while, thinking how different our backgrounds were. Mary was from a strict Catholic family, the youngest of three sisters. In her family the only legitimate reason for a woman to leave home was marriage. Her sisters had stuck to the formula. But Mary had rebelled by sleeping around even before she left high school. She once told me she had auditioned guys in bed before considering going out with them. I, on the other hand, had always been with Lenny. Even in high school I was already loyal to Lenny. In fact, I had been thought of as somehow superior by my peers because I had a relationship with an older man. I had started sleeping with Lenny at age fifteen.

The picture Mary was working on was of a little girl sliding down a rainbow. Beneath the rainbow, lollipops grew like flowers. The outlines of the whole picture were there but, because Mary worked one color at a time, only pieces had been filled in. Nothing was complete. There were several colors in the rainbow, pieces of lollipops, and one fluffy white cloud. The sky was still empty. The little girl was just the shadow of an outline. I sat there winding the blue thread around my fingers.

"Tongue tied?" Mary finally asked.

I was thinking about the cure. I had two bags left. I rubbed my arm. Even though it was still summer I always wore long sleeves now. I worried about an inspection. The department didn't check cops for drug abuse routinely, but you never knew when you were slated for a surprise inspection. Just the thought made my heart pound.

"If you had a good time, why do you look like you just lost your best friend?" Mary questioned as she changed threads.

I thought about Errol and the way I had neglected to tell him the truth. If I could be honest with Mary, I would feel better.

"That Baker kid, my first collar, he hung himself in his cell Sunday night."

Mary stopped sewing and looked at me. "It's not your fault."

She sounded like Errol, but for her I had a response. "I went to see him Sunday to get more information about my brother's girlfriend and I asked him about Cobra."

"Cobra? Don't tell me you're chasing him too," she said, turning half her attention back to the needlepoint.

"Errol thinks Lenny's connected to him."

"So why would that make Baker hang himself?"

"I don't think he did. I think somebody caught on to the fact that he was talking about Brian, and they killed him to keep the cover-up in place."

The end of my sentence was punctuated by her yelp of pain as she pricked herself with the needle, and we both studied the pinpoint of blood on her finger.

"Does Errol know this?" she asked, sucking her finger.

I shook my head. "No. I can't tell him. But I asked him to take me out to Reedman's tomorrow night because I want to buy a car. I can't find Sunny on foot. Will you come with me? I don't want to be alone with him. I don't want him to get romantic."

"If you really believe Baker was murdered, you're in danger too. You don't know what you're in the middle of."

"Will you go to Pennsylvania with us?"

It was very important that she say yes. But she ignored my question. "You're crazy," she said. "You're worrying about a car when you should be worried about your life. And you don't want to be alone with the one man who could probably help you."

I got up and walked to my side of the room. My badge glistened on my night table, and my piece lay next to it. I thought about Errol—I didn't want him to love me. I picked up my badge. It was so much lighter than it looked, and yet it had taken on so much weight in my life. Errol was right; I didn't want to lose it, not for anything. I did want to be a cop, and I didn't want to be powerless ever again. I caught myself pacing like Lenny always had when he was afraid of losing. Mary moved the needle faster, trying to control her anger.

"I don't like using people," she said. "Why don't you tell Errol what you want the car for?"

"I can't tell him. I have to solve this thing myself. If I tell, I might lose my badge."

"But if you're right about Baker, you might lose your life."

I stopped pacing and cut the conversation short to head for the bathroom and the cure. Her words followed me as I shut the door between us. "You're using him and it's not right."

I had the feeling she wanted to say "You're using me," but she didn't quite dare. I locked the door and while I ran water into the tub, I sat on the bathroom floor and took my coffin out from behind the commode where I had last hidden it. Then, I very quietly used myself. I poked the needle into my arm until the blood came up. Then I felt better. I turned the water off and nodded out. I saw myself hanging in that cell instead of Baker. What could he have told me that was worth killing for? How far did this conspiracy against my sanity reach?

From the nod I fell down the continuum to

oblivion. I lay in the cut of nothingness until it gave birth to nine heads. They were writhing from one angry reptile stem, crawling to encircle me. The faces were junkie faces, their eyes belonging to the victims of my search. I loaded a Magnum and began picking off the eyes—iris, pupil, retina. Every splattered eye was replaced by two, until my reflected hate opened like a mouth and consumed me.

The next day after work we left the city. We took the Lincoln Tunnel and the route through the Jersey flatlands with tank farms and chemical factories that ate oxygen, making it difficult to breathe. Conversation was slow getting started until we found our topic: life at the station house. Errol and I laughed at Mary's imitations of the men. From that we got onto high-school sex. Mary and Errol had a lot in common, similar stories of groping, blushing, and longing. I couldn't join in. Finally, Errol asked, "What about you? Were you always this virginal? Is that why you have no war stories?"

Before I could think of a witty reply Mary giggled and said, "She was betrothed at twelve. That's tribal life on the Lower East Side."

I saw Errol's grip on the wheel tighten but otherwise he showed no reaction. "That's behind her," he said tersely.

Mary stopped giggling and looked into my icy eyes. I wanted to rap her in the mouth. I was sandwiched between them on the front seat, and I wondered what else she was about to blurt out. I turned the radio up. Mary turned it down.

"I worry about her. Sometimes I think she's trying to go backwards," she said seriously.

"I hear she has trouble sleeping." Errol added. I had a strange sensation that they had had this conversation before and that it was being repeated for my benefit.

Mary looked boldly into my face. "I don't see her doing much sleeping. Her bed is usually empty."

Errol glanced at the traffic in the rearview mirror. "What are you up to, Conroy? How many more secrets do you have?"

"We're your friends," Mary said flatly.

"What is this?" I tried to laugh it off. But nobody else joined in.

Errol pulled into the passing lane. "Don't throw away your whole future for a past that's gone."

After that we just fell silent. It was an angry silence. I was mad at them for prying, and they were mad at my refusal to talk. Errol accelerated to seventy miles per hour. The car filled with the smell of burning rubber and rotten eggs. Finally, in Pennsylvania, the conversation was resurrected as we all noticed how the summer had yellowed the trees and scorched the grass.

Reedman's was a carpet of cars that stretched as far as the eye could see. All sizes, all makes, all years. I had never had my own wheels and I was excited. I wanted something small, not a gas guzzler, with a stereo. I sat in a lot of cars, and Errol looked under a lot of hoods, before we finally decided on a Toyota. I counted my cash and handed it to the dealer. He put dealer's plates on the car and we headed back to the city in two cars, Mary riding with me. As soon as we were on the highway, I lit into her. "You had no business telling him that stuff. If you wanna know what I do at night, ask me."

She fidgeted with the radio dial. "I know what you're doing. You're out there playing undercover, trying to get your ass killed." She didn't say anything about skag, and that was a relief.

I changed the subject. "This car has a nice feel to it."

Her comeback took me by surprise. "You shouldn't spoil what you have with Errol by hiding the truth from him. You two really fit together. I wish I had something like that."

Errol's head was dancing in the car in front of us. He had put on his Walkman and was enjoying the drive.

"He's okay," I said. "But there's nothing happening. Just because he isn't a sadist like your partner doesn't mean I have to love him."

"You're so out of touch with yourself you don't even know your own feelings. You should see the way you look at him. No wonder you've got him cross-eyed and crazy."

"I could never get into a cop, especially not the one I ride with."

Even though she said it very softly, her answer cut a little deeper than I would have wanted it to. "Maybe you just don't know what loving a man is all about."

CHAPTER THIRTEEN

A couple of days later when we were back on twelve to eight, we decided to check out the squatters. It was an overcast night, and in a darkness that was almost as thick as fog it was starting to drizzle. I didn't even see a moon. I had finished the stash under my mattress and now I had no escape. No cure. I felt a depression was closing in, and I didn't feel well. But there was no time to see the squatters and no time to brood. A call for backup came over the radio.

"Ten-fourteen get over to East Sixth Street *tout de suite*—assist on burglary."

I expected Errol to hit the siren but he didn't since there were very few cars in the street. In moments we were in front of 412 East Sixth Street, where we spotted Mary and Sevinsky's squad car. We parked and ran to join them.

"What's going on?" Errol questioned.

Mary winked although we didn't say anything to each other.

"There's five guys inside," Sevinsky said. "They made it right past the Paramount guards, cracked open this here truck, and made off with fifty grand in equipment. They took it through one of these abandoned buildings through the backyard onto Seventh. That's where they ran smack dab into us, so they hightailed it back over here. Now we got both blocks barricaded." He was talking very fast. "They gotta be in one of these buildings. Let's split up to cover our bases. I'll take 412, Conroy take 410, Mary 414, and Stutz 416. I've called for more backup to come on Seventh Street just in case they make it back across." Sevinsky sucked loudly on a tooth. "They're armed and dangerous."

"Be careful," I whispered to Mary as we split up.

Fortunately, 410 was populated, and the staircase seemed moderately well lit. On the first floor landing a prune face with two bright gray eyes peered from a door that was ajar. A finger pointed up. "I saw them," came the whispered voice, and then the door closed. I ran. The farther I climbed, the darker it got. The hallway light bulbs had been smashed. The fifth floor was very dark. The partially open door to the roof creaked on its rusty hinges. I pulled my piece and released the safety catch, then kicked the door all the way back. The beam from my flashlight moved across the rooftop like a small search light, catching the raindrops as they fell into black puddles on the black tar.

I stepped out quietly onto the rain-soaked roof. There wasn't a single star in the sky. I heard rustling and cooing, and my light found the outlines of a pigeon coop halfway across the roof. To my right a circular water tank stood on stilts. The slight drizzle created a moving gray curtain, and its rustle filled the air. I crossed the roof to the pigeon coop. I sloshed through unavoidable puddles and water seeped from my shoes into my socks. Something fluttered. I placed my face close to the wire mesh and aimed my flashlight. Inside, pigeons hid in their own wings. A silver metal box gleamed in the dark inside the coop. Raindrops bounced off it in quick hard taps, and I could read the word "Paramount." Footsteps. The pigeons cooed. The footsteps seemed to be headed for the water tank. I followed. The rain got heavier. I thought I saw feet under the tank but I wasn't certain.

"Police!" I said. "Stop where you are." As I scanned the roof with my flashlight, I heard a menacing chuckle. I grabbed my radio and called Sevinsky in the next building. No answer.

The skeleton of the scaffolding that had transformed Sixth Street into Little Italy blocked whatever light might have been rising from the streetlamps below. The scaffolding shuddered as if someone had pushed it hard. I moved as close as I dared to the roof's edge and studied the inside of the scaffolding. Was anyone hiding there? Or trying to climb back down? I was contemplating my next move when I heard sirens over on Seventh. Several car doors slammed hard, fast and loud. Backup had arrived. "All right, hold it right there! The party's over," someone yelled.

I felt a sharp pain in the back of my legs and my knees buckled. My body lunged forward. For a moment I tottered on the roof's edge, and then I fell. My gun flew from my hand as the scaffolding slapped me across the chest. I curled around it and grabbed hold, clinging like a child on a monkey bar. My gun landed on the fire escape below. I studied the scaffolding, its surface slick with rain. Could I climb back up? My arms were heavy, my hands studded with splinters that stung like needles. I could aim for the fire escape and let myself drop, or I could scream for help, alerting whoever had pushed me. I decided to let myself go. The fall to the fire escape just a few feet below seemed very long until the cold metal hit my knees and elbows. I lay there soaked to the bone, listening to several sirens wail at once.

"Toni! Toni! Where the hell are you? Toni!"

Something in Errol's voice told me this was more than a cop calling his partner.

"I'm okay, I'm up here behind the scaffolding." I began the climb down. When I got to the first floor, I loosened the last ladder from the fire escape and lowered it to the ground. Through the silver sheets of rain, I saw Errol below me, his shape blurred by the water in my eyes. When my feet hit the pavement, his sigh thundered in the raindrops.

"Holy shit," he said. "I was pissing in my pants."

"Somebody pushed me off the goddamn roof," I panted. Now that it was over, I felt my fear.

"Did you see who?"

I shook my head. "Didn't see anything. Thank God for that scaffolding. It saved me."

"Who the hell could it have been?" he asked. Thunder cracked above. As we made our way back to the squad car, I saw Mary running back to her car. She was soaked.

Mary yelled, "They got 'em all over on Seventh." She got quickly into her car. A few minutes later Sevinsky came out of 412.

The rain was so heavy we couldn't see beyond the car windows. It hit in huge drops that splattered as if we were sitting under a waterfall. We sat staring at each other. The running water whispered all around as if the world outside had stopped. I wanted to say something but didn't know what it was. His blue eyes were gray in the silver light and full of words he didn't speak.

Finally he broke the silence. "You're going with me to my brother's wedding, aren't you?"

I had to laugh. "Is that all you can think of at a time like this?"

Suddenly, the uniform didn't matter. He pulled me close, ran his fingers through my soaking hair, and kissed my face all over. I nibbled on his lips then showed him my palms. They were red with welts where splinters were buried under the skin. Errol moaned as if the splinters were in him. Then he began removing them, one by one, using his fingernails and even his teeth. Some came out and some were buried too deep. When he couldn't get any more, he played with the ignition. The car coughed once or twice, then I heard the starter catch and the engine turned.

All through that week, it rained heavily. In the drops that whispered around me, I saw that roof, the scaffolding, and Errol's wet face. On my day off, I decided to follow the dead file to Atlantic City. I wanted to see this Bianca Navarez, who had been with Lenny the night of the fire. Maybe there was something she hadn't told the cops, something that wasn't in the DD5.

It took a little over two hours to reach Atlantic City. During the drive, I heard a news report on a large fire in Hoboken, New Jersey. A child had been killed, but the firemen had pulled the mother from the blaze. She had tried to run back into the fire. When the cops wouldn't let her, she struggled with a bluecoat and killed herself with his gun.

Was I doing the same thing . . . only more slowly? In the solitude of the car, raindrops sliding down the windows like so many tears, I counted the countless tragedies of this world and marveled that we chose to live at all. Outside, leaves shuddered in the trees and bent under the weight of the rain.

I recalled a day earlier in the week. Mary and I had been housecleaning. We had pulled out the stove and the refrigerator to clean under them. Amidst grease and small pieces of rotting food lived a whole tribe of roaches. Big ones, small ones, several with egg sacks, and even an albino. I grabbed the roach spray and put my finger on the button. They ran. I followed. Some died on the spot and others got dizzy and fled in futile circles. One tried to make it onto my sneaker but couldn't get up. It flipped on its back, legs running in the air, furiously fighting death. Then, as if hit by an electric current, it twitched and folded in a position of prayer. Was all that running involuntary?

The answer came in the whisper of racing tires on wet concrete. It was simple: life wants to live—all life. I faced my guilt. I wanted to live despite Kelly's death. I faced it fully, an old, old pain. I wanted to mourn and be free of it. But I could not.

I entered the outskirts of the town that calls itself a city. It looked like it was dying too. Through the gray drizzle, I saw that the old houses had once been lovely. I parked in front of a turn-of-the-century rooming house with a large porch and a circular turret. There were no curtains in the windows. The VACANCY–NO VACANCY sign dangled in the breeze, too washed-out to read. I checked the address, then got out of the car and ran through the steady rain and up the house's rotting front steps. I knocked on the front door and stood back to wait, watching the rain grow heavier. As it fell from the awning solid as a sheet, the world beyond became a pleasant blur. I knocked again, harder this time. In the sky above thunder rolled.

I tried the door knob. It turned and the old door fell back, revealing a parlor with furniture covered in white sheets. I shut the door and stepped farther into the room. A fading straw rug oozed under my feet. I was captured in a blue-cracked mirror on the wall. Inside a glass web, I was broken into a kaleidoscope of pieces. The smell of mold filled the empty spaces of the room.

"Looking for someone?"

I turned. A shaking white-haired woman said, "We're closed." Despite the tremor in her ancient voice, I heard a young girl, and I wondered if the wrinkles and the liver spots were merely a disguise. I offered her a view of my badge. She squinted at it. Her trembling didn't alter its pace.

"I don't need the Certificate of Occupancy any more," she said, and fluffed the sheet on the couch. Then she studied the chairs as if seeing the people who had once sat there. The sheet hovered in the air before floating onto the couch's contours. She patted the furniture soothingly. The young eyes in the old face turned to me. "What did you really come for?" she asked as I put my badge away.

She sat her old body slowly down and smiled, revealing a perfect set of teeth. I didn't know if they were false or not. I sat next to her and watched as she fidgeted with her hands. I speculated about her reaction to my next question, but I had to ask. I counted the spots on her hands for a few beats, then spoke.

"I'm looking for Bianca Navarez. I understand she used to manage this place."

She brought her tiny hands to her little mouth, and her miniature body shivered. Looking more and more like a child in disguise, she laughed and said, "The Albatross. It's called The Albatross."

I didn't know what she meant.

"The rooming house, the sign is gone now, but we called it The Albatross. My husband named it." She touched my hand. "He was a sailor and to him a home on land was an albatross. But for me, it kept me busy." She clapped her hands together, seeming to lift from the couch. "A-h-h-h, the people. You wouldn't believe how interesting they all were. Each in their own way. Some stayed just days, and others were here for years. No matter how long or short the stay, we always, all of us, had our meals together and afterwards there was brandy and Scrabble and talk."

She studied the ghosts in the room again. I was afraid to interrupt her reverie. Finally I asked, "What about Bianca Navarez?"

"She's gone," she said. "They're all gone now."

"Do you know where she went?"

She shook her head. "I had to let her go because of that New York boyfriend of hers. He was only here once a week but that man was a monster. He'd always con the guests into an after-dinner card game, poker or black jack. He always won. Every week he took everybody for every dime." She ran her fingers through her thinning white hair. "I never understood why they played with him. Everybody knew how it would end. But every week he'd have them believing different, eating out of his hand again. I told Bianca he had to stop coming, and she told him to stay away. That didn't stop him. That man always did just what he wanted to do. Every Wednesday he'd show up on the doorstep and she'd let him in again."

I twisted my fingers in my hair and watched the rain wash the windows and run like a river down the awning. A thick musk filled the damp air, and I was having trouble breathing. The flavor of Lenny's treachery seemed foolishly to matter.

"When did you last see this guy?"

She began playing with the corner of the sheet, readying to speak, obviously enjoying the presence of a listener.

"He came here very late one time. Everyone was asleep. He pounded on the door yelling her name over and over until she let him in. I heard them arguing until she let him come up to her room. I could hear her crying. Then it was very quiet. In the morning he was gone."

She lifted one of her little fingers parenthetically in the air. "That Bianca had a beautiful body. She never liked the beach, said it was too sandy. She used to tan in her bikini right in the backyard!" The old lady placed a finger thoughtfully to her lips. "That week her back and her stomach were black and blue. He must have beat her up pretty bad. The son of a bitch was smart though. He never touched her face."

She smoothed the sheet over the couch as if to say this story is finished. Her eyes went to the rain that shadowed the windows. "Come to think of it, he did come looking for her one time after that. I lied for her like she asked me to. Told him she had moved to Florida. They got casinos there too. She used to work the tables. That was where they met—at the tables. But she came to work for me to get away from all that."

The rain tapped the tin roof in a rapid melancholy serenade.

"Where is she now? Do you know?"

Her face twisted in a question. "You don't mean her any harm do you?"

I assured her that I did not. She threw her little hands up and offered, "The Golden Nugget. She's at the blackjack table. Tell her I said hello."

I headed for the boardwalk, which was about a block away from The Albatross. By now it was about one in the afternoon and there were no people in the streets. I climbed the steps to the boardwalk and saw the angry waves hit the sad and empty shore with fast fury before being sucked back into the sea. The beach was covered with cabanas that were like multicolored tents in the desert, the sand brown and red with rain. I didn't know where the Golden Nugget was, but it was certain to be along this walk. I followed my feet. The giant hotels—Bally's Park Place, Caesars, Atlantis—loomed like castles over the ocean. Even though it was daytime, mammoth neon signs blinked in sync, red, gold, white, blue, a garish contrast on the colorless gray sky. Then I spotted the words "Golden Nugget" as they flashed in gold, signaling a wonderful and fancy party in progress.

I stepped into the lobby, shaking water from my hair. Beneath my feet the rug was thick and scarlet. I followed a long staircase that led to music. When I reached the top, I looked out over an enormous pit full of people, tables, and one-armed bandits. I had the sensation of looking down on an anthill, except that the ants were people and they were gambling. Despite the light, the music, the cocktail waitresses dressed like bunnies, and the staccato fall of coins on metal, the people didn't look like they were having fun. They seemed to be desperately toiling at jobs they hated. Once in a while a face would light up, and a quick hand would gather a multicolored pile of chips. But instantly, the pained concentration, the clenched fist, would return.

I listened to the cacophony created by alternating panic and hope. At least twenty floor managers in tuxedos circled the floor. I descended the winding staircase that led to the brightly illuminated gambling pit and headed for the nearest tuxedo, debating whether or not to use my NYPD badge in Altanic City. I decided against it.

"Excuse me," I stopped a passing manager. "I'm looking for Bianca Navarez."

I searched his gray eyes for a reaction, expecting to be asked to state my case. He didn't even look at me. He simply pointed his finger mechanically and said, "Table nine."

Since he hadn't even glanced at me, I felt no need to thank him. Table nine was just a few feet away. Four men and a woman, their backs to me, sat on tall stools, each intent over a hand of cards I could not see. Towering over the players on a platform was a cinnamon redhead with high Aztec cheekbones and eyes so dark I could not distinguish iris from pupil. Her wavy hair was pinned back in an unruly chignon. She wore tuxedo pants and a vest with no blouse. She shuffled, dealt, and collected cards quicker than I thought anyone could move. I stood there paralyzed by her self-contained beauty, wondering if she'd been Lenny's woman while he and I were husband and wife. Or had she come later? I had to remind myself that the answer no longer mattered. I stepped up to the table and stood there for a while. Bianca gave me one look and no more. The players didn't notice me at all. I waited at the foot of the platform where she stood and I said, "I have to talk to you."

Without blinking, she looked down. I was ready for her and showed my badge. We both knew it was the wrong badge. But I said, "I could make enough fuss to cost you your job."

Anger flashed in her eyes and a line creased the center of her forehead. Her hands never stopped dealing. "I'm off in twenty minutes." she said. "Meet you in steamroom twelve in the health club on the twentieth floor."

I wandered through rows of one-armed bandits. People feverishly inserted coins, one after the other. At intervals one machine or another spit out enough coins to keep the players playing. I found myself rattling the change in my own pocket. Which was my lucky machine? I was hoping that my real luck would come when I spoke to Bianca.

There were no clocks anywhere in the casino. No one seemed concerned with time, whether it was day or night. Though it was early afternoon, many of the women wore evening gowns, and men were dressed for a night on the town. I could no longer resist, I thought, as I rattled the four quarters in my pocket. I fed three of them to one of the bandits and pulled its arm. Three oranges lined up and a hail of quarters filled the bowl. Maybe ten dollars. I tried my last quarter but luck didn't strike a second time. I pocketed my winnings and headed for the health club.

The attendant wanted my room key before letting me in. I flashed my badge and said I had an appointment with a guest who had a problem. My tone implied that I did not intend to answer any further questions, and the attendant handed me a key and towel. She hadn't noticed or cared that my shield was out-of-state. Inside the locker room I undressed. My arms were needle-marked and bruised. I put my clothes in the locker, keeping one arm close to my body, hiding the other under the large white towel the attendant had given me. I left my purse and my piece in the locker.

Through the glass door, I tried to see into the steamroom. The condensation on the other side of the pane made it impossible. I went in as the heavy door closed slowly behind me. It was a long, narrow, white room with tiled walls and two tiers for sitting. I sat in the corner on the top tier and watched steam rise from a rock pit. The room enveloped me in a damp caress. I pulled my knees to my chest.

After a while, the door opened. The steam was so thick that I couldn't see her until she stepped deeper into the room. Then she emerged from the veil of steam naked as the day she was born. I just crouched there hugging my knees to my damp chest. She took a wooden bucket from the floor and filled it with cold water from a tap. Then she threw the water over her head. It cascaded down the length of her body, glistening silver over cinnamon flesh. I imagined Lenny making love to her. I saw his hands on her thighs, her breasts, all the places, the same places, where he used to touch me. And I heard him whisper the way he whispered to me, those words that unlocked every lock.

My presence didn't seem to bother her in the same way. She studied me quietly, as if she had been waiting, as if my arrival had been only a matter of time. She sat down beneath me. "How did you find me?"

I studied her pretty dark eyes and answered her question with a question. "You know who I am?"

"Want some?" She offered the bucket. I took it and threw the water over myself. It was so cold it hurt.

"You look like your brother," she said.

"You knew Brian?"

"Sure." She got up again. "He used to come down here with Lenny."

Just then, steam hissed from the rocks and obliterated her voice. Her mouth moved, but I could hear no words. I watched her fluid movements, recalling her smooth dealing of the cards. How long had she and Lenny been lovers? And why was it still important to me?

The steam stopped and her words emerged. ". . . Brian was Lenny's sidekick. Lenny didn't really like him but he told me he was looking after him because you asked him to."

When she said that, the warmth in the long thin room became an uncomfortable heat. The tile seemed to burn my flesh. But I didn't get it. I was too wrapped up in the idea of Lenny's sexual treachery to get it. "You knew about me?" I asked. "You were seeing Lenny while we were still married?" I watched a rivulet of water descend from my thigh onto the tile.

"I was into him long before I knew him for what he was. I used to sleep with him before you were old enough to. . . ."

She drew another bucket of water and splashed herself. The water glistened on her breasts like gossamer threads. She shuddered. Droplets of condensation on her face gave it an ethereal glow. "It came as pretty much of a shock to me when he told me he was going to marry some kid ten years younger than him. I shouldda stopped seeing him then, but brains were never my long suit."

I sat like a rock on the tile and studied my toes. "If he's such a prick, why did we both love him so much?"

"My answer isn't yours," and she shook her head in frustration. I thought about how laughs are shared and misery is always so intensely personal, and I watched her wipe the condensation from her brow. "Why did you come?" she asked.

I answered with another question. "Did you hear about what happened?"

"You mean the fire?"

I nodded and told her about the dead file and that she was in it as Lenny's alibi.

She looked puzzled. "Alibi? I thought the cops just routinely wanted to know where every family member was that night."

"Some of the neighbors heard him threatening me. He said I couldn't leave him without paying. But you put him in the clear."

"Are you saying that you still suspect him?"

"No . . . but Kelly and Brian were murdered, the fire didn't kill them."

An odd combination of sadness and shock shrouded her face. "How horrible," she whispered, and then just sat there looking wilted. She seemed so honestly compassionate that I lost all reservation and began talking. I told her about Brian's toxicology report, my search for Brian's girlfriend Sunny, that Brian had gotten her started on drugs, that I thought she had the answer, and that her life on the street made her a difficult find. I didn't mention what happened to Baker, or how I'd been spending my nights.

"So Lenny supplied Brian and Brian supplied Sunny," she said.

I had been thinking how each of us had been brought down by our love, and then her words really sank in. "What?" I whispered. "What did you say?"

"Lenny supplied Brian and Brian—"

"Lenny supplied Brian?" I interrupted.

She looked at me strangely. "I just told you that. I've told you twice now. What did you think I meant when I said Lenny took care of Brian?"

I bit so hard into my lower lip that a drop of blood oozed onto my tongue. "But Lenny doesn't do skag."

She shook her head. "Of course not. He deals."

Then I put two and two together. "Lenny was dealing even back then?"

She didn't say anything. I pulled my knees closer to

my chest and laid my head on the sweating tile, hoping the silence would never end.

Then she spoke. "You're letting him kill you too."

Steam billowed toward me like a rolling cloud and scorched my heart. Her words bounced from tile to tile—"Kill you too . . . too . . . too."

"What are you saying?" I asked.

Again she didn't answer. Finally, I forced myself to ask, "Are you saying he killed Kelly?"

My eyes searched the mist between us for an answer.

"I doubt that even Lenny is that sick." she began. "He was in Atlantic City that night, but he didn't get to The Albatross until around two in the morning. He made me tell the police that he had been with me all evening. He told me about the fire and that you would blame him even though it wasn't his fault. He was shaking and crying about the kid, and I believed him. But looking back, maybe some deal of his went sour and your brother and your kid got caught in the middle."

I was suddenly too angry to breathe. Why hadn't she told the cops the truth? How had Lenny bought her silence? Then I remembered the old woman at The Albatross. "Did he hit you that night?" I asked.

Now Bianca seemed stunned. For a moment she studied me as if I were setting her up. Then she shrugged. "Yeah, but that wasn't to keep me quiet, it was later when I told him I couldn't see him anymore."

The tile in front of my face was sweating profusely. I rubbed my hands over it, releasing the many water droplets that quivered there. They fell to the floor in racing rivulets.

"What are you saying then? What do you mean, he's killing me too?" In the heavy dampness my throat suddenly turned so dry I could barely speak. I pushed my next words out. "Who else did he kill?"

She nibbled on her lower lip and sloshed her hand

in the water bucket, tilting her head to the left then to the right. "He almost destroyed me. I tried to get away from him so many times, but he just wouldn't let go. He used to laugh when I told him the relationship was killing me. As long as he was around, I could never be open to meeting someone else, someone really available for me." She raised the bucket to her lips and drank the cold water. Then, pouring some water over the fullness of her breats, she sighed deeply and slid closer to me. I felt my nakedness on the tile bench. Weary and numb, I was empty of emotion. She said, "I'm telling you this so you can free yourself, not to hurt you."

I sucked the salty sweat from my lips, rose, and walked to the glass door. It was covered with condensation and I could not see out. When I turned back to her I was barely able to distinguish her contours through the thickness of steam.

"I've been free of him a long time." I said. "I left him a couple of weeks before the fire."

She looked down at her feet that dangled from the bench. I could just make out the deep red glisten of her toe nails.

"Hate controls more than love does," she said. "The fact that all you care about is revenge means that he's got you by the short hairs." Drops of sweat shuddered on her flesh. "When we made love he'd always talk about addicting me to him, to his tongue, his dick. He was a very considerate lover, he always wanted me to get off. All for the wrong reasons. Not to give, but to take, to control."

The heat began to scorch my skin and I felt a burning sensation on my inner thighs. I looked down at my pubic hair studded in quivering, glistening water droplets. I flashed back to Lenny's lovemaking. My nipples were taut and erect. "Meaning?"

"Lenny would say anything to get what he wanted.

He's a human vampire. He feeds on people's dependency, and now he's turning you into a junkie."

She was looking dead at my arms, and I didn't see any point in denial. I rubbed the purple-blue bruises that seemed translucent in the heat. "Lenny has nothing to do with this. He doesn't even know I've been using," I said.

"Of course. You're well trained to self-destruct. You didn't live with him all those years for nothing."

"What about you? Are you afraid of him?"

She shook her head. "No. He knows if something shady happens to me, a letter will go to the 166th Precinct about his dope dealing. As long as he doesn't know who has the letter, I'm safe."

A chill ran up my spine. Despite the heat of the steamroom, I was suddenly ice cold. I told her about the Dragon, how expensive and posh it was, how it had opened shortly after that fatal night. As I spoke, I kept opening circles in the glass door. As soon as my fingers removed the condensation, it would return. The naked women exercising on the other side of the pane became shadows.

"Do you have any idea where I could find Brian's girlfriend?"

Steam belched from the heated rocks and rolled around the room like a cloud before a storm. She shifted on the tile and shook her head. "No. I don't. But you're better off dropping this thing. Live your new life. Lenny will hang himself eventually."

A golden crucifix gleamed between her cinnamon breasts. Thinking I had to get the hell out of there, I said, "I don't have that kind of forgiveness in me."

CHAPTER FOURTEEN

I left Atlantic City way over the speed limit, weaving in and out of traffic without even bothering to lie to myself. I was sick. The steamroom had cleaned the last of the skag from my pores, and I was sick. Even after all that sweating, and after a cold shower, my skin was damp and itchy, and my nose was running. I yawned with regularity. I didn't want to think about Lenny dealing back then, or about him supplying Brian. Those nights when he came home late, when I had suspected him of being with other women, had he been out there dealing? What kind of an idiot was I? How big had my blind spot been? I headed for Harlem and the cure—pretending that nothing else mattered.

After trying unsuccessfully to cop in Harlem, I headed for El Barrio. It was dusk, and the neighborhood was bathed in the blue haze of streetlamps, and the orange glow of an occasional cuchifrito stand. Tropical aromas laced themselves with the smells of decay, damp concrete, and old garbage. Salsa, guguanco, and merengue drifted from storefronts and windows as children played in the streets. Adults sat on stoops or stood on corners waiting, as they always had, waiting for a rescue that was never going to come. I passed Robert's Place on 103rd Street and wondered if I should try to cop there. I parked the car and stepped inside. Even if Sevinsky was still hanging out at this joint, it was too early to worry about it.

The place was almost empty. I stepped up to the bar and ordered a draft beer. Next to me two guys were rapping politics, low and intense. But I could hear every word.

"The guy is a poverty pimp from the word go. That's all he is. You can vote to put him in the City Council if you want to, but he ain't no Messiah."

"He promised me a job."

"That's what I mean, exactly. Some dudes pimp whores, others pimp workers."

The listener shook his head, "I don't get it."

"Look, City Hall is scared shitless of people like us. They're scared of this whole goddamn neighborhood. So they set us up like a goddamn banana republic and put a fascist like Mendez in charge of the natives. He runs us, and they run him. He delivers jobs to guys like you, and you deliver your vote. Social programs, my ass. It's all pimping."

"He said some commissioner named Mulwihill was gonna make sure this neighborhood gets funding, and I was gonna get electrical contracting work in all the buildings we rehab with that funding."

"Yeah, Mulwihill's selling contracts for votes like it was going outta style. He's a sleazy fuck. He used to be an ambulance chaser. Then he married some rich bitch whose family has been in politics forever. Next thing you know he's appointed Special Commissioner for Economic Development. Mendez is his tool."

As the two men ordered another round, I downed my beer and tried to figure my next move. When the bartender came back, I pushed my empty glass toward him and decided to be direct. I leaned forward and said, "I'm looking for Cobra's thing."

He acted deaf. "Another draft?" he asked.

I repeated my question. "Do you know where I can get Cobra's thing?"

He leaned against the low sink and began washing a glass on a circular brush that jutted up from the brown dishwater. He held the glass up, examining its spots. "I don't know what you're talking about," he said. "And even if I did, we don't do narcotics in here."

He took my empty glass to fill it, but I raised my hand and stopped him. My plan was formulated, and the bartender watched my face go from darkness to light without another word. I peeled a couple of singles onto the bar and cut out. Even in the early evening, the bar was darker than the night outside.

I decided to head for 110th Street, where I had copped a few weeks before. Maybe, I thought to myself, just maybe, I'll find Nancy, and she'll let me watch the kid while she cops for me. But no such luck. She was not on the stoop. Three men sat there now, no women or children at all. I passed the stoop twice, then decided to ask for her. I looked up at the three sour faces.

"Seen Nancy?"

No one answered.

"I'm looking for Nancy."

The youngest, a Puerto Rican teenager in shorts, a T-shirt, and a red headband, looked off into the distance and answered me as if he were actually talking to himself.

"She ain't around," he said. His face shut down.

"Where is she?"

There was a long silence in which I yawned and listened to the crawling under my skin. My dilemma must have been obvious because the young man eyed me directly and said, "Cops got her last week. If you don't watch out they'll get you too."

I began walking away. No more words were necessary. Yeah, the cops might get me too, I thought. But not the way he had in mind. I was standing on the corner studying the wasteland all around when a squad car cruised by, moving so slowly that the driver caught my eye and we stared at each other. In his gaze I saw my illness and the reflection of my desolation. He was one beat away from calling me over, and I should have turned away as soon as I sensed his attention on me. I never should have let him catch my eye. I knew cops had a way of reading you. Every crime has an aura, a language of arms and legs. A junkie looking for the cure is the easiest crime to make, since the fear of being stopped before reaching the cure is in every move. Few ghetto dwellers looked as determined as a junkie looking to score. I knew it from the other side. Through that squad car window, people were like characters in a well-written play—you knew the motivation right away. Now the cops were reading me.

I was mesmerized by the coasting car and the ice blue stare of its driver. He was trying to decide whether or not I was worth stopping. The aroma of fear rising from my damp skin made me a tempting target. I couldn't break the glare that held us both. My feet wouldn't move. My knees were locked. If I could have moved, I would have started running.

Suddenly two large arms embraced me from behind. "Hey baby, how long you been waiting?" boomed a loud voice.

My heart pounded in my chest and I felt my tongue hit the dry roof of my mouth. The arms spun me around. I faced the chest of the teenager from the stoop, my eyes level with his lips. Through clenched teeth, he said, "Kiss me, babe. Kiss me and they'll go away."

I put my arms around his neck and placed my lips

on his. I locked my teeth against his tongue, but his breath invaded mine.

The cop looked away, and the squad car moved on. I pulled away from the kid. "Thanks," I said.

He shrugged. "Why don't you put some shade on what you're doing? You're standing there like a billboard."

"Do you know a blond named Sunny?"

He took another long look at me. I felt suddenly certain he would answer yes. But he shook his head. I studied the desolation that was Lenox Avenue, feeling it would be easier just to lie down and die. The evening's unusual stillness seemed to be echoing within me. The heartbeat that had jumped into my throat earlier was gone. Now I wasn't sure I had a heart at all. I couldn't feel myself breathing either. The tears that oozed from my eyes didn't mean that I was crying. I was hollow. I yawned, not even bothering to bring my clammy hand to my dry mouth. I was standing there thinking about just going home and waiting for the sickness to go away, when the squad car reappeared up the block. My heart began to beat again. I scratched my tracks and looked down at feet that still didn't move. The young stranger grabbed my hand. "C'mon," he said, "let's get the fuck outta here."

I tripped after his long legs as we headed in the direction of the park.

"How much bread you got?"

"Enough," I said.

"For both of us?"

I kept walking. "Hey, c'mon," he said. His voice grew louder as he flapped his arms in a gesture of frustration. "I just saved your ass from the man and now you don't wanna answer a simple question."

I let go of his hand and kept walking but he caught up with me quickly and he grabbed my elbow. I stopped and checked out the hard eyes in his soft face. His brows were arched, his lips full and angelic. It was a masculine face still cloaked in puberty, unshadowed by a beard.

"What are you really asking?" I said.

His face lit up. "I'll cop for you. I even have works. But you've got to take care of me too."

"A taste?"

He shook his head and played with the hint of a dimple on his chin. "Uh uh, baby. You've got to do better than that. . . . A taste is if you do your own copping and just use my works. If I cop for you, I want my own bag."

His almond eyes sparkled with thoughts of the cure. He was a sponger like Brian. I decided to take him up on his offer. But before I agreed I started walking again.

"I wanna go with you. Take me with you."

"Why?" he said. "Don't you trust me?"

I looked down at the Adidas sneakers on the sockless feet attached to long bare legs. "Something like that."

Under my clammy skin, every cell in my body sucked like the open mouth of an infant. Hungry, hungry for the cure. He smiled. "I have my works stashed not far from here. That's where I was gonna take you to wait for me. But if you want we can cop on our way over there. You wanna hand me the bills now?"

I thought about Brian again and shook my head. "When we get there, not before."

I followed him up the avenue to 117th Street. The August night was a congregation of people escaping the confining heat of their tenement homes by gathering outside, rapping, drinking, laughing, playing dominoes and dice. The winos talked intimately to ghosts or yelled obscenities at passing shadows. As soon as we entered the block, I spotted the cop man. He was leaning against a dumpster, a red hanky hanging from his back pocket. A steady stream of people made their way to his side.

They'd slap him five, and he'd reach down into his sock, then slap them five back, and they'd leave.

"Gimme the bread. How much do you want?"

"Three bags," I said.

He beamed and put his arm around me. I slipped the cash into his hand, then watched him cross the street and join the other vultures. He returned in minutes with a new bounce to his step. I wanted him to hand me the stuff right then but he wouldn't. Instead he grabbed my damp hand. I felt a mixture of nervous anticipation and relief and I breathed easier. We were walking fast now, not looking at each other, not even bothering to talk.

When we got to 103rd Street, I followed him down some broken steps to a padlocked iron gate under the front stairway of an abandoned building. He made sure no one was looking, then pushed the gate back with his foot. The padlock swung loose, not hooked onto anything but the gate itself. We took one steep step down to a rusting metal door. He gave it a kick and it groaned and fell back. Piles of damp, decaying garbage lined the narrow cellar hallway. He turned a corner and I followed him.

"Watch your head," he said, stooping to enter the boiler room. I did the same. Inside, several naked light bulbs illuminated centerfolds nailed to the wall—hard-core photos of women in lace and leather being whipped, beaten, chained, and fucked up the ass. Scarred and bleeding, they knelt with docile inviting smiles, their privates spread like clams on the half shell. The walls dripped with moisture. On the concrete floor half a dozen naked mattresses were lined up, unoccupied. Soot covered everything. Near the boiler, a bare-chested man lay with his mouth hanging open. His head was tilted back so that the whites of his eyes stared directly at me. The rattle in his throat was the only sound in the underground stillness.

In the center of the oblong space a pale thin boy sat

with folded arms and legs. His huge eyes popped from his head and filled the room. His hair was cropped within an inch of his scalp. The Rican I had come with stepped aside, giving me a fuller view of the space I had entered.

"Is this her? Is she the one?" he said.

The boy's haunted gaze rested unflinchingly on me. I felt the Rican at my elbow stiffen. I should have been afraid. They had made me for a cop or a sucker, and the game was up. The irony of it was that I didn't give a shit about anything but the cure.

"I don't know," the boy said in a surprisingly feminine voice.

"What your name?" he asked me.

"Conroy, Toni Conroy." I was sick and didn't feel like pussyfooting around. For what?

The boy nodded and the Rican behind me retreated.

"Hey, wait a minute! Where's my stuff?"

The Rican looked questioningly at the boy as if to say, "Do I have to give it to her?"

The boy nodded. The Rican pulled three glassine bags from his pocket. He handed me two and kept one. I turned them over in my hand. They were sealed with green tape.

"What about works?" I said, thinking about the coffin in my bedsprings. But I didn't want to wait until I got downtown. This seemed as good a place as any for the cure. "You promised me your works," I repeated.

The boy began to rise, his short, thin body hidden in an old gray sweatsuit. "Don't worry about it. Let him take his works. I've got my own. Let him go. I need to talk to you in private."

The junkie on the mattress by the boiler curled into a fetal position and he purred like a cat. I wondered if he was waking up. Behind me the metal door groaned as the Rican left. Then I heard the outer gate bang open and shut. As the youth came nearer I noticed the blond roots beneath the dark hair and saw that even the baggy fabric could not hide the curve of breasts. A small family of freckles adorned his nose. Huge blue eyes filled the fragile beauty of his face, a young face veiled from its own youth by ugly memories. I wondered what he had seen and why. It was a face like Brian's face, that same lost look.

On a hunch I said, "Sunny, you've changed your hair."

The S and M scenes jumped from the sooty walls into my eyes. I studied the rusty nails on which they were suspended. Brian had led her to this place, and now I was feeling the guilt. "You've been looking for me, and I've been running," Sunny said. "But in the end it was me who found you."

She pointed to the mattress and we sat down together. Under my clammy skin crawled a monstrous need. Everything seemed upsidedown. For so long I had thought of Sunny as the solution. Now I sat across from her concerned only with getting my hands on her works. "I'll give you a bag if you let me use your works," I said.

She looked puzzled. "I thought you wanted the guy who took your brother and your kid off the count."

For a moment I was afraid that she was about to provide the answer. I was afraid that I would have to hear it. Then there would be nowhere else to go and my search would be over, my purpose gone. It was the eventuality to which I hadn't given much thought.

"Your habit can't be all that bad," she said.

"What?"

"It's a chippie. You haven't been out here that long. You've been camouflaging your shit because you're on the force. Why don't you just go home and forget this bullshit. In a week you'll feel better."

"I guess you're right," I said, but I didn't mean it. I

was thinking that I shouldn't start begging. I should just get back into my car and drive home to my own coffin. I started to rise. Beads of sweat quivered on my upper lip. A million amoebas moved under my skin. My knees buckled a little, but then I was up. I wanted to walk out on the answer and substitute the cure. I was halfway across the room when she asked me a question.

"Don't you want to know what I know?"

I turned to look back at the desolation that separated us and to take one last look at her, the dyed cropped hair, the boyish disguise. "Who are you hiding from?"

Sunny lit a cigarette butt that she retrieved from the floor. "I've been running ever since that night."

The sleeping junkie stirred again. He made an ungodly sound somewhere in his throat, and then he farted. Otherwise it was completely still in this strangely unpopulated shooting gallery. Hot and cold ran through my body. I fingered the glassine bags in my hand, hoping my sweaty palm wasn't melting the contents. I was thinking I'd get off just this one more time, and then I'd never cop again.

I took a step toward her. The floor angled so sharply down that she became taller and I became shorter. "You wanna hit me?" I asked. "I have a lot of trouble finding my own veins."

Her whole face fell, like a child unjustly slapped. "I've been looking for you to solve this case so I can stop running! Now that I find you, you want me to hit you?" She flapped her delicate arms like a bird with no prayer of flight. "I can't believe it," she whispered hoarsely.

Since I had no real answer, I weakly took the offensive. "Are you telling me you're clean?"

She tilted her head right, then left, her shoulders came up and went back down, and all the while her sad eyes stayed dead on me. "I really loved Brian," she said.

I thought I might cry out then, loud and long and

crazy, and just leave all sanity behind. Instead, I swallowed the extra saliva in my mouth and spoke. "So did I."

She extricated a loose brick from the wall behind her, reached a hand into the hole, and pulled out a plastic sandwich bag, which she offered to me. "I'll give you my works, but you're gonna hafta hit yourself."

I took the works and a spoon neatly packaged in the sandwich bag and looked for a source of water. She pointed to a pipe at the far end of the cellar where the ceiling was so low you had to crawl to reach it. A large steady drip fell from the rusty pipe. I took the spoon, got on my hands and knees, and crawled over to the leaking pipe. When I got back, my knees were covered in soot and I felt it on my face too. I sat down next to her and started to cook up. She watched intently.

Her little tongue darted hungrily around her thin lips. "No, I ain't clean," she said. "But I wish to God I was." I knew what that meant, so I offered to share my stuff with her. After watching my trembling clumsiness, she volunteered to do the cooking. I began to tie up. "There was supposed to be a big payoff that night," she said, "and when Brian stole the money, the shit hit the fan."

She lit the match under the spoon and the stuff melted. She withdrew the flame and dropped the match. Then she held the spoon while I took my share. Because I was suddenly in no hurry for the truth, I let her take the lead.

"We were gonna run away together. He figured it was a routine monthly payoff and it would blow over."

I slapped my arm because the veins refused to stand up. I slapped it until it got red. I tried for a vein. She kept talking.

"We were gonna go to Arizona or California or someplace fresh where we could stay clean and Lenny would never find us."

I poked the needle in my arm. Had I heard right? My veins were rolling away from me. I pulled the needle out and inserted it again. Only when the needle had hit its mark did I dare ask, "Brian stole the money from Lenny?"

My blood rose in a thin red line. The dope cruised in softly like a kitten on little paws that cupped my heart in its fur. So when she answered "Yeah," I was able to bear it. She continued relentlessly to explain. "Lenny was paying off some cop, some cop in the precinct who would tip him off whenever a raid was coming, a cop they call the fat man."

I wiped the needle on my jeans and gave it to her. I said "The fat man?" as I watched her take care of business.

"Yeah."

Now my revenge had a name—a nickname—fat man.

"So what went wrong?"

"That night the envelope had fifty grand in it. Brian had no idea it was gonna be that much. Usually it was just a couple of grand. He just grabbed the payoff envelope from the hiding place behind the bar . . . Lenny had this hiding place behind the bar . . . you remember the storefront social club on Thirteenth Street?"

I remembered. My skin stopped crawling. Everything in me stood still.

"When Brian got home, to your place, he opened the envelope and freaked. He called me right away. We knew something big was up, and Brian had walked right into it. We were gonna leave town right then. But Brian wanted to wait till you got home from the restaurant. After that, we were just gonna hop a train and be gone. But I'm betting the fat man got to Brian before Brian could get to me."

"How did you know it was him?"

"It had to be him." she said. "He was Lenny's enforcer. Brian told me about him many times."

"Where is this fat man now?"

Her face went soft and free and young. She slumped forward and pulled the needle from her arm.

"I guess he isn't in the 166th anymore or you would've seen him. The grapevine has it he's still hot on my ass."

"So how am I gonna find him?"

"He has a tattoo."

She was so high that the words came from her throat with difficulty, as if she were underwater without air.

"The fat man has a rose tattoo on his right arm. Brian told me that once. The fat man always picked up the payoff. Once in the summer Brian saw this weird tattoo, a rose with a cobra wrapped around its stem."

When she said the word "cobra," I got stone-cold sober. "Do you think the fat man is cobra?" I asked.

She looked more terrified than before. "I dunno. I just know he's relentless—you know how a cop on the take can be. He's been after me for two years now. He came for me the night of the fire. He tore up my apartment after he'd paid his visit to yours, but he didn't get me because I was waiting for Brian on the roof across the street. I saw him, he's huge, he must weigh almost three hundred pounds and he has brownish hair."

"Did you see Lenny that night?"

She shook her head. "Find the tattoo and you've got the killer. Two years I've been running from this maniac. He's still out there asking for me. I can't figure out why."

I wondered something out loud. "Could it have been him that got to Baker?"

She was watching my lips as if trying to make sure she had heard right. "Did you say Baker? Larry Baker?"

I told her yes, that it was Baker who had told me about her and that he had died in prison. "Larry was with me that night," she said. "We were getting off together when Brian called. But Larry booked as soon as he heard what Brian had done. He didn't want any part of it."

Her eyes turned inward on a memory—maybe Baker's face the last time she saw it. Whatever it was, her terror became palpable. I actually thought I tasted it on my dry lips.

"So Baker's dead," she said. "Do you think he told the fat man about me? Is that why he's still on my ass?"

I had no way of knowing but I said, "The fat man must figure you know about the fifty grand. That fifty grand must have been for something big, something really big. Something big enough for a police cover-up."

The sleeping junkie moaned and stirred. His lips twitched. He seemed to be running, running from a nightmare. I wondered if I was asleep myself. Was I a character in his nightmare or he a character in mine?

Sunny's head bobbed slowly up and down, the blue eyes swimming in an enormous sea of white. "The fat man wants to kill me for something I don't even know," she whispered thickly. Then she leaned across the mattress, both her thin arms stretched in supplication. I thought about Brian starting her on the stuff. She scooted closer to me and grabbed hold of my arms, clutching me like a child clutches its mother. Fear darted like quicksilver in her eyes.

"I've got to get out," she said. "I've given you all I know. Help me get out. I need to get out. There's no place left for me to go in this stinking city."

Even high as I was, I must have looked skeptical because she added a promise.

"I'll stay in touch. I'll even testify for you, if you ever get the motherfucker to trial."

I took her small hands in mine, and we both tottered to our feet.

"How much do you want?" I asked.

"LA. I want to get lost in LA."

Soledad Santiago

The sleeping junkie scratched his balls and groaned. His legs twitched the way a bug twitches when it's dying. I turned from the sight back to her eyes and the door behind us. "My car's not far from here." I said. "I'll go get it. We'll go by my place. I'll get my cash card and give you some bucks. Then we'll see how soon you can fly out."

"Just like that?" She smiled wanly as if the offer were a dream destined to fade.

"Just like that."

CHAPTER FIFTEEN

I hit the light switch and faced myself. The walk-in closet next to the front door was completely covered by a one-piece mirror. I looked as if I had just climbed out of a sewer. My arms, legs, and even my cheeks were soot-stained. My waxen skin was accented by the greenish circles under my eyes. I thought I heard the sound of a whip cracking. A spiderweb spread between my eyes before they shattered, splintered, and slid down the wall, their fall punctuated by the tinkle of glass. Then my whole reflection dropped to the floor. Someone had fired a single bullet into the mirror.

Just before my knees gave way, I hit the switch, returning the room to the safety of darkness. I lay flat, inches from the sea of glass, then crawled to the window. On the roof, across the street, a shadow watched. Sweat dripped between my breasts. My face quivered. My breath rattling in my throat, I crawled to my bed and felt for my piece, its coldness comforting me. I crawled back to the window. The shadow was gone, the night outside silent.

I lay there clutching my piece, listening to the fear

thunder in my throat. My body, aching and damp with sweat, had no will to move. Mary was on night tour and Sunny safely on a plane to LA.

I lay there looking up at that roof across the street where oblivion stalked and at the sky above, which not a single star illuminated. Where were the screams of neighbors? Someone who had heard the gun shot. Someone who wanted me to live. Or a siren racing to my door. But nothing. No one. I was alone. The stillness around me deepened.

I rattled the locked window gates and crawled back to the darkness of my bed. I lay there thinking about Lenny and the fat man. How did the fat man know Brian had taken the payoff money? Was Brian the only one who could have taken it? Had Lenny sent the fat man to my apartment? I had the awful feeling that Lenny knew a lot more than he let on, and that he had kept quiet to protect his own ass. But even that didn't explain the police cover-up. Maybe the fat man had paid off Vogel, but why kill Baker and keep Sunny running? Something didn't fit. Still, I was close, awfully close. I was sure that it was the fat man who had fired at me from that roof across the street. My revenge was now so near that it was stalking me. Death felt as close as a lover awaiting my embrace. Just before I went under, I remembered Errol. His brother's wedding was tomorrow.

"What the fuck happened here?"

I opened my eyes to the sound of Mary's voice. Slices of silver mirror sparkled with morning light. A shimmer of light fell across her violet eyes. Specks of reflected sun danced around the room. I sat up. Her eyes were on the gun next to my pillow.

"Someone tried to shoot me last night," I whispered, as if it were a giant secret I had to keep even from myself.

"Did you call the cops?"

I got up. My knees were weak. My head hung as if my neck were broken. I felt a false smile scar my face as I tried a hollow answer. "I am the cops."

She waded through broken mirror to the window, its smooth surface marred by a clean bullet hole. "It came from the roof across the street," she said. "Only one try?"

I shrugged. "I guess he wasn't too determined."

"No, that isn't it. This is a professional killer, a sharpshooter. He got your reflection and he thinks he got you. That mirror saved your life."

Now that the initial shock had worn off, Mary began to get angry—angry at the situation, angry at me, angry at the danger I had manufactured.

"We've got to talk to somebody," she said tensely. "If you don't, I will."

That's when I got up and started talking fast. I told her about Sunny and about the fat man and his rose tattoo.

"Why can't we tell that to the cap?" she asked almost pleadingly.

I grabbed a broom and dustpan and started sweeping glass.

"The force had its chance and somebody killed the investigation. I can't take a chance on that happening again. I'm gonna find that fat man."

She opened a garbage bag, and I dumped some slices of the broken mirror into it and listened to the tinkle of glass on glass. Then I started sweeping again.

"I need a week," I said. "If I haven't wrapped it up in a week, I'll go to Internal Affairs." I was working fast and hard. She grabbed me. I flinched. Underneath the long sleeves, my blue and swollen arm ached.

"Please, Mary, please. I promise."

"What if this guy tries again?" Her voice was ice. She felt trapped by loyalty and friendship.

"We can stay at a hotel for a week. We can stay at the Martha Washington. I'll cover it."

"And then what?"

"If I haven't found him by the end of the week, we can go to IAD together."

She walked back to the window and looked out for a long time. "If I don't go along with you, you'll never trust anyone again." I shrugged because truth is truth. She sighed then and acquiesced. "Nothing's gonna happen in broad daylight." And then softly, very softly, she added, "I must be nuts."

Later we both threw some things into a suitcase. Neither of us said much. My nose was running, and I was yawning a lot. I had one bag left, but I didn't know how to get to it with her around.

"You working tonight?"

She nodded. "I'm safer out there in the street than I am in my own home." I detected a touch of bitterness. But I was now much too close to back down.

"I'm gonna drive us to the Martha Washington, and then I have to meet Errol for that goddamn wedding. I can't believe I promised to go to that thing."

She sat on the suitcase. I snapped the snaps closed.

"You should talk to him," she said. Of course, I planned to ignore her.

CHAPTER SIXTEEN

"What am I going to wear?"

"We're here in fucking hiding, and you can't figure out what to wear to a goddamn wedding."

Mary's face was so red it was purple. She was pissed. The truth was I couldn't blame her. She was stuck in a damn hotel room she didn't want to be in, she hadn't slept in almost twenty hours, her life was in jeopardy, and now I wanted access to her wardrobe

"You could've told me you needed a fancy dress before we left the apartment. I can't help you now."

"What about the white skirt with the white top and jacket?"

"It's too casual for a wedding. Besides, the bride wears white, not you."

I bounced on the corner of the double bed we would share until it would be safe to leave the cheap hotel. The mattress was soft and bumpy. I lay down and rolled immediately into a ditch in its center.

"It's a Chinese wedding," I said. "The bride is wearing red so I guess it's okay for me to wear white."

"You can dress it up a little," she offered grudgingly,

rummaging through the suitcase for her jewelry case. While she did that, I called Errol to tell him to meet me in front of the temple.

"Is there a reason I can't pick you up?"

"Nothing personal," I faked a laugh. I was about to concoct a story, but he didn't question me further.

I waited alone in front of the Buddhist temple on Mott Street. It was two o'clock in the afternoon, and the ceremony was to start momentarily. Errol came up the cobblestone street with the sun shining strongly behind him. He was tall, well built, handsome in a beige summer suit, and his gait was long and languid. He emerged from the glare with a mellow glow of his own and kissed my mouth. "You look great," he said.

"You too." He took my hand and opened the wooden door that led inside the small temple. The incense smelled of flowers. In an anteroom we took off our shoes, placed them with the others, and went in. A carved Buddha, sitting in full lotus, smiled under half-closed stone eyelids. Four of his fingers created two circles, one in each hand. Bamboo mats lay across the wooden floor. White lilies floated in the clear water of a shallow pool.

"Where are the other guests?"

He shrugged, not speaking.

I followed him to a garden where my question was answered. Some slippers lay on the threshold and we put them on. Under the cool shadow of a big-bellied Buddha, members of the family gathered around the bride and groom. She wore a red silk dress embroidered in flowers and birds, and baby's breath framed her purple-black hair. The groom wore white silk. A monk in orange nodded his bald head. Bonsai trees in a rock garden with hot pink azaleas and milky gardenias surrounded us.

"They wrote the ceremony themselves, in English

and Chinese," Errol said as we moved to join the other guests.

The sun was directly overhead. I could barely focus. I wanted something positive to come out of my mouth, but no words came to mind. He put his hand on my arm and winked. "Good preparation for marriage," he said. "Everybody speaks a different language, communication is kept to a minimum, and you can stay together for fifty years without ever getting to know each other."

"And everybody plays a role," I said, squinting at the few red hairs in his beard that glistened in the sun.

He brushed my cheek with his lips. I whispered, "I've been there."

The couple spoke to each other in a long alternating poem, sometimes her, sometimes him, sometimes together. A bird bathed with its own reflection, and as it sang, the sun moved closer to the earth and washed the ceremony in orange light. As the smell of flowers filled my nostrils, Errol's chest expanded with longing. I stopped hearing the words, but that yearning in him, I heard that. It touched something in me that took me backwards in time.

I looked outside, and the whole Lower East Side was covered in snow. I ran upstairs to Lenny's and used my key to get in. He was still half asleep. He reached up from under the covers and tried to pull me in.

"Lenny, Lenny, the snow's here. Today's our wedding day."

"That means I get to sleep with you tonight?"

I sat on his crotch and bounced up and down. "Yeah, tonight."

I had told Lenny that I wouldn't sleep with him any more until we got married. He and my mom wanted us to wait until I got older. But I got my way. I wanted to get married in the snow. Just me and Lenny. Then City Hall.

Soledad Santiago

The sun was bright as summer, and we were standing under the widest tree we could find in Central Park. The naked branches rustled in the icy wind. He slipped the ring on my finger and said, "Honor and obey." I shivered all over. The sun and the ice made rainbows.

I jumped into his eyes, which were black as a hawk's, and laughed. "Yeah, I'll obey you."

He stepped in close. "I'm gonna take you home and make you beg for mercy."

The nearing sun caressed my skin. My restless feet shifted. I felt the pebbles beneath my slippers move and Errol squeezed my hand. "Relax," he whispered, "it's almost over." Then he cupped his hand over my ear in an odd way that meant affection.

In the restaurant at 100 Park Avenue, the tables were all set. I searched for our place cards and noticed we were with family. People had not yet situated themselves. They stood around the mirrored restaurant with its painted golden Dragons on the red lacquer walls and waited for the arrival of the bride and groom. Errol switched our place cards with two names at the end of the table, far from his mother and father. We hovered near out seats.

"Want a drink?"

"Sure," I said, and he wandered off to the bar. The bride and groom arrived. The bride held one long-stemmed red rose. I thought of the fat man's tattoo. Where would I find it? What would I do when I did? One sick tear slid down the side of my nose. My hollowness filled itself with a need, and I felt alone. My cheek itched. I touched the shadow of the heart that my mother had left there and wondered if she remembered me at all. I hadn't seen her since she went to California with her new man, and that was years ago, right after

Lenny and I got married. I hadn't heard from her either—not even an address or a phone number. When she left, she left. The parents of the bride looked happy. I thought about my dad. Was he drunk in an alley somewhere, or had death rescued him a long time ago?

There was half a bag of stuff in my bra. I felt it scratch my skin and thought of my cure, that lie with deadly sweet arms. A lie about peace and warmth that seemed better than no answer at all. Errol surfaced at my elbow, and he put our drinks on the table. "Sit," he said. "Is that ghost still following you?"

We both sat down.

I was about to ask him what he meant when a rose came over my shoulder and it touched my face. The bride and groom were behind us. Errol and I stood to congratulate them. I kissed the bride's shiny cheek, wishing her all the best. Errol hugged his brother, George, who was a lot shorter than Errol and who looked like somebody's else's brother. A long moment passed before Errol let go, eyes glistening.

"I beat you to the altar," George said, talking to Errol but looking at me. "Is this her?"

Errol blushed. "It's her." Both sets of parents appeared and the bride and groom moved on. I studied Errol's parents and looked for a family resemblance. I found his mouth on his mother's face but nothing else. Errol had his father's height and coloring, but that was it. He introduced me.

Errol's father was a ruddy cop whose glacial eyes offset the small red veins that mapped his face. He reminded me of our precinct captain. After squeezing my hand, he slapped Errol on the back.

"Well, son, I hope this time you can pull it off, even if she is a cop."

The color in Errol's face deepened. His birdlike mother looked embarrassed and offered me a frail hand and a feeble shake.

"Don't mind George," she said, meaning her husband. "He's always trying to get a rise out of Errol."

Errol's father was telling him how many greenbacks the wedding cost. These two people seemed so unlike Errol that I couldn't imagine him as their son. I searched his mother's face for a clue. When I couldn't find it, I asked, "Why did you name him Errol?"

"His father hates that name," she said, one ear on the financial report her husband was giving. He bit off the end of his unlit cigar, and I asked her again. "Why?"

"Errol Flynn," she explained, "The Swashbuckler." She said it as if she were picking a laundry detergent.

The band struck up a tune I didn't recognize. The bride and groom danced, and Errol's mother wanly clapped her little hands. All the romance had gone from her life, and the dreams—if there were any—had died on the vine.

Errol winked at me. I took a closer look at him—his receptive gentleness, his steadfast determination to be a good and just person. It was all over his face, his compassion, his depth. He was worlds above his parents, and yet he treated them with a loving respect I had never seen in my own family.

The music shifted tempo and the dance floor began to fill. I watched the bride and groom, but my thoughts were with two people I had blocked from memory, mom and dad. I remembered how much they had once loved each other and how circumstance and weakness had turned it sour. A sourness that almost destroyed us all.

Perspiration dampened my body. My knees were weak. I tried to steady myself by holding onto the back of my chair, but I had to sit. Faces, eyes, mouths—the room was going out of focus.

I was wearing my best dress, satin and lace. I was fifteen. It was, in fact, my birthday. Because it had been forgotten at home, I had snuck up to Lenny's for a quiet party for two. We had champagne and lasagna from the Italian joint on Second Avenue. After we ate and toasted each other, we sat on the couch watching a ball game. My legs were across his lap. It was the bottom of the ninth and the Mets were sure to lose as he stroked my chubby thighs and said, "Why don't we move to the bedroom? Take off that pretty dress and lay with me?"

I watched a player slide into home plate. "I don't know, Lenny." I wanted to but I didn't.

"C'mon." He leaned down and placed a family of little kisses on the inside of my thigh. "A birthday present?" Then he stuck out his tongue like a dog for a biscuit.

I giggled. "But it's not your birthday, Lenny, it's mine."

He winked at me. "That's what I mean," he said. "I'm gonna give you the birthday present of your life."

I put my arms around him and gave him an Eskimo kiss. "I'm not ready for a baby."

"I know that babe," he said as he slid his fingers around my throat. "We'll just hold each other close, real close."

He rotated his hips up from the couch and placed my hand over the bulge in his pants. "See how much I want you."

I didn't know if I was scared or excited, but I stood up. He looked at me hungrily and reached his muscular arms my way. He was wearing tight jeans and a very white undershirt, his hair glistening blue-black. I thought about being his wife, having his baby, and moving out of mom's place to be with him. He licked his sweet lips. I said, "Last one under the sheets is a rat's ass."

He chased me to the bedroom. While I giggled in the dark, he unbuckled my belt, unzipped my dress and pulled it over my head. I slipped under the sheets and watched him undress. Then, as he came close I felt his

naked skin against mine and crawled into his open arms.
I put my face in the space between his flat hairy tits and
felt at home. He rubbed the cheeks of my ass and
nibbled on my neck. Then, he pulled my panties down
and I helped him take off my bra. I watched his beautiful
face as he took a whole breast into his mouth.

After a while he pulled back to look at me. "I love
you," he said, "and I'm gonna make you mine."

I wrapped my arms around his thick neck and felt
his whole body tense as I snuggled under him. We were
close, close as an arrow in a bow. His lips were purple in
the darkness and tasted like violets. He pushed his
hands between my thighs, feeling everything there—my
hair, my love lips, my insides too.

"What a cute little button," he whispered, and slid
down to touch it with his tongue. His tongue was slow
and gentle, so sweet I could hardly bear it. His hands
climbed my body, and he took my nipples between his
fingers. His nails dug into me.

I stiffened with pain. "Ouch, Lenny, ouch."

His tongue got longer and went into all my crevices
like he knew them, knew the pleasure hiding there. I
grabbed the pillow for comfort and covered my face with
it. Sounds were coming out of me that I didn't want mom
to hear downstairs. Not that she could have. He cupped
my ass, separated the cheeks, and brought me up, up
into his face. The sound that came from my throat was a
deep growl.

Then he slid up my body, his face glistening with
my juice.

"Do you love me?" he asked.

I shivered. "Yes."

"I want to be in you."

He got on his knees.

"I'm scared, Lenny, I'm scared."

"It's gonna be good, babe. You love me, don't you?"

I held him to me, feeling the strong muscles of his back. "I do, I do."

"Well then, happy birthday, babe." He rammed into me. I felt a white pain shoot through my abdomen, into my spine, up to the back of my head until it came out of my mouth in a high short shriek. Lenny pulled back, then thrust forward again. The pain took on a deeper color, I thrashed beneath him and bit hard into his shoulder. He pulled back and took my face in his hands. "I'm always gonna love you," he rasped.

And then, with his lips on mine, he moved in me slowly, sweetly, circling my center, until the line between pleasure and pain blurred and I begged him never to stop.

"T-o-n-i, T-o-n-i," my name surfaced in the sound of Errol's voice. I didn't know how long he had been sitting there. My eyes were watering and my stomach entered a slow somersault. Errol's pupils were getting bigger. He leaned across the table. "Have you thought about us at all?" he asked.

Sweat was beginning to wet my clothes. I told him that I couldn't think about anything until after the investigation. I really wanted to say that I was sick and that he was crazy. I wanted to scream. But the wedding party didn't seem to be the place to fall apart. I pulled every fiber together and said, "The ceremony got to me, and the champagne just finished me off."

Every cell in my body was in anguish. I leaned forward, feeling the bag in my bra on the table's edge. "We could be happy together," he was saying. "I can't believe you don't feel it."

I thought about my life in the street. I figured if I came clean now, his love would fade pretty fast. "There's a lot you don't know about me," I said.

"Whatever it is, Toni, it's okay. I've been with you every day for the past three months now, and I know the person you are inside. You needed that hate to keep you alive, but you can let it go now."

He lowered his eyes and shifted his cutlery around like a nervous kid. "I know it sounds pompous, but it's baggage from the past," he added. "Everybody has it, some more than others. But you're awfully young to be carrying such a big load. Let it go."

I smiled. "It's that easy?"

He bit his lower lip. "You're an adult now," he said. "You know yourself better. I'm a good choice for you." He spread his hands before him as if to say, "Please don't make it so difficult."

I shrugged to indicate he was asking the impossible.

To my right and to my left people were beginning to sit down. His side of the table filled up too. I greeted the people, thinking I had to get out of there.

"Be back in a second," I said as I pushed myself up from the table, feeling his disappointed eyes follow me. My damp body screamed with aches and pains that made me feel like my own grandmother. It was a long walk to the ladies' room downstairs. Women and girls primped in front of the huge mirror. A Chinese attendant, I thought she must have been eighty, sat holding a stack of white hand towels.

All the stalls were unoccupied. I took one. Inside, I removed the bag from between my skin and bra. Just in time. My damp skin was beginning to wet the cellophane. Snorting it was a little bit complicated. I was worried about being noisy. But the others were busy laughing. So I just pulled out a nail file and snorted up, noisy as can be.

Afterward, I stayed for a few moments, pulling on my clothes, trying to get it together. My head felt better, but it wasn't like shooting up. There was no rush. I promised myself that after tonight I would quit. I had found Sunny, so my excuse for running in the street had expired. Sunny was right—I had a chippie. With will power, I could be myself again pretty quick. But did I want to be myself? I dropped two quarters into the attendant's cheap glass ashtray and returned to the festivities.

The first course had arrived. As I approached, Errol's face brightened. I sat and downed a sip of wine. On the table between us, a flame floated in a squat glass bowl, clinging to a wick in a glistening inch of translucent oil. The flicker reflected in his eyes as he leaned across the table. "What is that white stuff on your nose?" he whispered.

My hand jumped to my face. I had neglected to check myself in the mirror. I shoved my fingers across my nostrils and played dumb. "Nothing."

I guess he believed me because he dipped his egg roll into the hot mustard and changed the subject.

"When did you decide you wanted to be a cop?"

"My dad left home when I was twelve . . ."

"Do you know where he is?" Errol interrupted.

I shook my head. "No. . . . Do you wanna hear my answer to your first question?"

He poured wine into my half-empty glass. "Yes."

"My dad's last job, the job he had just before he disappeared, was in a synagogue. He was the shabbos goy."

"He was what?" He had that look on his face as if I was a martian with wings. The man was obviously in love. He didn't put any shade on it anymore. But I pretended to be blind and kept talking.

"In the ancient traditions of the orthodox Jewish religion the faithful aren't allowed to kindle a flame after sunset. On Friday, that is. So, modern orthodox Jews don't hit a light switch, drive a car, or turn on the heat—stuff like that. The shabbos goy is the arms and legs. My dad was the shabbos goy on Hester Street. Monday to Friday he was just a plain super. After my martial arts classes I would go down there and hang out with him. I liked hanging out there. Anyway, these cops were on a stakeout. They had a wiretap operation in the basement of the synagogue. I watched them for a couple of months, and I dug the power. I decided I wanted to be a cop too."

"Why do you think you were interested in power?"

I didn't have the answer to that one so I just kept talking. "I remember when I told my mom I was gonna be a cop, she laughed. We got into an argument and she smacked me in the mouth. Boy was she pissed. She said it meant I wanted to be a man."

I neglected to mention that after that first impulse and the confrontation with my mother, I had forgotten all about being a cop until much later—when I needed a reason to go on.

"That's funny," he said. "In my family becoming a cop was the natural thing to do, and I didn't want to. So my dad called me a fag. He could never stop baiting me."

We looked at each other and laughed. I wasn't enough of a woman, and he wasn't enough of a man. I put my hands around the glass bowl that held the oil and the flame, wondering why stuff I hadn't thought about in years was coming up now. The flame stretched up tall and thin. It seemed to be gasping for air in the overcrowded room. Slits of yellow light gave Errol's pupils a catlike glow. He licked his fingers and sucked on a sparerib. Then he said, "I want a partner that's more than nine to five. We fit together."

The room around us slowed down as I watched his mouth. He licked his lips and kept eating. Despite the dope, I felt a sharp sense of desire. I shrugged it off and blamed him. "Stutz, you're nuts. You must be horny. The world is full of men who propose marriage every time they get an itch."

He stopped chewing as if I had just reached across the table to slap him. I was thinking how to redeem myself when his attention shifted to the space above and behind my head. I heard the words "telephone" and "emergency." He wiped his lips with his linen napkin and got up. "Be right back," he said.

I started wondering what the hell I was doing at this wedding. The waiter came with a new course, followed by the mother of the bride, who gave every woman one long-stemmed rose. I laid mine on the tablecloth next to my knife. Red on white. I caught the conversation in bits and pieces. Nothing made much sense. I took a long drink of water, then studied the thorns on my rose with an impending sense of doom. Errol's hand was on my shoulder. "Grab your bag, let's step outside."

I picked up my purse and followed him. He wove through the spaces between the tables and exited through the mirrored entrance. He walked to the edge of the sidewalk and studied the clock on a parking meter; he wouldn't meet my eyes. The glass in the pavement under our feet sparkled and danced in the light. He fumbled in his pockets as if they belonged to someone else.

"What are you looking for?" I asked.

"Keys," he said hoarsely. "Car keys."

Just then I heard the jingle of metal on metal, and he produced two keys on a rabbit's foot. He grabbed my hand and headed down the block in his long-legged way. I tripped along, my high heels hampering solid movement. "What the fuck is going on?"

"Don't let this scare you back into your shell. Mary's been hurt," he said.

A wailing siren punctured my thoughts. "What happened?" I asked evenly, but inside, I was already falling apart.

He shook his head. "We're going to Bellevue to find out."

"Hurt?" I sank my fingers into several thorns. The

rose's sweet smell made me slightly nauseous. I took his arm. My fingers dug into him. He did not pull back, and I did not release my grip. "She's not dead, is she?"

"No, she's not dead. She's in a coma."

CHAPTER SEVENTEEN

It was a long narrow corridor painted an institutional light green. We ran into the antiseptic smell that surrounds death in a hospital. A doctor dressed in white, holding a clipboard, was explaining something to the captain and the brass. There were at least a dozen cops. Sevinsky was there too. His hands moved to his flushed face again and again, and he seemed unable to stand still. When I got there, I asked to see Mary.

"We've been waiting for you, Miss Conroy," the doctor said. "The patient's family is out of town on vacation, and we thought a familiar face, a familiar voice might bring her back."

The doctor had a harelip.

"I tried talking to her," Sevinsky interjected. "But it didn't seem to help."

I couldn't take my eyes off the doctor's scar. "What happened?" I asked.

He had a slight speech defect, and my ears wrapped around his offbeat lisp. "A brick fell from a roof and fractured her skull."

I looked at Sevinsky, "Where were you?"

He answered without a flinch. "A few steps ahead of her. I didn't see it happen. We were on a burglary in progress. I ran up the stoop thinking she was right behind me, and then I heard the thud and turned around. She was laid out on the steps, and there was blood running from her head like a faucet. I called for an ambulance. Then I checked the roof. There was nothing up there."

He looked at the rose I still clutched in my hand. "I guess she's a goner," he said.

I thought about all the shit Mary had told me about this asshole and wished the brick had fallen on him. The doctor grabbed my elbow and pulled me into a room.

Mary was behind a wall of curtain surrounded by a ghoulish penny arcade of blinking and beeping machines, and there were tubes in her nose and arms. Her head was wrapped in a bandage, her face very pale and very still. Her lips had a bluish tint, but even now her cheek bones highlighted the simple beauty of her face.

"Did you shave her hair?" I asked stupidly.

"We had to."

Her arms lay at her sides. I heard the soft whistle of her breath. The steady beep-beep-beep of her heart went up and down on the monitor. "Can I touch her?"

The doctor nodded. "Talk to her. The familiar sound might pull her back. We tried with her partner, but it didn't work."

I gently traced the line of her cheekbone down to her chin, and took her hand in mine. "Mary. It's me, Mary. It's Toni."

She didn't move.

"Mary, I love you. I'm so sorry. Please come back."

The beep seemed to speed up on the machine. I kissed her hand and placed the rose on the bed. Her eyelids quivered, then slowly opened. The light in her eyes was distant, as if coming through a deep fog.

"Mary, can you hear me?"

She blinked a few times quickly. Her chest heaved under the sheet. Her lips parted. Mary's eyes opened, and I saw that she recognized me. She moved her eyes back and forth like someone communicating a message. I read fear, a terrible fear. The sound that came from her cracked lips carried no words. The scar on the doctor's face twitched. I could barely hear my own voice as the horror in me grew into a question. "Can she talk?" I asked him.

He shook his head, the scar moving from side to side. "It's difficult to know about the extent of brain damage just yet."

A sound rose in her throat. Her tongue went wild in her mouth and her right hand twitched. She pursed her lips and a rattle came out. A tear slid down her cheek. Her spastic fingers grabbed for the rose. The doctor put his hand on my arm. "That's enough," he said.

She clenched her hand around the rose, thorns and all. The doctor tried to pull her fingers loose. "It's good that she recognized you," he said. "That means there's hope."

Petals wafted to the floor. I wanted to stay, to find out what she was trying so desperately to communicate, but the doctor ushered me out.

"Are you sure it was an accident?" I asked Sevinsky in the hallway.

He looked up as if the answer was written on the ceiling. He scratched the back of his head. "There was nobody up there. I gotta figure it was a loose brick. Besides, why would anybody be out to get her?"

When he said that the cap and all the brass looked at each other as if to say, "Where'd he leave his IQ?" Sevinsky smiled like a halfwit and added, "Unless of course it was one of them who hates cops. They're all over the place."

Sevinsky was like a lot of cops at the precinct. They divided the world into "us" and "them." He figured

Mary had gotten hurt because one of them had gotten one of us, but I kept my thoughts to myself.

I made my way back down that long corridor to where Errol waited, thinking that it was no accident. I figured the same killer who wanted to chill me had made a try for Mary. Errol and I stepped into the elevator, neither of us speaking. The elevator went down, then opened onto a light green corridor. An orderly in blood-splattered white pushed a stretcher into the elevator. He was whistling a cereal jingle. The elevator door slid shut. Through the sheet covering the stretcher, I saw the outline of hands and the shape of a dead face. In my throat, a silent scream rose and fell. I tasted the faint smell of formaldehyde. When the door slid open again, we were in the emergency room.

Errol grabbed my elbow and led me through the carnage. All the hurt people had big eyes, eyes like a deer that's been shot, eyes that said, "I can't believe it. I can't believe I'm hurt. I can't believe I'm dying."

I heard the crying behind the dull curtains that separated cot from cot. Some moaned, others pleaded. A few mothers stood waiting. Cops waited too. Orderlies in white coats waited to deliver loonies to the psycho ward. The loonies had hurt themselves. The sane people had provoked others to hurt them. There were knife wounds, gun shot wounds, and broken bones. An average evening in Bellevue.

I followed Errol to his car, both of us still silent. I just sat there and watched him drive down the FDR and across to the Village. Finally, he said, "I'm gonna teach you how to bend that elbow. This is no time to be stoic."

We parked on Seventh Avenue, and I followed him to the White Horse Tavern.

"Dylan Thomas used to drink here," he said when we were seated by the window onto the avenue.

"He drank himself to death, didn't he?"

"Gin?"

I nodded.

"Be back."

I watched the window. The activity at the bar reflected on the pane like a pantomime. The backs of so many drunken losers hunched over glasses I couldn't see. Every once in a while the red glow of a lit cigarette deepened as unseen lips inhaled. A thin line of smoke circled the hollow shadows at the bar in a devilish halo. My eyes, my haunted face, floated over them all.

"Drink up," Errol said as he returned, placing a glass before me. I lifted it to my lips and obliged. I emptied one glass after another that way. I didn't even notice that he wasn't keeping up with me. I just kept drinking and watching the reflection of the bar on the window, an occasional elbow lifting, an occasional cigarette glowing. I watched them, and he watched me. It was a long while before I was able to look at him.

"I wanna go home now," I said finally.

"Okay, but I want you to stay with me tonight."

I thought he was crazy thinking about sex at a time like this.

"I don't want you staying at your place tonight. It'll make you nuts," he said.

It was as if he had reached into the cavern of my chest and broken off a rib. The pain cut up into my eyes. I looked away so he would not see into me and stood up to leave. When I pushed my chair in, I knocked it over. He picked it up and maneuvered me toward the door. I don't remember going to his place. But I got there and kept drinking.

I heard him moving as I slumped in a chair, but I didn't open my eyes. The wail of a jazz horn spoke from the lips of someone's heart—the beat wild with anguish. The tune was about love and loss.

"Who's that?" my numb lips asked.

"It's Miles."

Through his muted horn Miles Davis was singing

the sorrows of an unjust world. Errol sat at my feet as I brought liquid forgetfulness to my mouth. It was that way through the whole disc, sides one and two. Then the long silence began. I thought I was suffocating, so I got up and went to the window. The apartment overlooked Brooklyn's Prospect Park. In the dark the outlines of the trees and bushes seemed as deep and crazy as a Rorschach. He came up behind me and placed his arms around me. I turned to face his chest. His warmth came through to me. Heat on ice. And that was all it took.

I felt myself crack. A moan rose from me, up my throat, down to the floor. My knees gave way. I sank down against his torso, down his long legs, down to the floor until my eyes were on his shoes and wailing filled my ears.

Grief closed around me like a cocoon. He squatted and held me to his chest. The liquor carried me on a soft wave until I reached the crest, where it finally broke, and the sounds that came from me I buried in his chest, screaming the agony straight into his heart. Time passed that way until I soaked both of us in sweat and tears. The sounds that wrenched through me rose from childhood a thousand years ago. And I cried for Mary and the bitter consequences of a vendetta that had led nowhere. I had broken all the rules. My revenge had brought me down, all the way down. I rose to my knees, face dripping, eyes slit. I knew he was there, but I couldn't make him out. I ripped the white jacket madly from myself and stretched my two bare arms boldly toward the smell and feel of him. I think he was on the floor too. I put my tracks and bruises in his face—the proof that I was no better than the animals I despised.

I felt his compassion click over into a granite rage as he grabbed my arms and shook me with a violence I didn't know he had. His face bobbed before me like a strobe light. He seemed to be chanting. "What are you telling me? . . . What are you telling me?"

We both knew what I was telling him.

The sounds in my mouth tried to turn into words but couldn't. The bobbing of his head and the crazy fear in his eyes conspired to make me laugh. I doubled in half laughing. I had to hold myself. I had to slap the damn floor.

He was pulling on me, yelling something in my ear, pulling me to his chest, trying so hard to stop me from laughing that he was choking me. I couldn't stop laughing. I just kept laughing, sticking my arms in his face. It was a lunatic boxing match until finally he grabbed hold of my head with both his hands. There was a split second in which I didn't know what his next move would be—then he covered my mouth with his hands and cut off my air. His face was so twisted by anger and anguish that I barely recognized him. I felt the breath leave me as he became a blur.

He was saying something. I couldn't hear him through the waves that seemed to be crashing in my ears. I clawed at his face with my nails. I bit deep into his palm. He took his hands from my mouth and placed them around my neck. I expected him to choke me. Instead, he opened my mouth with his and tried to suck my tongue out. I bit into him. He yelped and let go. His blood was on my lips as he shouted, "How could you? How could you when dope has cost you so much?"

A horrible pity fractured his whole face. His eyes were moving back and forth over my arms. I watched his love for me fight with something else that looked like contempt. Suddenly, I wanted to hurt him. I wanted him to hurt as much as I hurt. I felt my eyes narrow into slits as I searched for potent words.

"I lied to you. I've been lying to you all along. I'm out there with the junkies every night."

He came toward me again. My whole body flinched as I prepared for him to hit me. Instead, he put his arms around me and softly started to cry. I felt the sadness rise and heave in his big chest. I held his face, he held my body, and he rocked us. His gentle hands massaged me, cajoling from me the miserable story of my nights in the streets.

Between hiccups and sobs I told all. I told him about Lenny dealing even when we were married and about the big payoff Brian had stolen. I explained about Sunny and how she saw the fat man that night. I told him about the cover-up that had cost Baker his life. Then I told him about the sniper who shot my reflection and probably tried to get Mary too.

He stroked my head, pushing the wet hair from my face, over and over again. He kissed my eyes, my lips. I tried to see him but I was too drunk. "Don't look at me like that," he said. "I'm not here to hurt you."

I lay there sniffing, breathing through my stuffed nose, feeling his warmth around me. After a while I got up and moved to the bed. He followed. My whole body was quivering from the sickness, oversensitive to everything.

"Make love to me," I said. "Do it now."

He reached for a tissue to blow his nose. "You're drunk, do you know what you want?"

I took everything off then started on his buttons. "Please," I whispered, "please, you'll be doing me a favor."

"It's not the way I imagined it."

I grabbed a tissue for my running nose. "Me either."

"Is it the sickness, is it making you horny?"

"Yeah, yeah I itch all over," I said.

"This isn't the way I want it. If I say yes to you now, in the morning you'll have your track shoes on again."

I unzipped his fly. Gently, he took my hand away. "C'mon, I'll give you a rub down and you'll fall asleep. Then we'll see how you feel in the morning."

Pissed, I gave him my back and felt his confident

hands search out the aches and pains in my muscles—my neck, my back, my legs—until I slid into oblivion.

When I woke up I was naked under his sheets, alone. Everything ached more than before. He was on a mat on the floor. I slid in next to him and cuddled against his back. After a while, he turned to embrace me. "How do you feel?"

"Awful."

He was in his underwear, his body warm from sleep, and I felt that he was hard. I put my hands there. "I'm sober now."

He smiled. "You sure?"

"Yeah,- yeah I'm sure," I whispered.

I helped him pull his briefs off. He brought his nakedness close to mine and massaged me gently. I lay there shaking and quaking, feeling him sense my need. His touch was certain, his kisses hot on my clammy skin. Our bodies sprawled full-length against one another as his hands helped me forget. I took his hardness into my palms and his breath quickened. I turned over to bury my head in the pillow, and he massaged my back some more.

"Is this how you want it?" he whispered.

I moaned yes, because I wanted to be taken, that's all. He reached for my velvet pocket and then slipped gently toward my womb. At first the feeling didn't reach me. I turned my head sideways on the pillow so that I could see his muscular body over me. He brought his lips to my ear and whispered, "I want you. I need you. I want you. I need you." The yearning tremor in that chant unlocked my heart and I started to let go. I slid my hand underneath myself, down to my clitoris. "Yes," he said, "yes, rub it for me." I pushed up toward him and a steady driving rhythm caught us both. His sweat trickled onto my back as he slid in and out of me slowly, surely, dissolving all memory. Everything in me melted. I began to sweat.

"I'm gonna come," he whispered, his lips close to my ear. "Come with me, I'm gonna come." When he said that I went off—like a current, like electricity on water. As he shot into me, I exploded. For a time my demons were silenced, and I again found sleep.

I woke up sprawled over him, feeling as if I had aged sixty years. He was snoring lightly, his arms and legs wrapped around me. I lay there pondering how I could get out of his grip without waking him up. I wondered how I was going to make it the hell out of that room. I knew if he woke up he would stop me. I wormed out gradually. Because I was on top, it wasn't that difficult. He moaned and shifted but kept on sleeping.

I was dressed, had my pocketbook over my shoulder, and was ready to make it, when I felt his eyes on my back. I didn't stop. "Boy, are you predictable!" he said.

The door was a couple of feet away. I turned my head slightly, just enough to see him behind me. "Don't try it," he warned.

I felt his anger rising up from the mat where we had fallen asleep together. He didn't make a move. My eyes were on the two locks I would have to open before getting out. Half of me was expecting him to jump up and punch me out. That was how Lenny handled disagreements. So when he did jump, a long scream shot through me, and I covered my head with both hands. Nothing happened. I heard him sigh an incredulous, "Oh my God." I lowered my hands to see him. He was spread-eagled over the door, blocking my exit. His eyes were sad. Last night's crying had left his face soft and puffy.

"I can't let you go, Toni. You've got to stay and kick. It won't be all that bad. But you've got to do it now before you get caught and ruin your whole life."

"My life is already ruined, and I don't give a shit. C'mon Mr. Macho, don't play God. Just get out of my way."

"You better stay and face yourself," he said. "You can't continue fucking around out there playing victim in the streets when you know goddamn well you're the man now. . . . You're a damn good cop—all you have to do is get comfortable with the power."

"Save the lecture." I shifted my weight from one leg to the other. "Save the lecture and open the fucking door."

"Can't do it," he said. I stood there hating him and hating myself more. The minutes raced by. His resolution was obvious. So I tried a different tack.

"Look, I want to do it but I want to do it alone. If I do it with you I'll come out of it hating you . . . and you'll hate me too."

He shook his head and smiled sadly. "I love you now, I'll love you later."

I walked back into the room just to get away from him a little. "What about the job?"

"I'll call us both in sick, the cap will understand . . ."

"I can't do it now," I said. "It's too much at once. I can't handle it. I have to find this guy by the end of the week or turn the investigation over to IAD. I promised Mary I would."

He stepped away from the door, not fully facing me. "Mary's in a coma," he said. "There's no point trying to keep that promise. First you clean up, then we'll finish the investigation together."

Every bone in my body ached, my skin was clammy with sweat, and my diaphragm pulled across my chest like a lock on my lungs. We stood there listening to trash cans being hurled into a sanitation truck down the street. I turned completely to face him. "Are you with me no matter what the consequences?"

"What do you mean?"

"The force . . ." I began. Then there was a long pause as we both pondered the meaning of what I was about to say. "If you get any deeper into this investigation with me, and we get caught, it could cost you your job."

The sanitation truck crushed glass and metal. He looked at me in a mournful, longing way. "We won't get caught. We can't afford to."

Trash cans crashed on concrete. Someone cursed.

"The consequences could be even worse," I said.

He left the doorway and moved toward me. He took me by the shoulders and asked me to spell it out.

"Okay," I said. "When I find the fat man, I might . . . " My voice broke off and there was a long pause as we both filled in the blank.

Outside, a Siamese cat cried like a baby. I had been hiding from my own intention for a long time.

"I'm still with you," he said. And I knew that I would have to stay.

CHAPTER EIGHTEEN

I was on a bed by a window. Every other wall in the room was lined with books. Outside the window it was night. Across the room a refrigerator hummed, then stopped. Inside, all the lights were on. I thought I was in purgatory or dead or both. Errol slept on the rug. His mouth was hanging open. I wasn't sure if two or three days had passed.

I looked out the window at the park below. Nothing moved. There was no fire escape, and I would never make it out the door. I decided to torture Errol. He was snoring slightly. His eyes were moving back and forth under his lids as if he were reading an invisible book. I crawled to him and hugged my body to his. He moaned and turned. With both his hands he pulled me closer. My leg up on his leg, I felt that he was hard. He woke up, face to face, eye to eye, his hard-on digging into my thigh.

"You want something?" he asked.

I was sick, horny, tingling, wanting, and hating him all at once. I quivered in his arms shaking my head back and forth, claimed by an unprovoked orgasm, until I started crying like a little girl. He stroked my damp hair. "I know it hurts. I know," he whispered.

My teeth were chattering, and the noise seemed very loud. My ears hurt. His face was changing so fast he looked a thousand years old, twisting and turning like a psychedelic painting. "I'm so sick, isn't there something . . ."

I folded into myself like the petals of a flower at night.

"How about a bath and a rubdown?" he offered.

He pulled me out of my clothes.

The corners of the room were closing in, the air vibrating before my eyes. The thought of water made me cringe. Bats and beasts populated the room with us. I was losing my mind or dying. My body buzzed, and I felt the amoebas crawl under my skin into my eyeballs. Errol's eyes rotated like two dead fish in a bowl of white jelly. "It'll pass," he said with gigantic lips, his voice low and slow like a 45 disc at 33 rpm.

I saw a magic marker on the floor near some books. It was thick and a dark, dark green. Slowly, I drew on my skin. Errol watched. Roses and snakes on my arms and legs. Snakes sucking blossoms dead and dying on the vine. Thorns on my thighs and breasts. Then my lips. I drew my mouth in green. He was quiet. I went to the bathroom and emptied out my guts.

When I finished I felt his hands on me, one holding the hair at the nape of my neck and the other at the small of my back, like a mother. I heard the water running in the shower and let him pull me in. He was still in his jeans. The water sliced my skin like glass, but the snakes wouldn't come off. I was slimy. He scrubbed me with soap. The snakes began to move, slithering down my arms, my legs, into the drain. I shuddered and moaned. He washed my lips, the taste of soap coating my tongue. As the last of the ink slid from my chin, he drank a kiss from my mouth. Finally, he stepped out of the shower, wet and sexy in his jeans. He offered a towel but I just shivered. Then he handed me a bottle of cough medicine.

"What's this?" I almost smiled. "I don't have a cold."

The vee came and went on his forehead. He shrugged apologetically. "It's got codeine in it. Drink it. It'll give you a break from the sickness."

My hand started trembling. I was afraid I'd drop the cure. I opened the cap for a taste. It was thick, vile, bitter, and Eucalyptus green. My stomach protested. My face contracted. I drank the whole thing down.

After that I dried off and followed him to his alcove kitchen, where he made peppermint tea. I sat there watching him and thought of Mary. He put the water on the stove and put the cups, spoons, and honey before me on the table. Then we sat together, watching steam rise from our cups. He told me about his family, his childhood, his love of books, his hopes for the future. I could tell he was trying to avoid talking about his feelings for me.

"In my family people didn't talk about their feelings," he said. "It was never violent, but it was always cold, silent."

I smiled. "We were the loudest family on the block."

"When you were getting married, I was still anesthetized by a serious TV addiction. Later, I discovered sex and chased skirts for a few years."

I felt a twinge of jealousy. He caught it too and added, "It was just another kind of escape."

As I listened, the codeine crept into my bloodstream, and for a while the ache and the chills left me. I held the hot tea in the cup between my hands. Then I talked about my own mistakes. Heavy words fell between us, but we laughed, a sad kind of laughter, laughter about ourselves. It was the dawning of a realization in me. I began to know my real feelings for him.

After that I couldn't sleep. I was too sick to sleep. The longer I was awake, the crazier I felt, and the crazier I felt, the more scared I got. Errol held me, listening to me babble. He let me curse him and never let me go.

CHAPTER NINETEEN

It was a Sunday morning when I knew the sickness had left me. Even before the light rose, I felt the dawn in my bones. Outside, the birds hidden in the leaves sensed it too, because they began to sing sweetly. I lay there feeling the absence of pain and the beginning of hope. Errol came in, carrying French bread and the Sunday *Times*. He sat at the edge of the bed looking as if he had won the lottery. I moved to give him a big hug and the loaf fell between us. I giggled, he shrugged, we tried again. This time the loaf fell the other way. With our arms around each other, I smelled the still warm, fresh bread. The early sun filled the empty spaces in my heart.

"The hospital says Mary's improving. If she has the will, she's going to start walking and talking any day now. You know her better than I do," he said. "Is she a fighter?"

I watched him get up and wondered what makes some people hold life tight while others throw it away. I thought about the many ways in which Mary was fragile and I wasn't sure. "I hope so," I said.

"Today, the precinct plays ball against Manhattan

South at a park upstate. There's gonna be a barbecue, and there's a lake for swimming. It would be good for you."

The birds sounded like a flute riff. I felt the easy movement of my joints as I moved around the bed trying to read the goddamn *New York Times*. "I don't think so," I answered.

Errol ground some coffee and we listened to the loud noise. "I buy this stuff from a co-op that buys directly from the Sandinistas," he said. "The problem is they gotta take the coffee to Amsterdam before they can bring it here. So the coffee is politically correct, but the taste is a bit stale."

He made me laugh. For him everything was politics and bleeding heart. I barely knew where Nicaragua was. Probably because I never read the *Times*, which I was struggling with now. It was too big and too heavy. The real estate section slid off the bed. I reached to retrieve it when the cover story hit my eye. It was about Village East, the largest complex of condominiums ever to be built on the Eastern seaboard, and the fact that the controversial development had created the squatter protests in our precinct. I read with interest. Deep into the story several paragraphs referred to the benefits package the Chilean developer had offered the community. Ten percent of the apartments would be low-income rental units for neighborhood residents. There would be a sports complex and an entertainment complex, and management contracts for both had been awarded to local businessmen. The entertainment concession had been awarded to Lenny da Rosa.

"What's going on? You seem mesmerized," said Errol.

I handed Errol the paper. I counted a few beats until he said, "Holy shit. Plain as day in the fucking *New York Times*!" He slapped the print. "This is it! This is it!

This has to be it! The payoff. How else would a guy like Lenny land something like this?"

We stared at each other. "That money Brian copped must have been earmarked for someone in City Hall, someone who could guarantee Lenny the entertainment concession," I said. "That means the payoff went where it was supposed to go—so Lenny must know about the fat man killing Brian and Kelly. He must have known all along."

The birds hadn't stopped singing.

I thought about that little girl's room down the long hall. Lenny was sick, sick with guilt. But it didn't stop him from being the scumbag he was. Then I said, "But why would the fat man be involved if all he did was tip Lenny off to dope raids?"

"There must have been something in it for him too."

Errol started reading the article again, as if the answer might be in there.

I stood up, thinking that most of the precinct would be at that picnic, and that the simple thing would be just to find out about this fat cop. Where had he gone? "Let's go to that damn ball game," I said.

He threw some shorts and a T-shirt into a bag. Then we stopped at my place, and I did the same. We decided to head out in separate cars to minimize the talk, which was probably already running wild in the precinct house. I had to promise not to make any moves on my own, though.

We got back into Errol's car so that he could drive me to mine, which was parked a few blocks from my apartment. It was hot as hell, and pretty soon we both began to glisten. I put a tape into the deck and adjusted the sound so that it was all around us.

I looked over at Errol. In the sun's midday glare the heat between us was scorching. He leaned back into the curved seat, driving with care, ease, and speed, his body alive to the music. He was wearing one of those mesh

T-shirts that showed his shape and the shadow of the hair on his chest. He shimmered in the hard sunlight. I was watching his parted lips, which revealed his unusually long teeth. His mouth was always slightly open, Elvis Presley style, and I was thinking that I wanted to reach over and nibble on the crooked curve of his upper lip. I felt myself dampen down below. "Here we are, lady," he said, breaking my thoughts. He stopped the car.

"Well, gimme some directions," I told him.

"We're going up the Henry Hudson to the Sawmill and then the Taconic. It's easy. Tailgate me."

He reached over and offered me his sweetness. I took his lips, then said, "Later," climbed out and made my way to my own car. It was a ninety-minute drive. When we got there, he joined the ball game and I went for a swim. Neither of us really knew what we were looking for.

I was on the raft watching the sky and the water. The lake was gray and still as glass. I lay there thinking about the *Times* article. I was wondering if Lenny had sent the fat man to get Brian. Now that it was pretty clear that the payoff had benefited Lenny, it didn't make much sense to believe that the fat man had acted on his own. I figured it was time to go to Internal Affairs and let the law take over. The future seemed clear as a crystal ball. I had kicked more than drugs—I had kicked the past itself. The odds were, Lenny would get his. All I wanted now was to get mine—I thought about Errol's love and admitted to myself that he was the real thing.

The clouds above were still as cotton candy. After a while they began to move, and everything changed. The sky went liquid light. The waves ran azure in the wind. The cold nibbled my wet skin as I heard the gasp of lungs behind me. The surface of the water broke and splashed me. I figured it was Errol kidding around. He went back down. I figured he'd come up when he needed air. Then I heard a knock on the bottom of the raft and my heart knocked too.

Sevinsky shot up right in front of me, laughing like hell. I was rattled. He was so shaken by his own laughter that he slipped off the raft while trying to climb on. I got his profile and noticed that his eyes seemed focused on the shore where you could see the ball game through the trees.

"Scared you, didn't I, Officer?" he asked.

The wind suddenly stopped. I didn't bother to answer him. The mere sight of this guy filled me with hate. The light hit the water hard as ice. There was a glare in my eyes that blurred my vision, and I sat there hating him for sitting there while Mary lay in the hospital. I wasn't mad at God anymore. I was just asking myself what kind of crap game was it where the dice were loaded in favor of assholes like him. Through the silence, I heard the rustle of leaves and the game in the distance.

The light around us was so pure I saw the liquid over my own eyes—over the aperture over the hole to the optic nerve to the back of the brain—I thought I was seeing that. And I thought that was why tiny white worms crawled all over his wet body. For a second, I thought he had been in the water too long, but then in a blinding flash I realized who he was. His entire body was covered with stretch marks. "Lose a lot of weight, fat man?" I asked.

He put a hand on my wrist so I couldn't dive away.

"This isn't a roof, it's not your usual MO," I said.

He laughed that ghoulish laugh again. "Look at the water, Conroy. It's smooth as a mirror."

Then, as I tried to figure my next move, he grabbed me firmly by the roots of my hair. "You're not getting away this time," he said as he pitched me forward into the water. I took a deep breath and shut my mouth tight.

As I plunged, I managed to kick his gut. Because he wouldn't let go, he fell on top of me. His weight drove me down fast and hard. I saw the muddy bottom. It looked soft. His head hit my shoulder, I grabbed him by the hair. Now we had each other.

The sun's rays beat on the water, casting an eerie greenish hue over his skin. He was trying to bring his other hand toward me, but his flailing and the weight of the water worked against him. Shiny bubbles raced from his head for the surface; they clung to his mouth like iridescent fish. His face was close to mine, the eyes wide open, and I saw his horror rise as he realized that I was better at holding my breath.

One naked plant with slimy, waving arms reached for me. Locking my legs around Sevinsky's neck, I grabbed hold close to the root. My lungs threatened to force me to the surface. Then, as his arm passed before my eyes, I saw the tattoo. It was small and exactly as Sunny had described it. The open-mouthed Cobra threatened to eat the rosebud. My power doubled with rage. I would hold that root as long as it took. Even through the murky water I saw him begin to go blue. His pupils eased up, and the eyes went milky white. The little silver bubbles clinging to his mouth broke free and drifted away.

In his desperation he stirred the mud beneath us. The water became dark. He kept on trying to pry my legs from his neck, but I held tight. His fingers weakened, his face opened wide, and he screamed the loudest scream of his life, but there was no sound at all. I hung around him like a necklace. The water swallowed his last breaths, and he stopped moving.

I let go. My body shot itself up. When I hit the surface, water broke around me like a liquid glass. I ate the air. It hurt like hell, like a knife wound in the gut from the inside. That's what breathing again was like. I treaded water for a while to help myself catch up to my breath. Then I crawled back onto the raft, throwing one leg up first. I just lay there, feeling the weight of the universe full on my lungs. The sky looked like rain and a storm was moving in. I watched the water, waiting for him or his ghost to surface.

A storm cloud moved in the west. I figured if there was any justice out there a bolt of lightning would strike me down. Adrenaline raced through my body like sixteen highs at once. I was grateful to my body. Damn! I had had no idea I wanted so much to live. There was a tight sweet pain in my throat. A gratitude. A simple gratitude. And I was determined to shake off guilt before it tried to nest in. I was done with guilt. Done with trying to be God and make all the pieces fit. On shore there was lots of cursing going on. I thought about all those cars pulling out at once and that I should try to beat them.

What about my promise to Errol? The promise not to make any moves without him. The promise not to leave the park without him. Most of all, the promise not to bug out and go after Lenny.

The rain came down like a shower of needles. A few car doors slammed, but most of the men on the field were still fighting to finish that last inning. I was beginning to breathe like a pro again. I hadn't moved a muscle yet.

Rain fell down my face like tears. I rationalized breaking my promise to Errol. I did it by deciding not to kill Lenny. Instead, I would go home and get a tape recorder, hold my .38 to his head and get him to talk. Then I'd read him his rights. I could actually hear the click of the cuffs. I jumped in the water and swam to shore.

I trekked through the whisper of the dripping late summer leaves, the woods heavy with rain. I had left my car up the road. No one spotted me. I stepped into the extra jeans I had in my trunk without bothering to take off my wet underwear. The wet T-shirt I left on, too. I wanted to floor the pedal all the way back to the city. No chances though . . . I didn't eat any lights, and I seldom broke the speed limit.

To execute my plan I had to go to the apartment on Twelfth Street. I had to move fairly quickly to avoid Errol's catching up with me. I was sure he'd be hot on my trail once he realized I was gone. As soon as I opened the door to the apartment, the remnants of the shattered mirror and the bullet hole reminded me of Sevinsky. I thought of his face, green and silent in the water—maybe they'd found him by now—and put the chain on the door. The apartment seemed unusually quiet. The air conditioner wasn't humming, and even the street outside was still. From the closet, I pulled out the tiny tape recorder. It was extra sensitive. I had bought it for an arm and a leg, but had never used it. I kept it stashed behind the shoes. As I got up with the tape recorder I noticed a red halter dress of Mary's. I pulled it off the rack.

It was sort of a Marilyn Monroe dress with a tight waist, flair skirt, and halter top. I fixed my hair and put on makeup, especially lipstick. Then I took my over-the-shoulder bag—the good one—and placed the tape recorder in it. I was in the apartment no more than ten minutes before I headed out for the Dragon.

Something was different about the Lower East Side that Sunday. I couldn't put my finger on it though. Still I drove past the Dragon to check out Avenue D. From Tenth Street on, the whole damn avenue was cordoned off. Squad cars and ambulances and a limo with City Hall plates cut off access to the squatters' tents. People crowded the sidewalks, but they were so quiet I wondered if they were imaginary. I got out to take a closer look.

There were stiffs everywhere and chalk shadows where others had been. There wasn't much brass around since the precinct was still at the picnic. Mulwihill was being interviewed by a print reporter. Apparently some

generous dope dealer had given the squatters a party—
coke, smoke, skag. A few hours later all those who
indulged were very ill or dead. Mulwihill had this sick
look like he couldn't believe it himself. Flies buzzed on
the eyes and mouths of the stiffs. Some still had their
eyes open. One guy had a wine cooler in one hand and a
cigarette in the other. They all looked like wax figures in
the Believe-It-or-Not Museum. Forensics was gathering
empty cellophane bags from the filthy street, bags sealed
with green tape.

I decided to hit the Dragon from behind. I climbed
over the fence from a backyard on Eleventh Street. It
was a little tricky, but I managed without getting too
messed up. Then I simply climbed the fire escape to
Lenny's veranda and walked into his bedroom.

The first thing I did was place my piece under the
bed. I put it on the side where I used to sleep when we
were together. Then I sat down at the vanity. I fixed my
makeup, waiting for him, calm as ice. I was going to get
from him exactly what I needed. There wasn't any
question in my mind. No doubt. I hung my purse, with
the tape recorder in it, on the back of the chair just like I
used to do when we lived together. Then I waited. But
not for long.

In the mirror I saw the doorknob turn behind me.
Then him. Our eyes met in the mirror. I smiled as
sweetly as if time had stood still, and he registered no
surprise. He crossed over to me and his hands were
instantly on my shoulders, his lips on my neck. Inside, I
flinched. Outside, I made no move at all. I couldn't
decide if I should confront him immediately or first
soften him up.

"I'd have let you in the front door, too," he said.

I laughed, the sound ringing false in my ears. He
didn't seem to notice. I said, "Seems like more of a
surprise this way."

259

His eyes sneaked over to the bed. "More romantic, too," he added.

I reached back into my purse for my makeup case with the red stripes. As I grabbed it, I pushed a button with my index finger, the record button. He watched my every move twice, once in the mirror and once from behind me where he stood. But he couldn't see inside the purse.

I dropped my makeup case onto the vanity as if it belonged there. And in a crazy way it did, because he had bought the bedroom set I had dreamed of owning back in the days when we were together and always broke.

Our faces reflected harshly in the oval mirror but were softened in the black lacquer surface of the vanity. On the vanity sat a small bouquet of porcelain flowers, a china bowl with birds painted on its belly, and an antique silver-handled hairbrush. I pulled back the zipper on my plastic makeup case, turned it upsidedown, and scattered its contents. I lined up the lipsticks as if I were moving in. I felt him eyeing me but I never looked up. Then I picked up the hairbrush. He watched as I brushed my hair. There was something crazy in his eyes, something that scorched my soul, like a dry ice stare that was so cold it burned. My skin hurt. A chill climbed my spine. Two crimson spots grew on my cheeks and I saw them deepen in the mirror. I wondered did he? He rubbed his hands together.

"Any bubbly?" I asked. His tongue wet his lips. He went to the refrigerator in the wall unit on the far side of the room. As he opened the refrigerator, I placed perfume behind my ears.

He began working the cork with his fingers. It seemed to be pointed dead at me so I started to get up. He turned toward the wall.

"When did you decide?"

For a moment I thought he was talking about when

did I decide to set him up. Then I realized he was saying something else. "To come back, you mean?"

The cork popped. It flew across the room like a bird, crashed head first into the wall, and bounced on the bed. He followed it with his eyes, then gave out a satisfied murmur. He looked at me as if I were naked. "Wanna get the glasses?" he asked.

I hopped up like old times, tip toed across the rug, and brought him two long-stemmed glasses. I offered one to the mouth of the bottle and he poured. The foaming translucent liquid fell into the glass. As I felt his eyes on me, I was wondering if he had dispatched Sevinsky to execute me, or if Sevinsky had acted on his own. But Lenny's expression betrayed satisfaction only. He moved to the love seat against the far wall and put the bottle on the table. With a gesture of his arm, he offered me a seat. "C'mon sit down, let's toast each other."

I didn't follow. I wanted to stay near the tape recorder so I sat down on the bed. With my hands I caressed the silk spread invitingly. "No," I said. "You come over to me."

He raised an eyebrow. Now he did look surprised, but he didn't hesitate. He stepped over to me. I was eye level with his crotch, and I saw that he was aroused. I wanted to stand up but he moved first. He knelt at the foot of the bed.

"To us," he said. "To life after death."

His glass hit mine. The crystal tinkled loud, clean, and pure. In my abdomen a consuming white hate began to burn. I drank. He emptied his glass and pulled a joint from his shirt pocket. He put it under my nose. It smelled of strawberry. "I don't any more," I said.

He shook his head. "Just this once. Just to celebrate," he insisted as he put it in my mouth. Then, still kneeling, he brought up the flame on a platinum lighter with a flick of his thumb. As I took the first drag that lit the paper and then the reefer, the flame rose high and thin between us. It cast a copper glow on his beautiful face and cut through his pupils in a yellow perpendicular line.

I let a lot of smoke escape from my lips, not wanting to inhale too deeply, and tried to hand him the joint. His hands were on my thighs. He shook his head. "Na-a-aw, take a serious puff. I wanna see you get a real buzz."

As I pulled again on the strawberry-flavored thin line between my lips, I became mesmerized by that look in his eyes. Even though the lighter was closed now, and the flame gone, that streak of yellow light continued to oscillate in his pupils. I put the joint to his lips again. This time he took a long, deep drag. A red glow ate the pink paper, consuming it in a tiny flame. He pulled hard. Smoke rose like a mask over his face. I was inhaling it too, in every breath I took.

Lenny picked his eyes up from the joint. They rolled toward me. Then his long, thin tongue moved to wet his lower lip slowly, very slowly. I reached for what he was handing me, crawling backwards up the bed, my heart fluttering like a hummingbird. He undulated in my direction and unhinged his large square jaw.

The room became a pulsating neon sign, every object vibrating, closing in. We were reflected in the vanity mirror, and my eyes strayed to rest on our image—a cobra playing with a kitten. His lips whispered into my ear, "Open up. Open your legs bay-bee."

My claws rasped the bed. Lenny's skin kept changing. I reached my paw for his lashless eyes, and as I recognized his true essence, I realized that I had always known. "What did you put in the smoke, *Cobra*?"

His hard laugh fell over me like hail. He pushed my skirt up over my waist and slid a hand under me. I was trying to think. I guessed that it must be PCP and that it wouldn't last because I hadn't taken much.

"Aw-w-w kitten, you're trembling. C'mon open up.

I'm not gonna hurt you. Besides, I'm not the whole Cobra—Sevinsky and me together, that's the Cobra—two heads, not just one."

I struggled to come down. The neon room lost its intensity and became a murky green. I thought I was back underwater, back holding my breath, back fighting Sevinsky, ready to kill to save myself. My lips were fuzzy. If I could talk I might get him to back off. The words came out deep and slow.

"What are all those bodies doing on the street?"

He froze above me like a statue. I smelled something pungently nauseating. "What street? What bodies?"

I pushed more words up my throat. "Avenue D, the squatters."

He laughed again. This time the peals fell with a caustic scratch. My skin began to burn. He brought a hand to the vee between my legs and rubbed while murmuring in my ear. "I guess it means the protest is over."

I let my right arm slide off the side of the bed. His breath was hot and icy all at once. He reached under my panties. My heart turned over.

"What about Brian and Kelly? Why them? Why did you kill them?"

He was set to lower himself into me. "It was an accident, baby, a tragic accident."

As I felt the first stab of him in me, I found my .38 under the bed and released the safety catch. I brought the piece to his gut. The tables turned. His eyes popped out of his head, and he went soft. I felt sanity return.

"Kneel," I said. He obliged; I stood and hovered over him.

"Now, I want you to tell me exactly what happened that night."

His shoulders started to shake. I moved my sights between his eyes. He began to weep.

"It was an accident. I swear to God it was an accident. We just wanted the money back, and Sevinsky got carried away."

Twenty years left his face. He looked younger than I had ever known him.

"Don't shoot. Two wrongs don't make a right."

I wanted to rap him in the mouth. Where did he come off using words like right and wrong? But I held myself in check.

"What about Kelly, answer that, Cobra, what about Kelly?"

"She woke up and started screaming, so Sevinsky put a pillow over her face to shut her up."

My finger was itchy on the trigger. I got off the bed and moved behind him to place the barrel against his neck, nice and cold. I felt it chill him. His hands grabbed at his face.

"I didn't know she was gonna die so fast."

He brought his hands back down, pulling on his fingers as if they were removable.

Gently, I eased the barrel back and forth. Goose-bumps raced up his spine until finally a loud sob fell from his mouth.

He folded his hands as if in prayer. "I had to set the fire, I had to, the whole deal would've blown if I hadn't."

My finger tried to ignore my brain. It tried to pull the trigger. But I held on.

"So you killed your own child."

He shook his head back and forth, hunching into himself and sobbing like a little boy.

"No," he said, "No, I didn't kill her. When I lit the fire, she was already dead."

A beam of light from the chandelier danced on the gun barrel. An impulse traveled down my arm. Something in me was dying to pull that trigger and put him out of his misery. I was still fighting the PCP.

"Who was that payoff to?"

He took his head into his hands as if it was a thing, a bowling ball, to roll down an alley. He was procrastinating, I guess, because he knew there was no more fancy footwork. It was straight down the line to the simple truth. I traced his spine with the piece. His sobbing let up a bit. I could hear his heavy breathing and I could hear him think. He was wondering if this answer would be his last answer. When the gun returned to the nape of his neck, he sighed and seemed to resign himself.

"The payoff was to Mulwihill, the Special Commissioner for Economic Development. Sevinsky knew him from Centre Street back in the days when Mulwihill was an ambulance chaser. We knew Mulwihill would grant the entertainment concession so Sevinsky aproached him and he bit. Finally, after two years, everything is falling into place, and you go off the deep end."

"How did you get Vogel to lie to me?"

Lenny hesitated. I let the gun breathe gently on his last vertebrae and he started talking again. "Vogel was up for retirement and we sweetened it for him with a condo in Florida."

I just stood there locked into the hate between us. He turned evil eyes over his shoulder. "Why don't you just blow my goddamned brains out so we can both meet in hell?"

I bit the inside of my cheeks and sucked fiendishly. I gave him a bitter smile. "Because I want you to have your day in court."

It was a mistake, though. I should have played by his rules. Because when he realized I didn't want to shoot him, he wasted no time. I didn't even see him move. In one turn, he punched me in the belly and had the gun. Now he was on top.

"Now I'm gonna hafta do Sevinsky's job for him," he said.

"You sent Sevinsky to kill me?" I wasn't surprised. I wasn't even frightened. I was calm.

I didn't try to move. For the record I said, "You wanted that concession so bad you watched Brian and Kelly die. You killed all those people out there to end the protest, so the development could continue on schedule, and now you want to kill me."

"I'm going to win this round. It would have been easier if you just came back to me. But you made your choice."

"You'll get caught."

"I doubt it. The cops are pretty dumb. Look at you."

He kept the gun on me and pulled a syringe from a drawer in the vanity. It was full and ready to go. He took off his belt, then put the gun down and knelt to tie me up for my hot shot. As he picked the gun up again, there was a loud shattering noise behind us. Lenny turned. Errol came through the French doors, glass splattering like rain.

I gave the gun a karate chop. In one instant it turned off me onto Lenny and fired. There was a flash of light, then the top of Lenny's head flew off. He was still on me, but his head was gone.

The shot ached in my ears and the hot smell of blood filled my nostrils. I extricated myself from the carnage, expecting to die any second. I reached into my purse and gave Errol the tape recorder quickly, with red hands. Only then did I realize that I was untouched. The blood, like the guilt, was Lenny's.

When my ears stopped ringing, Errol was giving me Miranda. I told him to cut the crap. When it came to my rights, I knew them as well as he did.

EPILOGUE

As soon as the elevator door slid open, I was blinded by the lights. Reporters, photographers, and camera crews circled me like a single human octopus. There must have been about thirty of them—every paper, every radio station, and every TV station in the city.

"What happened in there?"

"Is it true they brought Vogel in from Florida and gave him immunity?"

"Did you see Mulwihill? How did it make you feel?"

I kept stepping. The camera crews were walking backwards to catch my every expression for the six o'clock news. My car was just across the street. Finally, I just stopped. "Look, you guys know grand jury proceedings are secret. Why not just wait to see what they vote?"

Across the street Errol approached in the golden halo of the autumn sun. All I wanted to do now was make it into his arms.

"I'd love to stay here and chat with you guys but there's somebody over there I want to talk to even more."

All heads turned. Now I had really given them a story. Still shouting questions, they watched me walk into his arms and recorded it for posterity. I didn't give a damn.

We drove to his place and fell into a long dead sleep. I awoke to the ringing of the phone. It was Mary. Fully recovered, she would be leaving the department to work in a special victims counseling center, but for now she was still tied to the precinct.

"WINS is reporting that the grand jury voted not to indict. You're off the hook."

"What about Mulwihill?"

"A seven-count bribery indictment. Your tape, together with Vogel's testimony, really hung him."

My heart was happy.

"One thing, though. This time if you want your badge, you're going to have to fight for it. The department is going to try you. They have to—there's been too much publicity."

"Thanks, Mary, thanks," I said, figuring I would make my own decision later.

As I told Errol his arms surrounded and lifted me. We laughed and cried all at once. He nuzzled his face between my breasts and then we tumbled together onto the bed. Two people never got naked faster. Near the open window a solitary bird reached a high sweet note, pure and far above loneliness.

"Partner or driver?" Errol asked.

"I'll drive," I said, and climbed on.

"Oh shit," he whispered, "Oh shit, this is it."

Later, when I was tired, we changed places.

ABOUT THE AUTHOR

Soledad Santiago was born Sábire Vural in Konstanz, West Germany of Swiss-Turkish descent. After immigrating to the United States at age twelve, she was a resident of New York City's Lower East Side for many years. More recently, she served five years as Deputy Press Secretary to the New York State Attorney General. Currently, she heads the New York press office for the State Comptroller.

Ms. Santiago has written for *The Daily News*, *The Village Voice*, *The New York Post*, *G.Q.*, *Penthouse*, and numerous other publications. Her play "Perdido," was produced by Woody King, Jr. at New York's Henry Street Settlement. She has also written for film and television in both Spanish and English. She makes her home in Manhattan with her children Leylâ-Linda and Rocky-Taino.

Kinsey Millhone is . . .

"The best new private eye." —The Detroit News

"A tough-cookie with a soft center." —Newsweek

"A stand-out specimen of the new female operatives."
—Philadelphia Inquirer

Sue Grafton is . . .

The Shamus and Anthony Award winning creator of Kinsey Millhone and quite simply one of the hottest new mystery writers around.

Bantam is . . .

The proud publisher of Sue Grafton's Kinsey Millhone mysteries:

BANTAM
SHOP-AT-HOME
C·A·T·A·L·O·G

Special Offer
Buy a Bantam Book
for only 50¢.

Now you can have Bantam's catalog filled with hundreds of titles plus take advantage of our unique and exciting bonus book offer. A special offer which gives you the opportunity to purchase a Bantam book for only 50¢. Here's how!

By ordering any five books at the regular price per order, you can also choose any other single book listed (up to a $5.95 value) for just 50¢. Some restrictions do apply, but for further details why not send for Bantam's catalog of titles today!

Just send us your name and address and we will send you a catalog!